Moments of Ecstasy

Sexy Stories Collection

VOLUME 29

22 EROTIC SHORT STORIES

JULI MATESON

Publisher's Note: This is a work of fiction. Names,
characters, places, and incidents are a product of
the author's imagination. Locales and public
names are sometimes used for atmospheric
purposes. Any resemblance to actual people, living
or dead, or to businesses, companies, events,
institutions, or locales is completely coincidental.

Moments of Ecstasy/ Juli Mateson. -- 1st ed.
Xplicit Press, an imprint of TLM Media LLC

ISBN-13: 978-1-62327-560-0
ISBN-10: 1-62327-560-1
eISBN: 978-1-62327-610-2

Printed in the United States of America

CONTENTS

CONTENTS

1 THE GREEN MAN FROM XENOT

The cool, crisp air rushed into my lungs as I scaled the rugged terrain; my breath came in gasps and my heart thundered in my chest. I could hardly see the down-trodden path that led to the top. I thought, "I had to run faster, or I'm dead meat." I could hear the thundering hooves of the "monster" crashing through the bushes. I was so terrified my legs refused to budge from the spot where I stood. I was paralyzed with a profound fear I had never experienced before.

The lush vegetation behind me parted, and my eyes stayed glued at the spot where the din was coming from. There was a loud crash, branches of trees broke, and plants were flattened as the emerging figure stormed its way through the lush vegetation.

Without warning, the "monster" appeared in the clearing. I stared straight into two luminous green eyes. I screamed my lungs out, until I felt my legs turning wobbly, and then I blacked out.

I awakened with an incredible feeling of languor and delight. There was a burning sweet sensation between my thighs, and I felt a sexual craving I never thought I could feel again.

I opened my eyes, languidly savoring the pleasurable sensations emanating from my groin. I screamed as I stared at the same luminous green eyes that had terrified me earlier. My screams were muffled as his green puckered lips covered mine. I continued to struggle, but he—I presumed he was a man because of his sexual preference—was so big that I could barely move from where he pinned me down with his frog-like arms.

He wasn't actually hurting me, and it was the "tastiest" kiss I have ever basked in, so I stopped struggling. His lips were soft and pliant, molding wonderfully with every crevice of my palate; his tongue teased the inner, sensitive areas of my mouth. His tongue was longer and more elastic, and he darted it into the soft, sensitive tissues of my inner cheeks.

When I looked deep into his eyes, they were actually the gentlest eyes I had ever seen. All the fight was gone from my body as I closed my eyes and basked in his delicious kiss. Then I felt the exquisite sensation in my lips connecting to the pleasurable sensation between my thighs. It turned me so horny; I wanted to beg him to fuck me hard. But I opened my eyes instead with considerable restraint. He was still gently exploring my mouth, nibbling my lips and the inner sensitive parts of my mouth, ever so gently.

I felt every nerve of my moist and eager vagina responding to whatever he was doing down there. There was delightful pressure on all my pleasure points I was ready to explode. I felt my clit was being adored, licked, and sucked, and my G-spot was feeling full ready to burst into one gigantic wave of orgasm.

"Fuck me hard, please," I whispered when I could no longer contain the burning desire in my cunt and my body; I was crazy with the sensations, which were about to burst from my body. He persisted, however, in teasing me farther. I looked down and saw an extra appendage sucking and licking my clit. I drew apart startled. What was that? The dizzying pleasant sensations though won over my surprise and I was back to moaning and writhing in wanton abandon in his expert hands.

One of his green fingers was inside my hot pussy playing with my G-spot, and his other "appendages" were caressing my labia.

With my lips receiving utmost pleasure and my cunt and clit being fondled, I was ready to climax.

"Oh please, fuck me now," I cried, pulling him feverishly towards me.

With a grunt, he mounted me and I was shocked to see his penis as big as a horse's, but it was too late for me to react, all I wanted was the fulfillment of the clamoring heat inside me. I wanted to feel his penis inside my yearning and moist pussy.

When he started pumping, I clung to his neck and cried in extreme ecstasy. His rock-hard huge penis vibrated inside me like it had some sort of electrical charge. I felt my pussy widening to accommodate his enormous cock fully. It intensified the delightful sensations I was experiencing. His green face was awash with a translucent gloss that glistened in the descending darkness as he sucked and licked my tits and lips and thrust his big gleaming manhood into my eager pussy. I could fill his throbbing tumescent penis filling every space in my tight but slick vagina. It was an unadulterated pleasure I had never known before.

I clawed at his back and thrust my groin as waves of pleasure inundated the core of my being. I groaned in the sweet, exquisite sensations coming from my pussy and tits. God! I could die right then and there and I wouldn't care less. I strained against him to meet his powerful movements; his dick had a green metallic sheen that looked beautiful against the shadows. It was strange that I had noticed this since I was going mad with my near-exploding orgasm.

"Oh, god! Harder! Please! Yes! Yes! Fuck me!" I screamed at him as my orgasm came again in big tidal waves of unexplored delightful sensations. I writhed and locked my groin against him and wrapped my legs around his torso, as I came again, and again, and again, savoring his vibrating big hard cock inside me.

We stayed that joined in a tight embrace for about ten minutes, while my juices slithered through my legs. I was satiated beyond words. But when he started grinding his pelvis into mine again, I felt my sexual desire coming back.

He was hard anew, his red, tumescent penis was again clamoring for my pussy. I was no longer afraid of this alien creature. If sexual power was the basis, he was more human than any man I had met before. He was manlier and knows how to pleasure me more than anyone.

I allowed him to run his fingers along the curves of my body, quivering as pure pinprick pleasures warmed my body. I sat up and pushed on him flat on the cool grass, and started to fondle his already angry cock. He growled like a tiger when I stooped to take him into my mouth. I licked the crown of his cock and slowly inserted my tongue inside the small opening on the tip of his penis. He growled and raised his head in surrender as my tongue darted up and down his shaft.

I held the base of his penis and massaged it with three of my fingers, my thumb applying firm pressure on his balls. My mouth went up and down the length of his dick as my fingers worked at the base of his cock. When I took him all in into my mouth and sucked him, he growled louder and snatched my hair guiding me up and down his throbbing engorged penis. He was so big now; my pussy became moist imagining that powerful delicious muscle inside me.

He shifted suddenly and stood up. He reached out for me and carried me in his arms with ease. He was standing on the soft mound of grass that we have lain in. It was nearing dusk, and eerie shadows were everywhere, but

I didn't mind. I was sex-crazed, wanting to feel him inside me again.

He held me by the waist and with one big thrust brought my wet vagina down his imploring rock-hard dick. I gasped in pleasure when his cock touched the base of my pussy. I was climaxing again after a few minutes, as he brought me up and down onto his fervid cock. I had my legs crossed tightly in is back locking him in as I clung to his neck and tasted his delicious tongue like a scrumptious dessert.

I thought he was done, but he was still so big and angry that it made me horny as well. He shifted positions and grabbed me by my ass. Then he was pumping again, taking me from the back. I felt my quivering ass absorb all the pressure. The incredible sensations came with his every thrust. I moaned in desire as I felt another orgasm building deep inside my cunt. God, it was heaven! Nothing could describe the miasma of intricate pleasures that coursed through all the tiny vessels of my seemingly sex-craved body. I had never been this horny. He aroused me so quickly.

I squealed in delight as my orgasm came. He pumped like mad until I have to scream again as a gigantic wave of fulfilled desire swept my body. He gave a guttural cry and arched his back as he pushed his dick deep into me and his hands fondled my breast. I felt a warm, glowing feeling spread from my pussy into my whole body. It gave me a comforting feeling, like I was in a cocoon filled with love.

He finally let go off me and put me down gently. I collapsed into the soft grass, my body satiated beyond what I had previously imagined. It was an extreme sexual experience for me. I lay there for quite some time with my eyes closed, just basking in my state of euphoria.

Perhaps, I had fallen asleep because when I opened my eyes, it was already dark with the moon slithering through the shadows of the trees. He was nowhere to be found. I felt a certain disappointment when I realized he was only chasing me to have sex. Where did he come from? He was definitely not human. He looks more like a green lizard with his pointed head and the extra appendage between his legs that had given such wonderful sensation to my clit.

Gingerly, I put on my clothes on and trudged downwards towards my modest apartment. I have lived alone since my mother died of myocardial infarction just a month ago. I neglected socializing the past months and spent time reading a book in the open air under a tree. Sometimes, I would descend a little bit farther into the mountain when I wanted to admire the spectacular view of the surrounding terrain and the blinking lights of the city a mile away.

The fresh evening breeze was playing across my face as I made the short descent. I felt rejuvenated, and every fiber of my body was singing with sexual gratification.

The following days, I felt on edge, and each slight noise made me start. I realized that I was yearning for him to come back. I could feel my undies becoming wet just with thought of him. At night, I often woke up and imagined all that had happened. It felt like some sort of dream, but I still had the bruises where his big green hands were.

After a week, I decided I couldn't simply sit back and wait for him to return. I packed a lunch basket, and put in the book I was currently reading. The sun was shining gloriously in the morning sky, and I could hear chirping birds from the distance. I hardly was aware of these though because I had one purpose in mind, to find him, alien or not, human or not.

There was a gnawing feeling of the embers of craving lapping the periphery of my consciousness. I felt horny, but I was trying to divert the stimuli of desire. I came to the bottom of the mound and stood there for a minute looking around me. I was expecting him to appear before my eyes without me looking for him.

"Hello..." I shouted and my voice made a hollow echo in the distance. "Hello, anybody there?" I called anew. Silence, not a human sound, only the "silence" of nature.

I decided to continue with my descent. Anyway, I had my lunch with me, and I could relax and enjoy the tranquility of my surroundings, as I usually did.

I arrived at the clearing where we made wild, passionate love. Nothing was disturbed. The grass was still soft and smelled of morning dews, and the surrounding plants around it served as a screen from any exploiting eyes.

I touched the bed of grass where I have previously surrendered my naked body, and I felt my desire building up turning into a wild conflagration. I lay down on the grass and closed my eyes. I pinched my nipple beneath my flimsy blouse. My other hand reached down my panties and with a sigh, I wiggled out of them. I hungrily discard the blouse as well and continued to fondle my tits and clit. I imagined him straddling me and penetrating me with his big hard cock and my pussy became moister. I caressed my clit with my index finger, caressing the area around my clit and fondling my nipples. I could feel my clit becoming engorged with desire.

I spread my legs and fondled and caressed, my now already tingling clit. I inserted one of my fingers inside my wet pussy. I moaned as my need for sexual fulfillment intensified. But where was he? Will he ever come back? Or was he just a product of my imagination?

How I wished he were there making love to me in the open air. I stopped frustrated as my thoughts meandered, and I couldn't seem to focus in achieving my orgasm. I was horny and frustrated and aching for him.

I ran the middle finger of my right hand up and down my clit, while my left fingers toyed with my hardened nipples. I closed my eyes again, and I could almost see his green translucent huge body mounting me. My pulses quickened and I frenziedly finger-fucked myself. In and out my middle and index finger went in and out of my yearning pussy, while my thumb flicked up and down my clit.

My nipples were so hard with desire then, and my pussy wet with an incoming orgasm. My fingers though were not enough to grant me that satisfaction. I had successfully masturbated before, but that was before I came to experience the ultimate pleasure that the green "man" has given me. Where was he? I wanted him to fuck me hard until I went mad with delight.

Frustrated, I stopped fondling myself and stayed on the grass, half-naked, waiting for him. I waited for an hour, for two hours, for three hours, but he did not come. I was angry with myself for wanting him—this alien—to show up, but my body betrayed me. I was helpless against the burning desire I had for him.

I went back home that day with a feeling of frustration and dismay. It was weird, but I knew I wouldn't give up until I would be able to meet him again. I was sure I would be going back the following day to wait for him again, hoping he would show up. I don't blame you if you call me a fool. You couldn't understand unless you were in my shoes.

And by the way, my name is Alexis, Alexis Purchet.

2 THE XENOTIAN ESCTASY

The week that followed Xen's departure was gloomy. I felt that the minutes dragged so slowly. I went about my activities the whole day like an automaton.

"I'll come back..." I can still remember his emerald eyes, vividly.

By the third day, I knew I couldn't spend the rest of my life without him. By the seventh day, I gave up trying to get him out of my mind. I kept going back, to our hidden spot in the mountain, to find him, but he still didn't show up.

During those nights that I had craved for his touch, I masturbated. One night, I slept under the tree, in my backyard, hoping he would materialize before my eyes. I made love to myself, imagining it was him doing things to my body. I fondled myself like crazy, rolling my nips between my forefinger and thumb. I imagined his mouth on my nips, as he sucked them, with gusto and his appendage, sucking and licking my clit and my G-spot, too. I moaned my pleasure and shuddered as my orgasm took over.

On the tenth day, I decided to look for him in the forest, for the last time, but I came back frustrated. Did he change his mind about me being his queen? Or, were all the events a product of my imagination?

I showered and stayed by the window, hoping against hope to see him again. I couldn't take my mind off of the kind of pleasure he had introduced me to. Just thinking about him made my pussy wet, with desire.

I must have fallen asleep, because I was awakened by a soft touch on my face. Yet, when I opened my eyes, there was darkness and just my heavy breathing. When I was about to drop into a deep sleep, again, I felt a soft caress on my thighs and I let out a sigh, I recognized that touch. He had finally returned. I let him have his fingers caress my body. I shivered, as pure pleasure spread from my groin to the rest of my flesh. I allowed the delicious feeling to spread through my entire body, as the caresses continued alternately in both my thighs. He traced the contours of my body with his kisses, from my toes, going up my legs, slowly and lingeringly. I abandoned myself to the pleasure he was giving me.

I woke up, in my bed, to the pleasant "noise" of early dawn. He was nowhere to be found. Perhaps, I have dreamed what happened last night. But, my satiated groin proved he had been there.

I was alone, again, and I felt disappointed to find him missing. "Perhaps, he has decided just to turn me into one of his Harems and not his Queen?" The thought cut like a knife in my heart. The emotion surprised me. Was I in love with him? I was certain I covet him, sexually, and I would accept his proposal on this basis, but love? I shook my head, denying what I truly felt inside. Whatever the feeling was, I was sexually sated. A sensation I thought I would never experience again.

I wondered, "Will I see him, again? Was he serious with his proposal? How long will I have to wait to be able to be with him, again?" I went back to sleep with these last thoughts.

I dreamt I was in a long tunnel, running after Xen, he was walking ahead of me, obviously, not hearing my cries. When I could not catch up with him, I slumped down, to the ground, and cried. Then, gentle hands were shaking me, urging me to wake up.

I woke up, relieved that it was all a dream and that I was in safe hands. Xen was holding me tenderly in his big, muscular arms. He looked into my eyes and said, "Don't cry, I'm here." I pinched myself, to see if I was dreaming again. The sting hurt.

I clung to him, then, knowing I would never let go of him.

"You'll never leave me like so many people I have loved did?"

The pain of losing both of my parents, just a year before, was still festering in my soul. They left me with a fortune, but I was lonely and unhappy.

"I would never leave you, now," he said through his eyes. "Remember, I want you to be my queen. Will you accept it?"

I hugged him close, not wanting to let go, again, and said, "Yes! Yes, a thousand times."

He kissed me lovingly, finding my tongue with his own and sucking it with his pliable lips that sent shooting pleasures to peripheries of my whole body. I wound my arms around his neck, as he carried me onto his lap, while we continued savoring each other's taste. His tongue was so delicious, I had to suck and nibble it like a hungry puppy.

He half knelt, as he shred the last clothing I had on, and positioned me atop his thighs. Our lips were still glued to each other, grappling with each other's tongues, biting lightly, on each other's lips and basking in the joys of kissing.

I closed my eyes, as his hands traveled the length of my body and came to a stop in my pubis. I knew he was teasing me, letting my arousal reach its peak. His appendage came out and the unadulterated pleasure began. While his right fingers were caressing the area around my clit, his left hand went up and down the length of my body, and would rest on my breasts, every now and then, to fondle my nipples.

His appendage, I didn't want to look at it, whether it's a tail or something, was giving me exquisite delight in my pussy. It was more than a cock, because it was elastic, and I could feel it sucking my G spot and moving inside my pussy, like something alive.

I arched my back and caressed the back of

his green head, as he grunted with pleasure, pulling me closer to him. All the unbelievable sensations coming from all parts of my body were incredible. It was like I was being made love to by several sex experts. I shuddered and moaned continuously, as my orgasm erupted quickly.

He was not done yet, though. He wanted to ram his enormous cock inside me. He lifted me up, by the waist with both hands, and groaned with glee, as he slammed me down, hard, into his tumescent ramrod cock.

I joined in with his groans of happiness, as we both moved to the blazing fire of our passion. I went up and down his cock, pressing my soles to the floor, as he lifted me up, with both hands. We were sweating profusely and our bodies glistened with the power of our passion.

I could feel his cock growing, bigger and bigger, as we slammed into each other's groins. The squelching sound of his big cock coming in and out of my tight, but moist, pussy, was making us even hornier.

His appendage has now inserted itself between our bodies, caressing both my breasts. This increased my pleasure even more. His mouth sought mine, every time I came down and grounded my eager pussy into his throbbing cock.

For a few minutes, we moved to that rhythm. We gasped and screamed, as we enjoyed the mundane pleasure that only extraordinary coitus could provide. We were like two speeding trains, unable to stop until we have reached our destinations. When I could no longer reign in the outbursts of incredible sensations, I cried in surrender, as out-of-this-world body vibrations took me to a heavenly place I only experienced with him.

My climax was so marvelous, I shouted his name out loud, over and over, until the waves of pleasure subsided and I collapsed against him, fulfilled and happy.

We stayed for a while, on the floor, naked and content in each other's arms.

"Will you accept my proposal?" He asked, again, through eyes. His green eyes mirroring the same intense emotions I felt at that moment.

Looking into his eyes, I knew I have now learned to love my green-eyed monster, and I was willing to cross the seventh seas for him.

Imagining him to be the King of some place was difficult for me, but it didn't matter anymore. I realized I loved him.

Xen stayed with me this time, after our wanton love making, and we had the chance to talk through our eyes. I never thought mental telepathy did work.

I was to go with him back to his kingdom. I would be his Queen. I learned that I would be the only female in his kingdom. How exciting can that be?

Misgivings crowded my mind, as I imagined the enormity of what I am getting myself into. When he saw my hesitation, he kissed me and all my niggling doubts disappeared into thin air.

I learned that he eats nothing but "grass", vegetables, and no meat. He thrives under the sun and in water. He must be another species of a plant, because he's green, as well. I smiled and he sucked on my lower lip, again, reading my thoughts.

When dusk was nearing, he told me to get what I needed for a week. I packed some jeans and t-shirts, and pocketed my cell phone. "You don't need that there," he said. I hesitated and thought. I had no friends, or relatives, to look for me. Only the household help would wonder where I've gone. I would tell them I'm going to the city for a week. They were used to my lifestyle. They knew I didn't want to be bothered, unless I summoned them. The house was so big, and the land area so spacious that I didn't get to see any of them, unless I intended to. They left me to myself most often.

My portion of the house was connected to my own little lovely garden, where I spent my afternoons. At times, I opened my gate and ventured into the mountain, to catch a breath of fresh air.

Xen and I held hands, as we departed the place where I spent most of my life, the home I had always known as a child. I felt it would be the last time I'll be seeing it again. Mariah, the housemaid, didn't seem bothered at all, when I called her up, through the intercom, and told her that I was going up to the mountain, for a week's hike.

Under the cover of the trees and the

descending darkness, we boarded a green "bubble-like" contraption that could barely contain his huge frame. I clung to his arm, as the contraption swirled and whirred, and we were up in the air.

Then, within the blink of an eye, we were in a huge, green throbbing edifice, shaped like a football. This was his kingdom and his loyal subjects were the green little creatures I had seen earlier. There were hundreds of them, and they all bowed their heads, as he carried me in his arms.

Everything around us was filled with lustrous, verdant plants that were different from the plants in my backyard. They were all gel-like, elastic, and "alive."

He brought me into a large room, where the bed was made of the gel-like plants. His bed was like a huge, green waterbed. It felt good, just lying there, and enjoying its softness.

His eyes were, once more, aflame with the fire of his desire. He was hard, again. He tore down my jeans and licked me where it counts the most, my pussy. Then, without notice, about a dozen of his subjects were around us. I tried to stand and cover myself up, but he pushed me down, gently.

They started fondling me and, after a few struggles and some encouragement from Xen, I gave up. I surrendered to their astonishing skill in pleasuring me. Two of them were on my tits, twirling my nipples with their expert tongues, sucking and caressing them, while the rest had occupied all spaces in my body, and were doing all sorts of things that made me ecstatic with desire.

Xen was exploring my pussy with his tongue and appendage. His tongue licked my clit, round and round, lapping the mound with steady pressure, while his appendage caressed the folds of my pussy. I climaxed, as his flexible tongue entered my clamoring vagina. His appendage transferred to my anus and adored it tenderly. I shuddered, as another orgasm wracked my body.

They kept on, with their pleasurable ministrations, sucking and fondling my clit and tits, licking my ears, caressing my thighs, raining kisses on my skin, until I came, again, for the third time. I felt so sexually satiated and fulfilled, but Xen was still as huge as a horse's, not yet satisfied.

When he saw I was aglow, with love for him and my sexual gratification, he finally straddled me and entered my already fully loved tunnel. I thought I was fully satiated, but when his angry penis entered me, I gasped, as my arousal ignited and I felt my flesh craving, again.

I still could not come to terms with how huge he really was, and how incredibly "delicious" he was. Whenever he fucked me, it was like I had a different kind of special "treat" that left me pleasantly astonished and that there is such a kind of unique carnal pleasure.

With each thrust of his cock, I felt the sensitive spaces in my vagina loved, and every nerve fiber responding to the strong and sucking action of his cock. He grabbed my ass and pumped harder, going all the way inside, as my cunt clung to his manhood, never wanting to let go.

"Harder, faster... babe," I screamed, as I felt a humongous orgasm ready to erupt.

My frenzied prodding made him more crazed with passion. He stood, then, and pulled me up, to a sitting position. He spread my legs. Our groins, still locked to each other, as he carried me to what seemed to be a table, and sat me there. He was standing, and my dripping pussy was totally exposed to his cock. When he lifted both of my legs with his hands and spread them wide, I moaned in excitement and eagerness. Then, with my thighs spread-eagled, he penetrated me and, oh, it was the most superb sensation I have felt in my lifetime.

He went in and out, grunting with pleasure every time he penetrated my juicy mound with his enormous cock. His appendage was rubbing my clit simultaneously. I felt several types of orgasms coming, some from his clitoral stimulation, some from my G-spot, and some from my vagina caused by his pulsating cock.

I strained to meet his thrust, as my climax was nearing.

"Fuck me baby, yes! Yes, faster... Harder..."

Then, everything broke loose, I howled and he gave out a guttural cry, as we locked our groins and allowed the mammoth sensations of delight and fulfillment wash our bodies with happiness.

The creatures stood back, watching, as their King conquered his Queen. They cheered when he roared like a lion, establishing his ownership of me. I smiled through my tears, as another orgasm carried me up certain heights of new mundane pleasure.

That happened months ago. Now, Xen and I have our little prince and princess. We named them Alexen and Xenlix. They have inherited their father's green skin and extra appendage, but they looked more "human" than their father.

If you happen to travel into the Pacific Ocean, we live in Xenot, underneath the huge boulders of the Mariana Trench. No one can see us, unless we want them to, because we live in our huge, green bubble world and blend with our surroundings.

I would say I don't regret my decision. Living with Xen and our adorable angels in his kingdom is heaven, because every moment is filled with multiple joys and pleasures for me and our children.

3 XEN AND I

The week that followed Xen's departure was gloomy. I felt that the minutes dragged so slowly. I went about my activities the whole day like an automaton.

"I'll come back..." I can still remember his emerald eyes, vividly.

By the third day, I knew I couldn't spend the rest of my life without him. By the seventh day, I gave up trying to get him out of my mind. I kept going back, to our hidden spot in the mountain, to find him, but he still didn't show up.

During those nights that I had craved for his touch, I masturbated. One night, I slept under the tree, in my backyard, hoping he would materialize before my eyes. I made love to myself, imagining it was him doing things to my body. I fondled myself like crazy, rolling my nips between my forefinger and thumb. I imagined his mouth on my nips, as he sucked them, with gusto and his appendage, sucking and licking my clit and my G-spot, too. I moaned my pleasure and shuddered as my orgasm took over.

On the tenth day, I decided to look for him in the forest, for the last time, but I came back frustrated. Did he change his mind about me being his queen? Or, were all the events a product of my imagination?

I showered and stayed by the window, hoping against hope to see him again. I couldn't take my mind off of the kind of pleasure he had introduced me to. Just thinking about him made my pussy wet, with desire.

I must have fallen asleep, because I was awakened by a soft touch on my face. Yet, when I opened my eyes, there was darkness and just my heavy breathing. When I was about to drop into a deep sleep, again, I felt a soft caress on my thighs and I let out a sigh, I recognized that touch. He had finally returned. I let him have his fingers caress my body. I shivered, as pure pleasure spread from my groin to the rest of my flesh. I allowed the delicious feeling to spread through my entire body, as the caresses continued alternately in both my thighs. He traced the contours of my body with his kisses, from my toes, going up my legs, slowly and lingeringly. I abandoned myself to the pleasure he was giving me.

I woke up, in my bed, to the pleasant "noise" of early dawn. He was nowhere to be found. Perhaps, I have dreamed what happened last night. But, my satiated groin proved he had been there.

I was alone, again, and I felt disappointed to find him missing. "Perhaps, he has decided just to turn me into one of his Harems and not his Queen?" The thought cut like a knife in my heart. The emotion surprised me. Was I in love with him? I was certain I covet him, sexually, and I would accept his proposal on this basis, but love? I shook my head, denying what I truly felt inside. Whatever the feeling was, I was sexually sated. A sensation I thought I would never experience again.

I wondered, "Will I see him, again? Was he serious with his proposal? How long will I have to wait to be able to be with him, again?" I went back to sleep with these last thoughts.

I dreamt I was in a long tunnel, running after Xen, he was walking ahead of me, obviously, not hearing my cries. When I could not catch up with him, I slumped down, to the ground, and cried. Then, gentle hands were shaking me, urging me to wake up.

I woke up, relieved that it was all a dream and that I was in safe hands. Xen was holding me tenderly in his big, muscular arms. He looked into my eyes and said, "Don't cry, I'm here." I pinched myself, to see if I was dreaming again. The sting hurt.

I clung to him, then, knowing I would never let go of him.

"You'll never leave me like so many people I have loved did?"

The pain of losing both of my parents, just a year before, was still festering in my soul. They left me with a fortune, but I was lonely and unhappy.

"I would never leave you, now," he said through his eyes. "Remember, I want you to be my queen. Will you accept it?"

I hugged him close, not wanting to let go, again, and said, "Yes! Yes, a thousand times."

He kissed me lovingly, finding my tongue with his own and sucking it with his pliable lips that sent shooting pleasures to peripheries of my whole body. I wound my arms around his neck, as he carried me onto his lap, while we continued savoring each other's taste. His tongue was so delicious, I had to suck and nibble it like a hungry puppy.

He half knelt, as he shred the last clothing I had on, and positioned me atop his thighs. Our lips were still glued to each other, grappling with each other's tongues, biting lightly, on each other's lips and basking in the joys of kissing.

I closed my eyes, as his hands traveled the length of my body and came to a stop in my pubis. I knew he was teasing me, letting my arousal reach its peak. His appendage came out and the unadulterated pleasure began. While his right fingers were caressing the area around my clit, his left hand went up and down the length of my body, and would rest on my breasts, every now and then, to fondle my nipples.

His appendage, I didn't want to look at it, whether it's a tail or something, was giving me exquisite delight in my pussy. It was more than a cock, because it was elastic, and I could feel it sucking my G spot and moving inside my pussy, like something alive.

I arched my back and caressed the back of

his green head, as he grunted with pleasure, pulling me closer to him. All the unbelievable sensations coming from all parts of my body were incredible. It was like I was being made love to by several sex experts. I shuddered and moaned continuously, as my orgasm erupted quickly.

He was not done yet, though. He wanted to ram his enormous cock inside me. He lifted me up, by the waist with both hands, and groaned with glee, as he slammed me down, hard, into his tumescent ramrod cock.

I joined in with his groans of happiness, as we both moved to the blazing fire of our passion. I went up and down his cock, pressing my soles to the floor, as he lifted me up, with both hands. We were sweating profusely and our bodies glistened with the power of our passion.

I could feel his cock growing, bigger and bigger, as we slammed into each other's groins. The squelching sound of his big cock coming in and out of my tight, but moist, pussy, was making us even hornier.

His appendage has now inserted itself between our bodies, caressing both my breasts. This increased my pleasure even more. His mouth sought mine, every time I came down and grounded my eager pussy into his throbbing cock.

For a few minutes, we moved to that rhythm. We gasped and screamed, as we enjoyed the mundane pleasure that only extraordinary coitus could provide. We were like two speeding trains, unable to stop until we have reached our destinations. When I could no longer reign in the outbursts of incredible sensations, I cried in surrender, as out-of-this-world body vibrations took me to a heavenly place I only experienced with him.

My climax was so marvelous, I shouted his name out loud, over and over, until the waves of pleasure subsided and I collapsed against him, fulfilled and happy.

We stayed for a while, on the floor, naked and content in each other's arms.

"Will you accept my proposal?" He asked, again, through eyes. His green eyes mirroring the same intense emotions I felt at that moment.

Looking into his eyes, I knew I have now learned to love my green-eyed monster, and I was willing to cross the seventh seas for him.

Imagining him to be the King of some place was difficult for me, but it didn't matter anymore. I realized I loved him.

Xen stayed with me this time, after our wanton love making, and we had the chance to talk through our eyes. I never thought mental telepathy would work, but I was dead wrong.

I was to go with him back to his kingdom. I would be his Queen. I learned that I would be the only female in his kingdom. How exciting can that be?

Misgivings crowded my mind, as I imagined the enormity of what I am getting myself into.

When he saw my hesitation, he kissed me and all my niggling doubts disappeared into thin air.

I learned that he eats nothing but "grass", vegetables, and no meat. He thrives under the sun and in water. He must be another species of a plant, because he's green, as well. I smiled and he sucked on my lower lip, again, reading my thoughts.

When dusk was nearing, he told me to get what I needed for a week. I packed some jeans and t-shirts, and pocketed my cell phone. "You don't need that there," he said. I hesitated and thought. I had no friends, or relatives, to look for me. Only the household help would wonder where I've gone. I would tell them I'm going to the city for a week. They were used to my lifestyle. They knew I didn't want to be bothered, unless I summoned them. The house was so big, and the land area so spacious that I didn't get to see any of them, unless I intended to. They left me to myself most often.

My portion of the house was connected to my own little lovely garden, where I spent my afternoons. At times, I opened my gate and ventured into the mountain, to catch a breath of fresh air.

Xen and I held hands, as we departed the place where I spent most of my life, the home I had always known as a child. I felt it would be the last time I'll be seeing it again. Mariah, the housemaid, didn't seem bothered at all, when I called her up, through the intercom, and told her that I was going up to the mountain, for a week's hike.

Under the cover of the trees and the descending darkness, we boarded a green "bubble-like" contraption that could barely contain his huge frame. I clung to his arm, as the contraption swirled and whirred, and we were up in the air.

Then, within the blink of an eye, we were in a huge, green throbbing edifice, shaped like a football. This was his kingdom and his loyal subjects were the green little creatures I had seen earlier. There were hundreds of them, and they all bowed their heads, as he carried me in his arms.

Everything around us was filled with lustrous, verdant plants that were different from the plants in my backyard. They were all gel-like, elastic, and "alive."

He brought me into a large room, where the bed was made of the gel-like plants. His bed was like a huge, green waterbed. It felt good, just lying there, and enjoying its softness.

His eyes were, once more, aflame with the fire of his desire. He was hard, again. He tore down my jeans and licked me where it counts the most, my pussy. Then, without notice, about a dozen of his subjects were around us. I tried to stand and cover myself up, but he pushed me down, gently.

They started fondling me and, after a few struggles and some encouragement from Xen, I gave up. I surrendered to their astonishing skill in pleasuring me. Two of them were on my tits, twirling my nipples with their expert tongues, sucking and caressing them, while the rest had occupied all spaces in my body, and were doing all sorts of things that made me ecstatic with desire.

Xen was exploring my pussy with his tongue and appendage. His tongue licked my clit, round and round, lapping the mound with steady pressure, while his appendage caressed the folds of my pussy. I climaxed, as his flexible tongue entered my clamoring vagina. His appendage transferred to my anus and adored it tenderly. I shuddered, as another orgasm wracked my body.

They kept on, with their pleasurable ministrations, sucking and fondling my clit and tits, licking my ears, caressing my thighs, raining kisses on my skin, until I came, again, for the third time. I felt so sexually satiated and fulfilled, but Xen was still as huge as a horse's, not yet satisfied.

When he saw I was aglow, with love for him and my sexual gratification, he finally straddled me and entered my already fully loved tunnel. I thought I was fully satiated, but when his angry penis entered me, I gasped, as my arousal ignited and I felt my flesh craving, again.

I still could not come to terms with how huge he really was, and how incredibly "delicious" he was. Whenever he fucked me, it was like I had a different kind of special "treat" that left me pleasantly astonished and that there is such a kind of unique carnal pleasure.

With each thrust of his cock, I felt the sensitive spaces in my vagina loved, and every nerve fiber responding to the strong and sucking action of his cock. He grabbed my ass and pumped harder, going all the way inside, as my cunt clung to his manhood, never wanting to let go.

"Harder, faster... babe," I screamed, as I felt a humongous orgasm ready to erupt.

My frenzied prodding made him more crazed with passion. He stood, then, and pulled me up, to a sitting position. He spread my legs. Our groins, still locked to each other, as he carried me to what seemed to be a table, and sat me there. He was standing, and my dripping pussy was totally exposed to his cock. When he lifted both of my legs with his hands and spread them wide, I moaned in excitement and eagerness. Then, with my thighs spread-eagled, he penetrated me and, oh, it was the most superb sensation I have felt in my lifetime.

He went in and out, grunting with pleasure every time he penetrated my juicy mound with his enormous cock. His appendage was rubbing my clit simultaneously. I felt several types of orgasms coming, some from his clitoral stimulation, some from my G-spot, and some from my vagina caused by his pulsating cock.

I strained to meet his thrust, as my climax was nearing.

"Fuck me baby, yes! Yes, faster... Harder..."

Then, everything broke loose, I howled and he gave out a guttural cry, as we locked our groins and allowed the mammoth sensations of delight and fulfillment wash our bodies with happiness.

The creatures stood back, watching, as their King conquered his Queen. They cheered when he roared like a lion, establishing his ownership of me. I smiled through my tears, as another orgasm carried me up certain heights of new mundane pleasure.

That happened months ago. Now, Xen and I have our little prince and princess. We named them Alexen and Xenlix. They have inherited their father's green skin and extra appendage, but they looked more "human" than their father.

If you happen to travel into the Pacific Ocean, we live in Xenot, underneath the huge boulders of the Mariana Trench. No one can see us, unless we want them to, because we live in our huge, green bubble world and blend with our surroundings.

I would say I don't regret my decision. Living with Xen and our adorable angels in his kingdom is heaven, because every moment is filled with multiple joys and pleasures for me and our children.

4 THE STIRRINGS OF PLEASURE
PART 1

The refreshing, cool water lapped my feet and slowly coursed through my body. I closed my eyes to savor the calmness that settled within me. There was silence, except for the smooth sound of water rushing down the stream that gave me a feeling of peace and contentment.

It was late afternoon and the sun was just settling down west, mirroring a shimmering orange hue downstream. The lush vegetation surrounding the stream looked surreal amidst the orange overcast. It was a lovely summer afternoon.

I had just come home from the university for a summer vacation. I went horseback riding in the woods and over the acres of pasture that I had grown in as a child. That was a passion I had never let go since I was 6 years old and through my teen years. I closed my eyes and basked in the calmness that nature exudes and thought how nice it was to be home again.

I opened my eyes to a handsome face, just inches from my own. Startled, I drew away and exclaimed, "who are you?"

"I'm Ron, and you?"

I stared at his full, confident lips and was jolted with the feeling of desire I felt in my groins. He must have read my thoughts because he inched closer to me and said, "I get that reaction very often. Am I that attractive?" And then he roared with laughter.

I felt his overwhelming sex appeal oozing that very moment and I turned a beet red realizing this. I countered however, "you must have read the opposite meaning of my thoughts."

"Hmmm, okay. If you deny it, then it's fine with me," then he laughed again. "Come, I'll tour you around," he said.

It was my turn to laugh.

"I own this place. I'm Arya, Arya McComb."

That disconcerted him, but only for a moment. "I apologize, Miss McComb. I imagined you to be a proper lady with all the frills and the coffered hair."

I smiled and allowed him to lead me. I was in a T-shirt and jeans and I knew I looked younger than my age of 25. I liked him, he was sexy, and I could feel I needed a good fuck. I was wet between my legs.

We walked a few steps into one of the shaded grassy areas and sat fully aware of the electricity of lust coursing through our veins. I looked at him and smiled, while I stretched my body seductively on the soft grass.

He needed no further prodding. He lowered himself on top of me and kissed me. His kisses grew hungry and his hands crept inside my undies to tweak my clit. His fingers went up and down the lips of my pussy, while his thumb fondled my mound of desire. His action brought smoldering and delightful sensation in my groin that was making me writhe with joy.

I opened my eyes still feeling the pleasures between my thighs to the darkness that was beginning to envelope the wilderness. The heat of his body against mine made me horny as his manhood felt so hard on my abdomen. From my pussy, his hands roamed my body and settled on my tits tweaking each alternately. His gentle caresses evoked emotions I couldn't seem to control.

The gratifying sensations heightened as my pussy moistened, eager to be satisfied. The delightful pleasure was out of my control as my arousal spread like wildfire from my pussy to the other parts of my body.

He must be about six feet tall with a lean and supple body. I felt his tongue raking mine, searching all the sweet points that his tongue can reach. I closed my eyes and surrendered myself to the heady sweetness that invaded my mind and body as if my desire has a mind of its own. I savored the unadulterated pleasure. Against my rational mind, my body responded arduously to his ministrations.

The slow sweetness that started between my thighs quickly suffused my entire being as he continued to explore my mouth, twirling his tongue with mine, nibbling my lips and the inner recesses of my mouth with tenderness.

I felt there was pleasure coming everywhere, from my mouth, my tits, and my pussy. It was making me crazy.

He went down to my vagina and I felt my clit getting all the attention, being sucked and licked and my tits being rolled between his thumb and forefinger so teasingly slow and gentle, evoking more sensation after sensation that I didn't know existed.

The overpowering sweetness in my mouth combined with the blazing feeling as every cell in my desire-swollen and yearning pussy basked at every contact it got.

I was lost to the most delightful feeling I ever encountered in my 25 years, and my pussy was so wet and wanting, screaming for fulfillment. I thought "Oh my god, I can die right now."

The desire kept mounting as he persisted on sucking and licking my clit and his fingers were inside me, reaching my G-spot and teasing it oh so expertly. I didn't know what to expect; I just wanted this fiery feeling to be sated.

I was writhing and moaning. Then, I felt him leave my pussy and I cried out for him to continue whatever he was doing down there.

He opened my legs wider and I was trembling from want. He held his dick and slid it up and down my pussy without really penetrating. The moment his dick touched my labia, I felt like a furnace, so hot and pulsating with desire.

I squirmed and lifted my butt to meet his

dick as pure sweetness and pleasure pervaded my whole being. I felt him insert his dick head in my pussy and pulled it out.

Again, he entered me pushing another inch deeper and pulling it out again. He did it the third time penetrating and pushing yet another inch deeper and slowly oh so slowly pulling it out creating a sensation so incomparable to anything I have ever felt.

The pleasurable sensation was so great I nearly exploded. This time, I felt him push so deep and the exquisite ecstasy I felt was beyond description. I was stunned with how "delicious" he was. I felt my pussy stretched to its limits to accommodate his rock-hard and so huge dick. It filled my pussy completely.

Slowly, he moved his hips in a circular motion that made his penis move inside my vagina, creating a friction that slowly replaced the pain with yet more intense pleasure.

I moaned with delight. I didn't know such pleasures existed. He pounded deeper and faster as he kissed me passionately urging me to unite with him as our tongues twirled and twined with each other creating blazing conflagration of passion, clamoring for fulfillment.

His swollen penis pulsated inside my pussy like it was ready to burst. I felt my pussy widen to allow his dick inside and tighten around it as he penetrated and reached my G-spot. It increased my arousal that transcended all else.

My body voluntarily arched to meet him, eager for more pleasure, wanting to reach the conclusion of this intense sensation. His dick went in and out my pussy that was already dripping with juices. He moaned and pounded more aggressively and quicker and quicker, his breath was labored. I felt like my sanity was leaving me.

I felt the gush of his juice inside me as I exploded shuddering with my delight and tears started rolling down my cheeks. No amount of words can describe the pleasure that I felt that moment. It was just pure and exquisite sweetness.

He slumped on top of me still with his dick deeply buried in my very core. I felt his dick still so large inside me. It was still hot and hard. I was a picture of sexual contentment, sated to the brim, but when he started to move inside me, I felt my desire stir once again.

I didn't believe I could get horny a few minutes just after an explosive release, but my body temperature was rising again. My pussy vibrated in anticipation of what was to come. I returned every kiss I got with more passion and pleasure as he explored my mouth eliciting moans from me. He took my tits in his mouth and licked and sucked and rolled it in his tongue.

He rolled on his back and I was on top. I took over and kissed him exploring his tongue reaching his pleasure points. I took his lips in my mouth and sucked and licked as I rubbed my pussy lightly. He was rock-hard again. He growled "yes, oh yes." My pussy was burning hot as flesh rubbed against flesh.

I was trembling as pinches of desire spread from my groin to the rest of my body. The exquisite pleasure racked my body as I persisted to rub my pussy over his dick. "Ah, it feels good, oh god" I murmured.

I traced his body with my tongue and caressed his abdomen. He thrust his hips up to meet my lips. I grasped his dick with my fingers and massaged it from base to tip while licking and sucking its tip.

He groaned and grabbed my head and held it as I took him completely in my mouth and moved my head up and down his dick. His dick was glistening and taut with his desire.

I squatted on top of him with my pussy on his mouth and his dick in mine. I squealed with delight as he adored my clit, licking and sucking. His fingers inside my pussy teased my G-spot.

The sweet sensation he was creating in my groin was mounting as minutes passed, but he persisted to finger my pussy and suck my clit with more vigor. The pleasure spiraled and I nearly had my orgasm.

I mounted him as he held my hips helping me go up and down his shaft. It was oh so sweet. I was a fiery sex goddess seeking sexual fulfillment and satisfaction.

"Yes faster, faster, harder" he growled.

Suddenly, he pulled away, stood, and carried me with him. He braced my legs around his waist and penetrated once again. I clung to his neck as he pushed me against a tree and fucked me with all his might. His thrusts were so powerful I screamed "oh god, yes please fuck me harder."

Huge waves of orgasm washed my body, but he continued to thrust his dick inside me, as I came again, and again, and again.

He growled his orgasm and I felt his body stiffen as he spurted his semen inside my pussy. Our combined juices trickled down our legs as we locked our groins together in ecstasy. After some time, he gently put me down on the grassy bank of the stream.

The following morning, I woke up to the bright morning sunshine in my own room overlooking the wilderness, and the vast pastureland just beyond. I was feeling refreshed and sated. Suddenly, the memories of last night came rushing back.

I felt my pussy starting to get moist. When I can no longer contain my desire, I went back to the stream and sat down where Ron and I made passionate love last night. The grassy bank bore no indication that we did roll and made love on them. The grasses were so fresh.

I went back to the house disappointed and growing more puzzled. I have been living with my dad for five years until he got married again a year ago and left me for California where he and his new wife built a new family that I was not part of.

My only companions were my horses and a couple who keep the house for me and care for the horses. I kept to myself. I was never one who enjoyed going out with friends. All of my time is spent at work and my horses. When I asked them where Ron was, they said he went to the city for some legal business. He was a lawyer. I learned my father appointed him as his corporate secretary. I missed him. I lay down on the bed willing myself to sleep.

Two weeks had passed after the incident,

but the memory was as vivid as if it happened an hour ago. I kept going back to the stream hoping he would come back soon, but to my disappointment, I was informed that he had to go stay in the city for a few weeks, for some important business.

It was a beautiful Saturday and I decided to cultivate my flower plot at the back of the house. It was almost three weeks now. I didn't notice the time until I felt tiredness overcome my body. I stretched underneath the tree.

I must have slept a long time because when I woke up the sun was setting down and coldness came breezing in. I felt my body ablaze with sweet feelings. I wondered if I was dreaming. I looked around; there was no one there.

My desire was mounting as the memories came back. I ran my hand caressingly over my thin clothing. I stopped on my nips and I unbuttoned my blouse and rolled my nips between my thumb and forefinger. My thoughts kept going back to the night he was having sex with me.

I imagined him touching my sensitive parts from my nips to my pussy. Licking and sucking my clit with fingers inside me. The tip of his dick teased my pussy, sliding it over my labia again and again. His dick penetrating my very core evoked the sweetest feeling that I've ever experienced. His big hard dick quickly pounding and humping that made me scream my multiple orgasms.

I closed my eyes and writhed as my other hands reached for my mound caressing and sliding over it. I pinched my clit rubbing it vigorously as my arousal mounted. I was moist and eager for yet another head-blowing experience.

I inserted a finger in my pussy and I cried out as the powerful sweet feeling suffused my pussy. I opened my legs wider, exposing my pussy to the dark night. I willed myself to believe it was him fingering me, teasing and penetrating, and my pussy got wet. I imagined his tongue forcefully sliding up and down my pussy then tongue my clit and sucking it. My clit was engorged with my arousal yearning for satisfaction and my pussy was eager to close around his dick.

I was going nuts as my arousal increased and I screamed as waves of orgasmic feeling that emanated from my now engorged pussy and spread throughout my body threatened to explode. I concentrated on imagining him fucking me so hard and fast, urging me to come "yes come baby, yes gush it out."

"Oh god, yes fuck me please" I prayed.

In my mind, it was his powerful and fast pumping and deep penetration that brought intense sensation and catapulted me to euphoria. Waves and waves of my orgasm racked my body until I lay down spent with so much juices dripping down my pussy. I was sated beyond imagination. This I thought is something I would like to experience again as I looked up in the sky and wished Ron would hurry back home.

5 THE STIRRINGS OF PLEASURE
PART 2

Beethoven music played softly at the background as I sat at a corner of a dimly lit bar on a beautiful summer evening. I was sipping a sherry and enjoying the cozy ambiance of the place. It was my first time to enter the renowned "Angel's Place" that I've heard a lot about. It was a haven found at the northern most part of our small town, away from the hassles of city life. It radiated an aura of peace, homely atmosphere, and friendly welcoming aesthetics.

It seemed to beckon to anyone passing by to go in, as if there was a billboard "come on in, you will be treated like royalty." That why I found myself listening to the soft music and drinking red wine all by myself. I was missing Ron and I was horny as hell.

A waiter approached me asking if I needed

anything more. I shook my head, leaned on the couch headrest, and closed my eyes as the music pervaded my senses. This is a place that allows you to be yourself and reminisce the past, a perfect place for someone who wanted to reminisce. It was an excellent hide away.

I observed the crackling fire on the fireplace. I closed my eyes savoring the tranquility I felt. I raised my feet on the throw pillows and rested my head on the couch. Anyway, the place is almost deserted. The divider was keeping me out of the view of anyone occupying the seats on the outer room.

I was totally concealed and was left alone by the bar staff. It was like I was in my own home with nobody to talk to. The only difference is that I could hear the occasional clinking of glasses as they poured drinks for their few customers.

My thoughts turned to the guy who had given me the most amazing sexual experience I ever had. Ron did not come back from the city. I learned later that my father fired him for the "affair" that we had. Did the trees around us have ears and eyes? I kept wondering.

Where was he? It has been months since the incident. I lost count of the days I was left wondering if I will ever see him again; the nights I yearned to feel his hands over my body and his lips on mine, the longing that nearly destroyed my sanity. My father was aware of my unbridled sexual desires and had tried to contain me by keeping me cooped up in the house.

I forced myself to refrain from recalling the memories of that night until today.

My heart beat increased and I felt my pussy respond as my thoughts of him run wild. It became moist as pleasure stirred in me. I smiled at how potent my thoughts of him are.

I looked back at the events of that fateful day when I met Ron and made wild, passionate love. I willed myself to veer away from thinking of him but it just got me frustrated. As minutes ticked by, I found myself yearning for his touch. I inserted my fingers underneath my panty and rubbed my pussy, surrendering myself to the pleasure building up in my groin. I was wishing he was there to give me the exquisite feeling and fulfill my cravings. The previous days I masturbated frequently to assuage my yearnings for Ron.

I rubbed my engorged clit faster and quicker as my arousal rose to heights beyond imagination. I was writhing and moaning as the sweetness intensified. I felt like a ball of fire, burning with my desire.

Then, I felt my lips being kissed so gently, I opened my eyes to the most beautiful man I ever saw. It was Ron! I was shocked at seeing him. Perhaps, I was imagining things because of my desire for him? I stared at him as he looked down at me with eyes as blue as the skies. I felt an upsurge of tender feelings, aside from the passion I had nurtured for him.

He picked me up like a feather and brought me to a room. Then, he stood there tall and sleek like a Greek god who just came down from Mt. Olympus. He had stripped naked; his penis was standing huge and proud. I stared at it and thought: "Was this the same dick that entered my pussy a few months back? How did my pussy accommodate a dick as big as this?" It must be 8 inches long and it was really huge.

I looked at his nakedness and a delightful feeling stirred between my thighs. My cunt began to get wet as I continued to stare at his glistening dick that occasionally trembles and seemed to be responding to my stares. He looked at me with those blue eyes as if begging me to open up to him. I was getting hornier every minute as he continued to stand there, waiting for something to happen.

The next moment, he held my face and brushed my lips with his thumbs. He replaced them with his lips and nibbled and explored my mouth, finding my pleasure points. His hands traveled from my breast down my mound to my eager pussy.

I felt suddenly shy as Ron pleasured me with his touch reaching out to my private parts. He knew me very well—where to find my most erotic parts and how to arouse me. I felt the rekindling of my arousal escalating with every flick of his tongue and pinch from his fingers. My pussy was responding on its own, tightening the muscles to close in on his fingers. Multiple waves of delightful sensations overwhelmed me.

He stood up and carried me to the couch and made me sit. He knelt down in front of me and spread my legs wide as he came down on me. I leaned on the couch as he licked my pussy over my panty. "Oh so sweet" I thought. The friction between his tongue, my panty, and my pussy was creating a sweet ecstasy that was making me crazy as I grasped his hair and held him there, pushing his face to my moist, hungry pussy.

He raised my legs on his shoulders exposing my now swollen and red pussy. He pushed aside my panty and traced its contours with his tongue, lingering on my clit licking and rolling. I relished whatever he was doing to me and writhed as a tsunami wave of pleasure ruled my body. It seemed it was not going to end there, as wave after wave of the sweetest sensations assaulted my whole body.

My clit was so engorged of want as it was adored, licked, flicked, and sucked, and my G-spot teased by his fingers. There was a series of ripples of unadulterated desire sweeping my whole being. I clipped his shoulder to me with my legs, while he lapped and fingered me.

"Ohhhh so good" I murmured.

His whole body glistened with sweat and his dick was so long and powerful with all its veins visible and stretched to the limits. It was all swollen. He moved forward and I gently touched his penis. It vibrated in my hands like it was a ticking bomb. I held his shaft at the base and I licked the tip with my tongue, tasting and licking it. I looked up and he grunted as he closed his eyes, savoring the sensations coursing through his throbbing shaft.

With the tip of his shaft in my mouth, I massaged firmly the base moving my hand up and down, and sucking and licking the crown of his dick. He grabbed my head and pushed me as he trembled of want. I took his dick fully in my mouth and started to go up and down with my mouth. My hands gently massaged his balls to synchronize with my sucking. It was so large and hard and quivering with his arousal.

"Yes, harder babe, harder, oh god" he groaned.

I increased my tempo, and suddenly, he pulled me up and let me kneel on the couch on all fours. He slapped my butt cheek and rubbed his dick on my pussy in a circular motion. He rubbed it on the surface of my pussy in mesmerizing slowness that I groaned and thrust back my butt into his face. His hands held me on my waist to steady my butt. I squirmed with delight. The sensation was so intensely sweet, real sweet.

I cried out "fuck me please, oh please."

He spread my legs wider and plunged his dick deep into the folds of my slick pussy until it was completely buried inside me. He started to hump wildly and it was heaven.

I can feel the fire spread from my groin to my body. I met his every thrust by pushing my butt toward him. It was so exquisitely delightful. I never thought it could be as blissful as this. My desire was out of bounds; my cunt was an inferno burning with intensity and craving for fulfillment. I can no longer control my desire. I was crazy with the powerful sensations ruling my body.

His dick has found my core, teasing it and rediscovering my other pleasure points inside my pussy—every nerve was burning. It felt like a furnace with all the sensations that was threatening to blow my mind. My pussy was crying out, as it tightened around his dick every time it penetrated me. As his dick entered my pussy and pierce my G-spot, the muscles in my cunt squeezed his dick creating a dizzying sensation.

He continued to tease my G-spot with his humps, pulling and pushing his dick faster and quicker. Faster, faster, and faster I grabbed the pillows and bit with the upsurge of my arousal. My orgasm came in huge tons of waves coming one after the other, assaulting my senses. There were explosions in my mind as I climaxed over and over.

I felt the sudden surge of his hot semen as he poured it all inside my pussy. The feeling of the semen flowing like lava in the recesses of my cunt heightened the sweetness and caused me to cum again. "Oh, yes" I cried in pleasure. It was pure heaven.

The strength of my orgasm left me so weak; I slumped on the couch face down. He was leaning on me with his dick still buried in my pussy twitching and vibrating as his orgasm slowly receded. His breath was labored with the intensity of the sexual encounter.

We collapsed on the bed and dozed off for a few minutes. Words were no longer necessary. I felt arousal stir inside me anew, when his dick rubbed against my thigh. Quickly, he became engorged and ready to pounce again. I felt my pussy beginning to warm when he straddled me and went in and out with his enormous penis. I couldn't believe I could easily be aroused minutes after a passionate sex.

"I love you, Lady McComb," he murmured passionately into my ears.

Ron embraced and kissed me tenderly as he made slow and gentle foreplay. I can feel the delicious sensation mount as he caressed my boobs from behind and rained kisses on every inch of my skin. After running his tongue from my toe to my thighs and up my tits, he gave me a mind-blowing cunnilingus.

He licked the area around my pubis, the lips of my pussy, before finally concentrating on my clitoris. I was crying as I climaxed from his fingers and tongue ministrations. It was one of the purest orgasms I ever had. After I climaxed, he fucked me again with vigor, in quick and powerful strokes that left me gasping and screaming with fulfillment. Then, we both groaned as we reached our climax once again.

He stood up and pulled me with him. He asked me to put on my clothes because we were going somewhere. I did as I was told. We rode on his Jaguar, and in a few minutes, I found myself in a beautiful hotel at the outskirts of our town. This was a place I've never been to. My dad would blow his top if he learned I was with Ron, but I realized now that I loved him.

We went into room 456, a suite that overlooked the wide garden and the forested area of the Mt. resort. It was a romantic and spectacular scene.

He looked at me lovingly, "Will you marry me?" he intoned.

I was shocked. Teary-eyed, I nodded my head vigorously and collapsed into his arms. I never wanted to be away from him again nor wanted to go back to the empty house again. I would go wherever he took me, I vowed to myself.

He removed my clothes slowly, kissing each exposed area hungrily. When the last clothing fell off my body, he removed his own clothes and happily melded his body with my own. We both sighed with pleasure as our bodies ignited anew with each other's touch.

He embraced me in all our nakedness. I responded eagerly as he kissed me so tenderly and carried me to the bath tub. He let me sit down on the edge of the bath as he continued to kiss me. He licked my nips and sucked them alternately. He was teasing all my pleasure points with his tongue, determined to make me go crazy for the nth time.

I gave in to whatever he was doing with my body and just savor all the delightful sensations I felt. I lay down on the marble top beside the tub as he teased my tits, my lips, and my cunt. He kissed me as he pointed the spurting strong warm water of the shower to my pussy. The force of the water aroused me more; it felt like I was being tongued, my body trembled as I lifted my butt to meet the water.

Then, he replaced the shower with his dick. I was nearing my orgasm by now. He took my lips in his as he penetrated me with ease and started to fuck me again for the third time in one day. He increased his tempo, raising my arousal higher with his every thrust.

Even then, the yummy sensations didn't diminish. It even increased as he found more pleasure points and knew how to make me moan.

"Yes fuck me harder, yes harder please."

I cried out as my orgasm overwhelmed me. I was bursting with my desire gushing out of my cunt as I came once, twice, and thrice; the orgasm kept coming like a tornado ripping me off my breath. The delicious sensation was so intense that it caused momentary loss of my consciousness. There was nothing there except the exquisite sensations that I felt. It was a sweet surrender as Ron crushed my lips with his and spurted out his semen in my pussy. We clung to each other and collapsed against each other satiated and happy.

He pulled me to him and I curled up to fit his body. He kissed my forehead and said "I love you Arya McComb, and I want you to look forward to life with me, as Mrs. Potter."

6 THE CLAMOR OF THE MOUNTAINS

Aganas stood looking down at the miniature huts at the foot of the mountain. He had carried a bundle of wood on his sinewy shoulders and had decided to take a rest on the mountain top before finally heading home.

It had been a hectic week in the fields and the "kaingin" (mountain farm) that Aganas wanted to be left behind so he could start working early in the morning, but his "ama" (father) and "ina" (mother) were insistent he had to welcome the visitors from town. He was the "pangulo" (head) of the youth in their village, and he had always been assigned that duty. He finally stood up and his muscles rippled as he lifted the bundle onto his shoulders.

When he arrived at the village, the old folk had already lined up at the riverbank for the visitors. The river surrounded the village, so it served as the portal of entry and exit for those visiting their far-flung village. It also served as their foremost bastion of defense against other tribes who wanted to invade their village.

There were only 300 families and there were no roads leading to it, except for a perilous man-made trail that skirted the two mountains from the town of Ginaang. The village was composed of brave men who did not hesitate to behead any person who entered their territory uninvited.

"There they are," the folk along the riverbank were pointing at the arriving group at the opposite bank. "I think they can't swim well," one of the men said to Aganas as the guide was waving his arms for help.

Aganas and the village men had no clothes on, except for G-strings, which covered only their most private parts, their penis and balls. Aganas stripped off his G-string and plunged into the river; being the tallest and strongest among the young men, he was tasked to help the visitors from the neighboring town to cross the river.

As he emerged from the swirling rapids, he saw her then; she was draped by the dazzling sun's rays, like a virgin on a pedestal, so pure and so lovely. Aganas blinked and stood momentarily stunned by the exotic beauty before him. She had a small, aquiline nose prettily perched above her full pink lips, and her heavily lashed, big, brown eyes peered at Aganas' naked body as he resumed walking toward her.

"I'm Aganas,"

"Lucy, here," she murmured and avoided his eyes, conscious of his nakedness, and he, oblivious of it.

Aganas was surprised that a town girl could be shy. From what he has heard, they were forward and liberated, or was she just pretending? She must be the exception. There were two more girls from town, with some of the village girls who studied in town.

"You'll have to let go of your heavy clothing," Aganas said to Lucy. "It will hamper our movements. The current is strong."

Lucy knew how to swim but she was not an expert; the swirling waters looked dangerous from where she stood. Silently, she peeled off the layer of clothing from her body. She hesitated when all that was left were her undies.

Aganas gave her a look that seemed to say: "discard those unnecessary strips of clothing, what are you ashamed of?"

Lucy knew nudity to the village people was part of their lives. She learned from schoolmates that married women, even when not bathing, go topless with just a "tapis" (a woven rectangular piece of clothing) around their waste to cover their private parts. There was nothing underneath the piece of material. When they bathe, they discard everything, without feeling conscious about their nakedness.

When she let go of the last piece of clothing from her body, however, there was a visible gasp of amazement from Aganas. She was a goddess, Aganas thought as he held his breath when Lucy's fair unblemished skin and taut, firm luscious breasts were revealed from beneath.

"Let's go," Aganas grabbed Lucy's hand and lead her to the water.

He could feel Lucy's warm, soft skin against his, and this sent shivers through his body. Aganas was unaware that Lucy was also experiencing the same electrifying sensations. Lucy felt like she was zapped by 1,000 volts of live wire.

The cold waters of the swirling river did nothing to assuage Aganas and Lucy's fiery bodies; the flames were slowly but steadily growing. Lucy was confident she could swim on her own, but the strong current swept her. Aganas expected this and was ready to pluck her out of the water with his strong, sinewy arms.

"Here, hold on to my back," Aganas hissed at Lucy. "There's no time to waste; the river is swelling."

It was still not raining, but the roll of thunder in the distance meant rain has already started upstream.

Aganas turned his back to her, and Lucy placed both hands on Aganas' shoulders. He felt her soft luscious breasts rest on his back and he was surprised at his reaction. He had never been so fired up with a woman's touch. Oh, such softness, he thought.

Lucy felt her breasts come in contact with the rough skin of his back and she felt her senses jolted; he had an animal magnetism that was difficult to avoid. Oh, how manly his body was.

"You'll have to cling on more firmly. You can't hold on in that position for long," Aganas said softly.

"Do you want me to stay in front of you?" she wanted to say, but she chuckled instead. The spot between her legs was starting to quiver with excitement.

Aganas turned around again and instructed Lucy to climb on his back like he was carrying her. The local folk were talking like there was nothing unusual happening. Lucy climbed on Aganas' back and wound her hands around his neck.

Lucy could feel her pussy warm against his rough skin. It was a sweet sensation that aroused her. Aganas, on the other hand, felt the warmth on his back and he felt his arousal coming. He had never been aroused this way before. In fact, he didn't even know that a touch of a woman's body would cause such sensations in him. Quickly, he swam further, submerging both their bodies into the water where no one could witness his growing erection.

Aganas was flabbergasted with how he reacted. He tried to control his emotions, but he was not able to. He had never been aroused with any girl that he had helped swim across the river, and he had done this a hundred times since he learned how to swim.

Both Lucy and Aganas were silent as

Aganas did the swimming, and Lucy just held on to her position behind him. Lucy could feel her clit rubbing on his back as they water eddied around them. She couldn't help herself but to increase the friction and enjoy the pleasure. She moved up and down his back in small circles, pressing her already engorged clit into his back.

Aganas was astonished. What was she doing? He was acutely aware of Lucy's movements on his back, and his erection was growing bigger. It was still a long way to the other bank, but it would be shameful to appear at the other side of the river with an enormous erection. In their village, a man had to know how to control and ease his erection. He may have had wet dreams and some masturbation, but at 18, he still had yet to experience to making love.

In the village, there were no formal marriages, but when a woman and a man consummate the sexual intercourse, they were considered married in the eyes of the village folk and Kabuniyan (God.) He had yet to find a girl who could raise his desire.

They were at the middle now of the wide river and still Aganas' erection was not subsiding but was growing bigger instead. Lucy made no effort to conceal what she was doing. She was now rubbing her tits back and forth against his back.

Aganas heard about town girls being forward but he was not ready for this. Obviously, Lucy needed a good fuck. He was a conflagration of passion too as his body responded to Lucy's erotic movements.

Aganas knew they could not appear on the other side with their bodies betraying what they felt. He knew they had to satisfy their lust. What was happening to him? He had always been a level-headed man, but he couldn't explain why he lost control of his body. He just wanted to fuck her long and hard.

He turned his head to rest an inch away from Lucy's. "Do you want to go somewhere else?" he asked hoarsely. Lucy could no longer contain her passion. She lapped his lips with her tongue and groaned, "Yes, yes, away from prying eyes."

In the descending dusk, they were just two blobs in the river, indistinct to the people on both sides of the river. The rest of Lucy's group was being helped by the rest of the men, and they were left alone. Aganas knew no one would miss them if they slipped quickly.

Aganas bobbed unobtrusively in the river's current and allowed himself to be carried downstream. When he was sure, they were a safe distance away, he swam to a bushy area that was completely hidden from people in the surrounding area.

By then, Lucy had shifted her back position to Aganas' front body and was rubbing her groin against Aganas. Aganas' penis was now as big as a horse's. He was so aroused; his face was a beet red and was trembling of passion.

When the water was waist-deep, he

carried her like she weighed just a few pounds and quickly deposited her on the fine, gray sand. Aganas was beyond control now. He mounted her and uttered a guttural sound as his rock-hard cock was enveloped by Lucy's slick and eager pussy.

Lucy moaned and cried in ecstasy as Aganas fucked her hard, going in and out of her pussy in fast and quick strokes. So, this is how it feels, heaven! Aganas thought. He never fucked a woman before because he didn't have any inclination to do so, but today, he lost all his senses over this seemingly timid woman. She was a tigress, meeting his thrust with her own grinding her pelvis into his and clawing at his back like there was no tomorrow.

He went in and out of Lucy's pussy, savoring each entry with his dick and enjoying the exquisite ecstasy that coitus provides. Aganas gave an animal growl as he ejected his thick semen into Lucy's tight pussy and collapsed against her.

Lucy came too, but she knew, there was still more pleasure she could get from him, if she could teach him right. She knew natives were not familiar with foreplay or the art of lovemaking. She learned from her friends that in the village, lovemaking was only deemed necessary to bear children.

From the distance, they could hear people calling out their names. They quickly disengaged and washed to erase traces of their fiery lovemaking.

During the night, there was a program prepared for the town visitors. Native wine and cakes were passed around as the young people danced and sang around a blazing bonfire.

Aganas was nowhere to be seen. He was hidden, far from the bonfire and was in a state of confusion. What made him do what he just did with Lucy? The implication is that he will have to marry her, if the village's rules are applied.

But Lucy was not a villager; the "pangat" (village leaders) would surely oppose it. And did he really want to marry her? Aganas shook his head and stared broodingly at the star-studded sky. Kabuniyan, what would I do now? He asked his God.

In the circle of the bonfire, Lucy was seated with the other girls. They were laughing as the kids tried to teach them the lyrics of the song. Lucy was looking forward to meet her Greek idol again. She likened Aganas to one of the Greek gods she had read in her literature class. He was good-looking, not the cute boy type, but the rough, brawny type. It was obvious, it was the first for him, but she would teach him, she was a master of that. This would make her short adventure more interesting.

Lucy was not a tyro in sexual encounters,

as she was a natural flirt and boasted about her sexual exploits to her friends. Aganas was just another sex adventure for her. She smiled to herself as she remembered how fast the native man caved in. That was an easy target, she reminisced.

She couldn't deny though that his cock was one of the tastiest she had ever encountered. Her pussy started to get wet when she imagined how she would do fellatio. The naïve man may die with the pleasure, he had never experienced before. She laughed out loud with the thought.

The night wore on with Aganas not showing up in the festivities. He was by the riverbank, watching absentmindedly the shimmering river in the moonlit night. He was still at a loss on how to react to Lucy once they see each other again. His penis reacted instinctively, hardening, whenever he went back to their wanton sexual encounter earlier. She must be some kind of enchantress, he murmured to himself.

Aganas was lost to his thoughts unaware that it was nearing midnight. He could hear the distant roar of laughter and song from the small plaza, where the program was held. Then he could see flickering torches and babbles of voices approaching.

"There he is," he heard his friend Naganag called out to the others. Naganag knew this was Aganas' favorite hiding place.

"Hey, we've been looking for you. You have to brief Lucy about the activities tomorrow," Naganag said.

Aganas face was impassioned as he turned and said, "Let them rest first, I can orient them tomorrow."

And with that, he left, not looking at Lucy.

Lucy was aghast. Why was he acting strangely? Was he afraid? He does not have to because I would not be marrying a native, she cursed inwardly. Who was he anyway?

"Hey, Aganas," Lucy caught up with him. "I can put off rest for a while; can you just give me a 5-minute instruction of where I can start tomorrow?"

They were all looking at him, waiting tensely. Naganag had never seen Aganas looked like he was looking now – lost.

When there was no answer after a few minutes, Lucy instructed the rest to go ahead. They left them standing there eyeing one another but not talking.

Without a word, Lucy caressed his penis against his G-string. Lucy smiled as Aganas cock sprang into life quickly.

Aganas was trying hard not to react and he pushed her feebly, but his arousal was like another entity on its own, growing and expanding until he gave in and allowed Lucy's hands to tease him.

Lucy felt triumphant, she was sure now, he was hers to command, just like her previous conquests, someone whom she would enjoy the moment and forget once returned home.

She pulled him farther into the shadows of the brightly shining moon and daintily freed his tumescent penis out of its constraints.

Aganas' cock sprang forward and he started to straddle her but she restrained him. She knelt and slowly ran her tongue around the crown of his penis. His body went taut and he growled like an animal as Lucy licked his crown and ran her tongue along the length of his shaft. She did this for several delicious moments, until Aganas grabbed her hair and thrust his cock in and out of her mouth. She then sucked him and caressed his balls and the base of his penis as he fucked her in the mouth. Aganas' growl of pleasure could be heard a few distances away. If the river was not rambling, people would have heard it in the plaza. Then he spurted his juices into her sweet, happy face.

7 THE CLAMOR OF THE MOUNTAINS PART 2

Aganas was not able to sleep the rest of the night. He could not forget the two pleasurable encounters he had with Lucy earlier during Lucy's arrival. He grew erect every time he remembered her tongue on his cock and his cock in her love tunnel. He felt like he was in some enchantment, and he could not get out of it. He cursed inwardly and bolted up.

He made himself busy and fetched water from the river and filled all the pots. His ama (father) and ina (mother) were already sipping coffee by the stone hearth. The small village was stirring to life. A rooster crowed and sounds of clucking hens were heard in the distance.

"I heard you'll be escorting the town girls around," his father intoned.

Aganas nodded.

"Why don't you bring Angaway with you? She would be able to help, too."

Angaway has always been his parents' selection among the young women in the village for him. In their far-flung village, fixed marriages were common, but Aganas felt that it was important he felt something for anyone before he would agree to marry. He felt only friendship for Angaway.

And he had stood his ground. His parents have been pairing him off with Angaway, every now and then, but he didn't feel anything for her.

What would Ama and Ina say if he revealed that he was smitten by the girl from town? Would they don their warrior bolos and cut off both their heads? The village people were notorious for cutting off heads with lesser infractions.

"What's the matter? You seem preoccupied," his ina queried.

"Nothing, ina. Okay, I'll fetch her," he replied resignedly.

Angaway could distract him from his lust for Lucy.

Angaway was visibly elated when he fetched her. She was all smiles and offered Aganas coffee, but Aganas was despondent. Why did he not feel the same emotions for Angaway? Perhaps Lucy was the angtan (demon) in disguise? He had to get away from Lucy before things got out of hand. He was aware that for Lucy, it was only a game.

When Lucy saw them, she did not hide her

feelings of dismay. Lucy was civil to them both but she rarely smiled when Angaway was around.

The group visited the primary care center, which was under construction – a square single room measuring 20 x 15 feet. Lucy was a nurse and had visited their village as part of a missionary mission to instruct the villagers on how to do simple hygienic procedures when preparing food, maintaining shelter, and taking care of simple health conditions.

Mandadawaks (quack doctors) had always been there to render herbal treatment, and people in the village survived. If the person died, it was because Kabuniyan (God) wanted him to die, for whatever purpose he had.

The group was busy going around and cleaning things up, and Aganas saw to it that he was not separated from Angaway. But, Lucy was more ingenious.

"Angaway, where can I pee?"

Aganas looked at Lucy furtively.

Angaway smiled and indicated an outhouse farther away. Angaway led Lucy to it. When they were alone, Lucy said,

"It seems you're fast friends with Aganas," she piped innocently.

"Yes, we have been childhood friends."

"Are you betrothed to each other?" Lucy was aware of the village customs.

"I...."

"Oh, sorry, I'm being nosy." Angaway's hesitation was the answer Lucy needed.

So Aganas wasn't betrothed yet. That was rare. Almost all of the young men were already taken. Her heart did a double flip. At least she would not have to deal with her conscience, she smiled, elated at the thought. Why was she so excited?

When they went back, Lucy asked Aganas if they could talk about the specifics of the incoming medical supplies. They went to a shady area under the trees and started talking. Aganas was aware that Lucy was up to something, but he didn't know what it was.

Angaway went with them. But she started to wander off when they started talking about how many boxes and what types of medicines were needed. Angaway was bored with such topics.

"I'll get some water," Angaway said and left.

Aganas wasn't able to stop her. He had no reason to. He could never tell anyone about what happened to him and Lucy. There would be hell to pay.

When Angaway was gone, Lucy surreptitiously pulled Aganas to one of the plant covered corners of the yard. Aganas was already engorged even before she caressed him. He gave a stifled groan of surrender as Lucy nibbled his upper lip and ran her tongue along his neck.

He was quickly aflame, trembling in excitement and desire. He could not hold his emotions any longer. He snatched her and captured her lips with his own. How sweet her kiss tasted. He sparred with her tongue as Lucy fondled him beneath his G-string and rubbed her breasts against his bare chest.

Just then they heard Angaway talking to

people and asking where they were. Aganas seemed crazed with lust; he no longer cared about anything else but to fuck Lucy.

He pulled her hand and urged her to run, as they ran farther and farther from the babble of voices. They stopped, their breath coming in gasps as they stared at each other and laughed heartily.

They were like two children who were deliriously happy because they have discovered what happiness means.

The small clearing was surrounded by lush vegetation, and there were no visible trails leading to it. This was another of Aganas' hiding places.

Lucy stripped in front of him as Aganas' cock stood at rigid attention underneath his G-strings. Once more, Lucy French-kissed him and grappled with his tongue as he hungrily sucked on her red, tasty lips. This is pure bliss, Aganas sighed with pleasure.

Lucy slowly released Aganas' cock from his G-string and knelt before him. His heart raced, anticipating the thrilling sensations he had previously experienced. All his resolve was gone now. All he wanted was Lucy's tongue, her pussy, and her body.

Lucy held his penis in her hands tenderly, licking first the tip and then going around the head, in gentle but firm strokes. Aganas had raised his head toward the sky as in supplication, while one hand reached for her hair.

Lucy slid her tongue up and down his shaft, and then round his balls, licking the sensitive areas between his balls and anus. Aganas growled and eased himself into the soft grass. He was wild with desire.

Aganas was lying down now. Lucy then sucked his penis into her mouth with soft, suckling sounds, as she bobbed up and down, giving the best blowjob she had ever given. She sucked as her mouth went up and then down, and her right hand massaged the base of his cock.

Aganas was writhing in passion and want. He wanted to fuck her hard. He wrestled her to the grass and began to mount her, but Lucy was quicker. She moved upward, so that Aganas' face came right to where her pussy was.

"Eat me," she cried in passion.

Aganas needed no farther prodding; he was a quick learner. Tentatively he brought out his tongue and lapped Lucy's labia. Lucy sighed with pleasure. Making love with this wild man is something different, she thought.

She then parted her labia with her hands and urged Aganas to suck and lick her clit. "Not so hard sweetie. Suck and lick it gently but firmly."

Aganas did as he was told. His tongue was firm but soft on her eager pussy.

"That's it sweetie, flick your tongue up and down on my clit. Then dart your tongue inside my pussy," she moaned as her arousal increased. Her clit was red now with engorged blood vessels ready to erupt.

Aganas darted his tongue all over Lucy's pussy. Her cries of ecstasy prompted him to suck and lick unceasingly like his life depended on it. Lucy's moans of pleasure heightened his arousal, and he was now ready to explode.

Without a word, he straddled her and thrust his ramrod cock deep into her as he grunted with joy. Lucy cried in glee at the pleasurable sensation of his enormous, throbbing cock inside her waiting pussy. They moved to the building crescendo of their passion, as their sweaty bodies collided and strained to meet the other.

Aganas had both hands planted on each side of Lucy as he humped hard and deep into her, feeling her vagina sucking him back again as he pulled out. It was extreme bliss for him. He savored each thrust like a kid enjoying his first ice cream.

Lucy had her hands around Aganas' neck and rose to kiss his lips, whenever he pushed forward; her thighs were spread wide and her legs were crossed at his back, providing him a wide entry to her pussy.

She could feel him filling her up with his enormous, tumescent penis. Oh, what indescribable sensations. It was more than anything she had felt before. It was more than heaven.

They moved faster and slammed into each other as the peak of their climaxes became palpable. Aganas was like a wild horse in heat, and Lucy was writhing and moaning wildly. It was an unstoppable ride now.

Then Aganas roared and slammed his cock deep into Lucy as she arched her back and locked her groin into his.

They held on for a few minutes, kissing

each other softly, until all their juices were depleted and their bodies sated. Then Aganas disengaged and sanity returned anew.

He sat and caressed her pale, smooth skin with his rough fingers. "Why are you doing this to me?" he asked her.

"I'm not sure," she replied. "All I want is to feel you next to me, fucking me hard and long."

No one had ever fucked her that hard, and that long, Lucy realized, and with a sweet, delicious cock as big as a horse's. That must be 8 inches long!

"That's all I want to do too," Aganas had to accept the glaring fact confronting him.

When they went back to the center, there was no one else, everyone had gone home.

They ate some of the food left behind, and when they were full, they became horny again. Aganas was beyond caring now of whatever consequences his actions may cause among the elders.

He led her in a secluded place in the river. A part of the river branched into a small, shaded lake that made it a perfect haven; there was a small waterfall that cascaded beautifully into the small pool of water. If you wanted to make love, it was the perfect place to be. There were shrubs and verdant trees all around it, making it unseen by common passers-by.

Aganas loved adventure and he had discovered several hiding places. This was one of them. This was also great when hiding from invaders from a different village.

They undressed and ran to the cold fresh waters to swim. The middle portion was deep, so they frolicked in the shallower waters.

Lucy was feeling horny again. They were like two lovers on their honeymoon; they couldn't get enough of each other.

Lucy pressed her wet body against Aganas' and ground her groin against his, in deliberate, circling motions. His cock needed no farther prodding; it sprang to life and paid homage to its queen.

They stood there half submerged in water, tasting each other's lips, running their hands on each other's bodies, savoring the delight of foreplay. Lucy guided Aganas' hands to her erotic zones and guided his fingers on how to stroke her breasts, caress her clit, and play with her pussy.

She fondled him as well, caressing and massaging his penis like some fragile bird, light but firm, sensual but playful. She could feel her arousal reaching its peak as Aganas finger-fucked her and played with her clit.

She pushed down Aganas' face to her breast, and when he sucked her nipples alternately while finger-fucking her, she moaned and thrust her pussy toward Aganas. Seeing her frenzied need for him, Aganas raised her into the air with both arms and then brought her down toward his throbbing, rock hard penis.

They both groaned as his cock slid into her pussy. He held Lucy's buttocks with both of his hands, as he lifted her up and down, her juicy pussy sliding warmly and tightly into his pulsating cock. The movement made a squishing sound like somebody walking in a water-sodden shoe. The water made their movements smooth and added a unique sensation as his cock slid into her pussy.

Lucy had both hands around his neck, and her legs were crossed tightly behind his back as she moved with his rhythm. The water splashed around them when Aganas thrust her into his waiting and eager cock, while she rotated her groin and moved with his rhythm. The water helped Aganas carry Lucy, but she knew, water or no water, his muscular arms would be able to carry her weight anyway.

Lucy could feel her orgasm nearing, and she cried for Aganas to go faster and harder. Her senses were reeling; she was wild with passion as she went up and down him, kissing and nibbling his mouth every time she came down.

Then she locked her pussy on to his cock as she climaxed, and waves and waves of pleasure coursed down her body. Aganas had not cummed yet, and she lifted herself again after a few seconds and continued fucking him in a standing position. He was breathing hoarsely, and his face was suffused with passion.

Lucy came again after a few seconds of his thrusts. She was mad with delight, unable to contain the deluge of sensations coming from her groin.

Then he came, and he let out a load grunt as he withdrew his cock and squirted his semen into Lucy's stomach.

Lucy, however, knew she was safe and

grabbed his penis again as she savored the ebbing waves of her sweet orgasm.

It was late afternoon and they slept in each other's arms on the soft grass at the shaded area of the lake. Aganas was so happy; he had never been so happy in his whole life. It was a totally different emotion for him. They snuggled against each other, and napped, tired but totally satiated.

Lucy felt the same way, but she was sure it was because Aganas was a different lover compared to her previous conquests. I will forget him once we return home, she concluded.

When they woke up, it was getting dark. Aganas' cock was again engorged with passion, with Lucy's smooth, velvety body snuggled against his own. Lucy kissed his mouth and his neck, raining kisses on his rough, swarthy skin. Then she slid down her chest and kissed and licked every inch. She sucked his nipples as her hands shot up to fondle his cock.

Aganas' hands were busy too, pinching and rolling both of her nipples between his two hands. Lucy was now licking his abdomen, darting her tongue slowly around the area above his groin. She faced toward his cock, while she let her pussy rest against Aganas' face.

Aganas was surprised at first, but he

understood quickly what Lucy wanted him to do. He could see Lucy's dripping pussy just above his mouth. He licked her then and he was surprised that her juices tasted even tastier than before.

He licked and sucked her clit as she sucked and licked him too. He wanted to give back the ultimate pleasure she was giving to him. It was such delight he would never let go, he thought, pure unadulterated pleasure.

They made foreplay very slowly, savoring each touch, each sensation coming from their mouth, tongues, and fingers. Then when they could not contain themselves any longer, Lucy mounted him, and Aganas felt again another type of pleasure from this position. Lucy is his goddess, able to bring him pure ecstasy and joy. He groaned in delight as Lucy, rubbed her pubis against his, as she rode him proudly.

He reached for her tits as they bounced wantonly with her movements. He pinched her nipples and rolled them between his fingers as she became breathless with lust and slammed her tight pussy into his fiery manhood.

With Lucy on top of Aganas, she moved up and down, sometimes slightly leaning forward to grind her clit into his groin. She dropped for a kiss now and then and sucked his tongue as the sensations grew stronger. There was urgency now in their movements as their groins slapped together to reach their orgasm.

They climaxed together and clung together as their juices mixed with one another in passion and sexual fulfillment.

Aganas didn't want to think of anything else.

8 THE CLAMOR OF THE MOUNTAINS PART 3

After their bodies were sexually sated, Aganas and Lucy were glowing with fulfilled desires as they walked back to the village hand in hand. When they were near the plaza, Aganas pulled Lucy close and whispered, "We might not get another chance."

He pressed her to the ground and kissed her as he lifted her skirt and fucked her hard and quickly, Lucy's legs were spread wide and her moist, tight pussy squeezed his cock with exquisite sensations.

He lifted her buttocks and knelt, as darkness surrounded them. The only light came from the twinkling stars from the distance and the glow of torches from the nearby village.

Aganas couldn't seem to get enough of Lucy – her lips, her smell, her warmth, and her sweet and delicious pussy. He pulled out his cock and stooped down to lick her and fondle her breasts. She moaned and cried for him not to stop. He sucked her clit and tongued her pussy as her juices started to ooze with an incoming huge orgasm.

He mounted her again, lifting up her two legs as he thrust deep inside her with a loud and savage grunt. He quickened his pace, moving faster and harder. In and out he entered her, unmindful of everything around them – not the pebbles underneath their bodies and not the rough ground they were in. Their orgasm was building into a crescendo that exploded simultaneously as they searched each other's mouth and basked in the glory and joy of sexual intercourse.

"We've got to meet late tonight," Aganas said. "I can't bear to be without you."

Lucy did not reply though, because she was not sure if her emotions were as intense as his. All she knew was that she had never been so sated in sex with anyone else.

Aganas brought Lucy to the guest hut, where she was staying with the rest of the girls from town. People were waiting for them. Murmur of voices and anxious cries charged the air.

"Where have you been?" It was Aganas' father glaring from the door of the hut.

Aganas was speechless; he had never lied to his ama and he couldn't start then.

"I took Lucy around for some sightseeing," he replied cheerily.

"There are fascinating places here in your

village," Lucy seconded.

Aganas' father didn't answer but his face was a mask of thunder. He said to Aganas, "We'll talk at home."

When they arrived in their hut, Aganas' father didn't wait for him to sit down.

"I know what you've been up to, son. Don't deny it. You've been frolicking in forbidden territory with this woman, haven't you?!" he yelled at him angrily.

Aganas didn't reply.

"You know that this is not permitted in our tribe to have relationships with those outside our circle," he glared at Aganas.

"I love Lucy, Ama," Aganas whispered. "If she'll accept me, I would like to marry her."

Aganas' ama looked at his son with shock. He vehemently shook his head and stated, "No, you're not going to do that, and that's final!"

Aganas tossed and turned on the floor that night. Sleep was a luxury he could no longer afford. He tried twice to slip outside, but his ama was on guard, making sure he did not leave the hut.

When morning came, the red-shot eyes of Aganas were visible proofs that he was not able to sleep. He intended to visit Lucy no matter what the consequences were. He walked to the door.

"Where do you think are you going?" his ama blocked his path.

"I'm going to visit Lucy," he replied, not looking at his father's eyes.

"They've left last night, son. You better

attend to the seedlings in the fields."

Aganas' heart seemed to be physically torn into two. His chest seemed to burst with agony.

Without a word, he left the house and trudged absentmindedly to Lucy's guest hut. The sad expression on the village chieftain's face said it all. Lucy was gone. They had it all planned when they found out Lucy and Aganas had been missing for a day.

Aganas trekked to the rice fields absentmindedly. Lucy was gone and the world seemed to end for him. He had never been in love, and now that he was, the separation was more than he was able to bear.

He worked at the field like an automaton, lovesick, and missing Lucy. Whenever he remembered her, there was a gnawing feeling of yearning within his body, within his soul. His arousal always came to the fore.

By the end of the day, he was sure he couldn't go on the following day unless he saw her again. He was bent on following Lucy to town tomorrow, no matter what it took.

When Aganas returned home, he could hear the merrymaking even before he reached their hut. He was surprised to see Angaway seated between his parents.

"There you are," his ama pulled him beside Angaway. His ama was indeed a great strategist. First he found a way to send Lucy home prematurely and then had invited Angaway. He was not pleased; however, he was angry. Village children have been always married through fixed marriages, and apparently his ama thought he was no exception.

"Your ina and I decided that it's time for you to settle down," Aganas' father said. His eyes glinted with triumph.

Angaway looked at him shyly. Aganas had a soft spot for his childhood friend, but he realized he would always think of Angaway as a good friend and nothing more.

"Ama, please don't decide rashly. Angaway and I have to talk," Aganas pleaded.

"What's there to talk about? This has been the plan all along. Get ready for your engagement tomorrow."

In front of all the guests, Aganas was not able to say anything against his ama's firm pronouncements. He was still his father.

When all the guests had gone, and he and Angaway were left behind, he looked at her imploringly.

"Don't say anything," Angaway said. "I know you would never cherish me as a wife, as you do Lucy. Go to her tonight, while there's still time."

Aganas was speechless and in tears. He hugged her tight then. "I care for you as a childhood friend," he said. "And you'll always have a special place in my heart."

Angaway was in tears too, "Just promise me one thing," she intoned.

Aganas nodded.

"Promise me, make a vow that if ever you discover that you're not happy there, come back to me," she said through her tears.

"I promise."

Aganas had already formulated his plan. He would be trekking the mountains tonight so he could reach town before dawn. He was anxious and thrilled to be with Lucy again. It would be an arduous hike during the night, but he was ready to cross the seven seas for Lucy.

His ama eventually snored; sleep must have caught up to him. Aganas tiptoed to the door and slipped away into the moonlit night, skirting in the shadows of the trail leading to the river.

The river shimmered eerily as he pulled his G-string and swam to the other side, with the moonlight showing him the silhouettes of the opposite riverbank. After he had crossed the river and started ascending the mountain, he lit his torch and ran all the way to mountain crest. His father would surely send a search party once he noticed his absence.

Aganas was a seasoned hiker and it took him only 2 hours to reach town. Where would Lucy be? It was still early, but a few people were already awake, getting ready for the day. He asked directions to Lucy's house from some people sitting by a small store in the roadside.

What would he say to her? Would she still care? He was afraid to think about it.

The house was a mansion overlooking the hills below. It has a lovely manicured garden and a sparkling small pond that added serenity to the ambiance of the place.

Aganas suddenly felt naked amidst the cultured surroundings. In his G-strings, he suddenly felt uncivilized. It was the first time he had given attention to his ethnicity. Would Lucy accept him as he was? His firm resolve vanished and he turned around to go, when a scooter stopped beside him.

"Aganas?" It was a familiar voice.

He turned around and stared straight into the round, black eyes that he had been yearning for the past days – Lucy's.

Aganas wanted to run and crush her into his arms, but Lucy appeared so made-up he hesitated.

Lucy did not though, she ran into his dusty, nakedness and clung to him like she would never let go.

"I thought you would never come for me," she sobbed into his bare chest.

He crashed her then into his chest.

"Please don't cry. I came as soon as I could. I missed you so much," he kissed her well-coffered hair.

Lucy, her pulses racing, raced back to the scooter and instructed Aganas to hop behind her, and they sped into the distance.

They went past the town's center and raced toward the mountains on the town's outskirts.

Every fiber in Lucy's heart was taut with excitement. She had been in love affairs before but had quickly forgotten them after a few days. This time she realized during the short period of Aganas' absence that she has finally fallen in love.

Aganas held Lucy tenderly and basked in the fresh smell of her hair, the warmth of her body, and he could feel his arousal starting to show.

Lucy turned around, winked, and kissed him full in the mouth.

"Hey, look at where you're going," Aganas whispered through his breathlessness.

They finally stopped at a modest house atop a hill overlooking a large, green plantation of sugarcane.

"This is our farm house," Lucy said, and led him inside.

Once inside, they wasted no words and groped for each other hungrily and excitedly. He tore down Lucy's clothing and his eager lips sought her nipples, while his hands fumbled with the zipper of her jeans.

Lucy did not bother to untie Aganas' G-string. She inserted her hand inside the sparse cover of Aganas' cock and released it. It was already engorged and standing at attention. Lovingly, she caressed and fondled it while she kissed whatever skin was exposed to her lips.

They were gasping with desire and delight, and when Aganas carried her to lie on the bed, she clung to him excited at the prospect of foreplay. Aganas was a fast learner; he knew what Lucy's sensitive areas were.

Aganas stared lustily at her creamy body lying there, waiting to be adored. He started kissing her lips, drawing her tongue out with his own, nibbling her lower and then her upper lip. He sucked her tongue as he let his fingers tease her pussy with gentle upward and downward movements. Lucy gasped when he finally focused on her clit with his thumb, while the rest of his fingers ran up and down her labia.

When Aganas kissed her neck and went farther down to her breasts, she closed her eyes and reveled at the miasma of sensations he was creating. This is heaven, she sighed.

Aganas continued nibbling her right nipple, while her left tit was fondled and twirled in Aganas' right hand fingers. She could feel his big erection rubbing just inches above her love tunnel. Oh, she couldn't wait to have that enormous, delicious cock inside her.

Aganas was ablaze as well, wanting just to fuck her long and hard, but he wanted her to be satisfied too, like he had been in their past lovemaking. He went down farther with his lips and tongue, kissing and licking her skin until he was above her pubis.

Lucy groaned in anticipation; she was ablaze now with passion. She cried for him to eat her. He stooped and teasingly licked and tongued the area near her clit without coming in contact with her mound of pleasure. Lucy groaned feverishly.

Aganas ran his lips on her thighs, the insides of her thighs, and then the labia of her moist pussy. He sucked and licked until Lucy cried out and thrust her hips forward to allow his easy access to her clitoris.

As soon as Aganas' tongue flicked her clit, she moaned in pleasure.

"Please don't stop," she groaned.

His tongue licked and sucked her clit, while he had his fingers going in and out of her vagina. Lucy writhed and cried with ecstasy as her arousal increased.

Hearing her moaning in pleasure intensified Aganas' arousal too. He was now ready to fuck her like she had never been fucked before. When Lucy's juices of pleasure started to flow, he mounted her then. Towering like a Greek god over her, he spread her legs and thrust his hot, pulsating penis into her wet pussy.

He grunted with pleasure as her vagina enveloped his penis in a hot cloud of love and passion. He grunted lustily in utter joy. God, how he had dreamt for this moment in the past few days!

He withdrew his engorged penis and then slowly entered her slick pussy again, savoring each exquisite sensation coming from the movement of his cock coming in and out of Lucy's tight and slick pussy.

Lucy was whimpering with each thrust, grinding her groin against his own. Her eyes were closed and her face was suffused with passion.

"Fuck me hard and long, babe," she urged Aganas, lifting her buttocks even higher.

This drove him crazy, and he stooped down to kiss her agape sensuous lips while he slammed his dick into her, driving her wild and screaming with delight. He went in and out, ramming his cock deep into her, shaking her body and making her spread her legs wider in wanton delight.

She urged him not to stop but to go harder and quicker. And he did. He was unstoppable then as he slammed his penis hard into her, increasing the tempo. Their sweaty, fiery bodies moved together in unison, reaching out for an explosive orgasm that was hovering in the horizon.

In and out he fucked her until they arched their backs together, screamed in delight, and locked their groins together as their huge orgasms mixed in one joyful union.

When they awakened, they made love again. They rolled and wrestled on the wooden floor, exploring each other's sensitive, erotic zones. They seemed not to get enough of each other.

"We'll have to do something about your hair. You have to blend in with the crowd, so no one will notice you," Lucy said as she kissed him.

Aganas had never allowed his hair to be cut, but with Lucy he could do anything for her, even give his life for her sake.

Within those incredible moments of being together, Aganas came to know more about Lucy. She was not the happy-go-lucky woman he previously thought she was. She had a generous heart. He learned that she came from a well-to-do family, but she volunteered for the missionary work in their village and donated even some of her money in the health care of the village children. Aganas knew he loved her no matter who or what she was. There was one big problem though, her parents would never agree to their relationship, a relationship between a member of the fiercest head-hunting tribes and a town girl. Lucy knew this too but she was praying for a miracle. She knew then that she couldn't live without Aganas.

She touched his face tenderly and began cutting his hair.

Afterward, they rummaged in the small kitchen and cooked and ate whatever they found edible. They were walking around naked and teasing and caressing one another as they pottered around the kitchen. Dusk had settled in and they cuddled under the warmth of the blankets as they caressed each other's sensitive areas and pleasured each other.

Each knew by then what the other was most pleasured by, and they were willing to be adventurous. Lucy got Aganas to kneel and enter her from behind. He was a beast once he was aroused. He captured her and owned her like a slave during those times, and she flourished in his ruthless but gentle love.

Aganas humped mightily and held on to Lucy's buttocks as he drove his hard, tumescent cock into her slick vagina. Lucy met his thrusts with her own frantic backward pushes and their flesh slapped against each other producing a rhythm of sound that drove them more insane with desire.

Lucy cried in extreme delight as Aganas went faster, easily pulling her toward him, in an increasing tempo of lust and love. With one last hard thrust, he roared like a lion and slumped on her back as her climax claimed her too, making her scream his name.

9 THE CLAMOR OF THE MOUNTAINS PART 4

They slept entwined in each other's embrace, feeding on each other's love. They dozed off to sleep, satiated and happy. They were startled to wakefulness when shrieks and shouts reverberated from the distance. From the window they could see fire blazing in the horizon.

"What's happening?" Aganas asked Lucy.

"I don't know. We have to get back home now."

They dressed quickly and rode the bike toward town. There were several houses burning, and people were running into the forest in panic.

Lucy grabbed one woman and asked her what was happening. The woman's eye grew wide in fear, "The Angwans are attacking us. They were looking for you."

Aganas was in shock more than Lucy. His villagers had finally come for him, and they did it in utter terror. Village folks had started tribal wars for trifle reasons, and he was willing to suffer the consequences.

They were there waiting for them, Aganas' father, and the rest of the men folk of the village. It happened so fast Aganas stayed frozen from where he was.

One of the men grabbed Lucy by the waist and brought the blade of the bolo to her neck. Lucy's eyes were wide with terror, and all she could do was whimper.

"Son, we don't want to shed blood here. Please come home and we'll forget about everything. Your union could never happen."

Aganas knew that the man would not hesitate to get Lucy's prized head should he refuse to go with them.

Lucy was crying now, leaning weakly on the man and trembling all over –his beloved Lucy. Lucy's parents were guarded by the other men and they were crying in one corner.

"Okay, okay," Aganas replied, crushed. "Let go of her."

"Promise by the blood of our forefathers that you would no longer see this girl," his father commanded.

Aganas nodded dejectedly. They had nowhere to run. They would hunt them down no matter where they went.

The man released Lucy and she slumped weakly to the ground. Aganas ran and crushed her into his arms. The men allowed him to carry Lucy as he brought her inside the house.

"I'm sorry, my love. I will have to obey their wishes for now. Don't ever forget me. I'll come back for you." Aganas kissed her trembling lips as he wept as well.

The following day in the village of Angwan, a big wedding ceremony was being prepared. Aganas and Angaway were to be wed.

"I'm sorry, Aganas, I tried talking to them but they would not listen," she whispered to him, her voice reflected her anguish.

"It's not your fault," Aganas replied sadly.

Whenever there were wedding ceremonies in the village, everyone was invited. It was a village affair of about 300 families. Sometimes, two pigs or a cow or carabao were butchered for the occasion. There were taddok (dancing), ullalim (solo singing), and salidummay (group singing).

Basi, the native wine, was free flowing. Native cakes abounded, and the butchered animal was cut into small pieces and boiled in a large wok. There were no condiments added to the meat – not even salt. It was boiled in plain water until cooked, and that was it.

Aganas and Angaway danced the salidsid (courtship and wedding dance), and the village folk cheered with joy as they watched another powerful union between two clans. After their dance, the pangat (head of the clan) gave his blessings, and they were brought to the "padok" (the love hut) where they were supposed to make love while the festivities are still ongoing around them.

It was believed that the union should be consummated on the night of the marriage so that abundant blessings would follow. A Gobi (sex doctor) would examine the woman afterward to make sure this was accomplished, and Aganas' father made sure he had one ready.

As soon as Aganas and Angaway entered the hut, they collapsed on the floor, not knowing what to do.

"What would we do? The Gobi will surely find out why," Angaway cried. "Please don't do it, if you don't want to."

Aganas knew that if he would not consummate his marriage with Angaway, there would be hell to pay. Angaway would be considered an outcast, not being able to arouse her man enough to penetrate her. The elders would also force them into the act before the elders.

"We don't have a choice, Angaway," he closed the distance between them and held her hand.

Angaway had a special place in Aganas' heart but he had no lust for her, but he had to do it. Unknown to Aganas, Angaway loved him more than anyone else. She had always yearned for that spot in his heart, but she knew that spot belonged to Lucy.

In the shadows of the flickering torch in the corner of the room, Aganas closed his eyes and groped for Angaway. His hands encountered hard, rough skin. He opened his eyes to stare at her. She had her eyes closed and there was so much joy in her countenance that Aganas realized she loved him.

Why is fate cruel, Kabuniyan? Aganas thought. What a joy it would be if he had fallen in love with Angaway instead.

He was startled from his train of thoughts when he felt Angaway's hand groping for him in return. And he closed his eyes and thought about Lucy.

He kissed Angaway and it was just like kissing a friend. She kissed back breathlessly, whispering his name in the darkness. Then her hands were releasing his cock from his wedding garments.

It was still soft but Angaway showed no indication she noticed. She got the love oil given by the Gobi and spread it lovingly on his cock. With the fingers in her right hand, she enveloped his shaft and moved her fingers up and down in firm, gentle strokes.

Aganas' eyes were closed and his hands were idle at his sides as he allowed Angaway to arouse his sleeping manhood. Her gentle caressing fingers continued to go up and down his shaft, masturbating him.

The Gobi said she should not apply extreme pressure, "Your touch should be like a feather touching your skin – gentle but steady and firm," she had said to Angaway.

Her right fingers teased his cock, while the left fondled his balls.

Aganas thought of Lucy – Lucy's sweet pussy. How pleasurable it has been making love to her. The thought of Lucy made his cock harden instinctively.

Angaway smiled through her tears, at last her man is aroused. Aganas tried to put Lucy away from his thoughts because he respected Angaway, but Lucy's lips, juicy and slick pussy, kept flashing as Angaway fondled and caressed her. She was seated beside him, while he was lying supine on the floor.

He was finally ready; his cock was engorged and throbbing with lust. He gently pushed her onto the floor and mounted her. His oiled dick slipped slowly into her pussy, and he took a deep breath as he felt her tight virgin vagina.

It was the first time he experienced pleasure that night not because he was thinking of Lucy. Angaway was so tight, he could feel his cock gripped tight producing exquisite sensations that he grunted in pleasure. He heard a moan from Angaway.

"Am I hurting you?" he stopped, his cock gripped tightly by Angaway's pussy.

"No, no, don't worry, I want you deep inside me," she replied hoarsely. "Please thrust your cock inside me."

Aganas, hearing Angaway's urgent and lustful pleading, moved in small rotating movements to make his entry easier.

Angaway clutched his back and prodded him on, thrusting her groin against him. Her full, firm breasts glistened with sweat. Aganas reached out and took one nipple into his mouth. Angaway moaned and had spread her legs wider.

As Aganas sucked her nipple one after the

other, he inched his penis deeper and deeper into her. There was a cry of pain and pleasure from Angaway as she clawed on Aganas' back and then held on his buttock to grind it into her own.

They were panting heavily now and uttering guttural indistinguishable words as they fucked hard to reach their orgasms.

Angaway's tight pussy brought inevitable sensations to Aganas, much as he denied it. But, there was a big but, he did not feel the soul-drenching arousal and fulfillment he felt when he was with Lucy.

Angaway was now writhing and grinding her pelvis frenziedly into his. Her pussy loosened up a bit as her juices mixed with the oil. Aganas felt his cock being sucked back deliciously every time he pulled out and he closed his eyes as his orgasm exploded and he rammed his cock deeper into her.

Angaway's climax came a few seconds after his. She clung to him and arched her back as delightful sensations coursed through her body. Then they held on to each other thankfully, with the realization that everything in the village would be fine then.

Both of Aganas and Angaway's parents were bursting with pride as the young couple started with their village life. They were hoping for a grandson soon, and it made them happy that someone would continue the lineage even after they were gone.

Aganas and Angaway went on with the daily toil in the village. They attended to the fields and the kaingin (mountain rice plantation) simultaneously. It was what village life was. People woke up early in the morning and toiled day in and day out in the fields so they could have enough harvest to eat three square meals a day.

Although Angaway wanted to make love more often, Aganas rarely had the strength to do so after work from the fields.

Aganas' thoughts were filled with Lucy, thoughts that not even distance and time could erase. There were times he thought of Lucy in his sleep, and he would wake up with his cock throbbing and aching with desire. During those times, Angaway would feel his erection and eagerly fulfill his need on his own.

Aganas thought about Lucy. When would he seek her? He knew it was impossible at the moment to do so. It would surely spark a tribal war. He did not want to endanger other people's lives just so he could fulfill his desire. How was she?

Days passed and then months. Aganas' and Angaway's parents were anxious to have a grandchild. They started giving Angaway fertility herbs.

In the village of Angwan, a couple had to produce offspring for the marriage to be considered successful. When unions are not gifted with children, both couples are free to search for partners who could give them one.

It was almost a year but Angaway had still not conceived. Aganas did not know if he should feel happy or not, but he had hoped their union would succeed for the sake of Angaway.

His duty as a husband had now started to lessen his desire for Lucy, but not his love for her. Should he inform Lucy now that she could go ahead and live a life of her own? That he was not able to keep his promise? Would two people's love be enough to sacrifice all the people around them? Aganas knew the answer was no.

The Gobi visited them more frequently to give pointers and herbs to Angaway, but all of these were useless.

One night, after they were done eating, Angaway sat beside Aganas by the stone hearth and lovingly leaned on him.

"The Gobi has given me a new herb. Can we try it?" Her eyes begged him to say yes.

Aganas nodded and they splashed ashes on the flickering fire and stretched their naked bodies on the bamboo floor.

Angaway took the herb and chewed on it before spitting it out and placing it at the tip of Aganas' flaccid cock. He felt the stirrings of an arousal, but his manhood was still asleep.

Angaway stooped to spread the herb's juices on his cock. She ran her tongue on his shaft, spreading the concoction from his crown down his balls. Aganas' penis inevitably responded, and his fingers went down to her crotch.

Angaway was holding his already hard cock in her fingers while still running the herb's juices from her tongue to his penis.

Aganas had rarely thought of Angaway's satisfaction during the rare times that they made love. He did the act to ease his lust and to fulfill his responsibility as a husband.

That night he felt guilty that she always tried her best to make him happy, while he rarely made the effort.

When Angaway stooped down again to take his cock into her mouth, he pulled her legs and spread them apart on his face. Angaway stammered in her surprise. Aganas never did this before. They were in a 69 position and this position was unknown among the villagers. Lucy had taught him well, Aganas thought, and his heart ached with the thought, but he knew he had a responsibility to Angaway, too.

Angaway was jolted in pleasure, as Aganas' tongue flicked over her labia. How good that felt, she admitted.

Aganas' tongue ran over her labia and up her pubis to rest in her clit. This he did over and over until Angaway had to stop sucking him for a while to savor the dizzying sensation. Oh, how delightful it felt, she thought.

Then she went back to licking and lapping his dick, exploring every inch of it like it was her favorite food. She groaned now and then rotated her pussy against Aganas' face. She was hyperventilating, making strange sounds of pleasure that reverberated around the small hut.

Aganas inserted his tongue inside Angaway's already moist pussy. It was still tight as it had been, only moist. Angaway moaned her ecstasy and clutched his cock.

She was on fire, bent only in satiating her passion. She hurriedly pulled Aganas on top of her and spread her legs wide as he thrust his pulsating manhood into her deepest depths. Angaway writhed and clung to his back as he fucked her hard and long. In and out he fucked her, relentlessly and fiercely.

With every thrust he did, his cock was warmly sucked into the tightness of her tight but wet love tunnel. They moved to each other's rhythm, savoring the pleasure of the exquisite friction of Angaway's tight pussy with his own enormous cock.

Then they both came simultaneously as their juices blended with each other, while they shuddered with incredible pleasures of sexual gratification.

That perfect sexual union that night, however, still was not able to bring them children. There was something wrong. Kabuniyan (God) did not want them to be together, or he would have blessed them with children.

It was evident then, Aganas would soon be betrothed again to someone who would be able to give him children. Angaway cried most of the time, thinking about her love for Aganas.

Aganas felt pity for her. He had formed a certain fondness for her that was difficult to explain, but village customs were the law in the village.

Angaway joined the alangtan, a group of women who were considered as icons of dedicated service. She had been resigned to her fate when the Gobi stated that there was no hope for her. Aganas' parents were searching for another girl for him.

Aganas, however, told them firmly that they should let it rest first, as all girls were now betrothed to someone, so that was how life went on for him for 3 months.

Will there be tomorrow's rainbow? Aganas was not sure anymore.

10 THE CLAMOR OF THE MOUNTAINS PART 5

The feeling of remorse that Aganas felt because of his separation from Angaway was shortlived when he saw her happy and contented being one of the dedicated single girls. At least she chose not to wallow in the "failure" of their marriage, according to village customs. She has chosen not to become a pariah.

In the village, there were no longer suitable girls for Aganas for they were all now betrothed to someone. Aganas' parents did not have any option but to search for a suitable partner for him outside of their village.

Aganas was encouraged to attend barrio fiestas (celebrations) in neighboring villages with which they had a peace pact with. He, however, had no interest in other women. He thought of Lucy more frequently. How was she? Did she marry? They have had no communication whatsoever since the night they had made wanton love more than a year ago.

Aganas had the burning desire to know how she was doing. Angaway was not able to rekindle the same passion that he had only felt for Lucy.

It was a weekend when Aganas and a few of the men were tasked to buy some basic commodities for an incoming fiesta. Aganas knew he had to see Lucy and know how she was doing.

They hiked for two hours in the mountainous terrain and arrived before lunch at the town proper.

"I'll look for some supplies at the town center," he excused himself from the group.

When he was away from their sight, he ran all the way to Lucy's house and hid in one of the nearby bushes. There were no people outside, and the neighboring houses seemed to be empty as well. Perhaps because it was lunch time. Lucy's scooter was there in front of the house. It seemed like it was just yesterday that he had rode that scooter. The memories of that ride and the event that followed brought a familiar, aching sensation in Aganas' crotch.

He waited for several moments observing the yard when the door opened and Lucy came out of the door. For a few seconds, his heart stopped beating. His pulse raced, and his breath came in gasps as he stared at the woman, who had meant the world to him.

He still was not able to understand how she could create these powerful emotions within him. God, how I love this woman, he realized then. And he had previously thought he had gotten over her.

Lucy was striding toward the scooter; helmet in hand, when there was a loud wail from a child. He came running down the road, flailing his arms in the air, shouting, "Mama, mama...wait."

Aganas witnessed all this, like he was in a trance, like it was a scene from another world, another dimension. Then the young tot clung to Lucy's neck laughing, as Lucy smothered him with kisses.

She married! Aganas stared in disbelief at the boy. His heart felt heavy and he turned to leave.

"There, there, Aga" he heard Lucy saying, "Don't give lola (grandmother) a hard time. Go inside now."

Aganas stopped in his tracks. Aga? Aga? Was he named after him? Was he....

His heart did a double flip, as he heard Lucy's scooter bark and start.

Then she was right in front of him, before he could turn away. Their eyes met and Lucy's mouth fell like she has seen a ghost.

"Aganas?" she whispered.

Aganas was uncertain whether to run to her and hug her, as his heart dictated. Was she married or not?

"Are you married?" he queried, as they stared at each other a few feet away.

Lucy's eyes were brimming with tears, "You said you'd come back for me, so I waited."

Aganas was in tears as well. All the longing and emotions he felt for this woman came flooding in to stifle his words.

He crossed the small distance between them, and they clung to each other tightly as they kissed. They were hidden from the houses but if someone arrived from the road, they would surely see them.

"Come." Lucy revved the scooter, and they sped toward the place where they had made fiery love more than a year ago.

There in the farm hut, Lucy told Aganas that Aga was indeed his son. Aganas knelt before her and apologized for leaving her alone to tend for their son and for not going back earlier for her. Everything would be fine now, Aganas assured her, but they both knew that there is still the question of tribal customs. Lucy was a girl from town. That would be a problem.

They did not care, though, as their bodies touched and responded to each other's warmth, like a violin to its master. Lucy's body was clamoring for his touch.

Aganas already had a huge erection, an erection that was as hard as rock and as big as a horse's. He realized how he had missed her. He unbuttoned her blouse, and his hand went to each of her breasts alternately as his lips pinned hers, exploring and sucking her tongue, nibbling her lower and upper lip.

Lucy's hand caressed his cock beneath his G-string. It was throbbing with desire and screaming then for Lucy's pussy. Aganas' hands crept to her groin too, and it gave him satisfaction that she was already wet.

The long months of longing for her touch and love made him mad with desire. He straddled Lucy with his hands planted on both sides of her as he thrust his craving penis into her eager pussy. He grunted pleasurably when her pussy enveloped his cock in a tight embrace.

Lucy moaned and crossed her legs across Aganas' back as he pumped in and out. Slowly at first, savoring the exquisite sensations caused by the friction of their penis and vagina. Then hard and quicker.

Ahhh, Aganas' movement started to increase in tempo as he deliciously pushed in and out of Lucy's slick pussy. He was breathless and beet red with passion as he went in and out with his dick.

Lucy was crying with pleasure, urging him to fuck her harder. He brought his mouth down and sucked her nipples on both breasts and then went back to her lips to search for her tongue with his own – not ceasing in humping her hard and deeply.

Lucy screamed as her orgasm was hovering, about to explode. Then Aganas pulled her up and sat her on his lap as he continued fucking her hard. They were both facing each other, with Aganas half kneeling and supporting Lucy's buttocks with his lap.

Lucy had her legs crossed behind him while she, in turn, moved up and down toward his huge, beastly penis. Aganas held her on the hips with both hands and brought her up and down to his waiting cock.

They strained toward each other as they increased their pace and move to the tempo of their own wild fire of lust and passion.

They kissed, savoring each other's tongue, as their groins slapped against each other, and hungrily devoured each other in ecstasy.

Finally, they came simultaneously in a huge wave of sexual gratification that left their bodies shuddering in utter pleasure and felicity. It was ultimate heaven for both of them. It was even better than their previous lovemaking.

After disengaging, they napped naked, in each other's arms. They made love again when they awakened.

Aganas explored Lucy's body with his tongue. He kissed her nape and trailed his caressing fingers with his tongue. He was all over her body, his fingers fondling her clit as his lips and tongue roamed her erogenous zones. She had taught him how to give pleasure, and he was paying homage to his teacher.

Lucy felt her body respond instinctively to its master. She no longer desired for any man's touch but Aganas. She had finally arrived home and she knew that her previous flirty nature was at its end. Aganas and Aga's love was now her road to forever.

She surrendered herself to him, crooning in pleasure as one of his hands fondled her nipples, and one was caressing her pussy. His lips were glued to her own as her body arched and twisted in response to his touch, in a delirious state of pleasure.

When he pressed his fingers against her G-spot, she cried in joyful anticipation. Then Aganas let his two fingers slide in and out of her vagina in slow, deliberate movements, applying pressure to the spot just below her pubic bone.

The sheer pleasure coming from Lucy's different erotic areas – her mouth, breasts, and pussy – was so intense that she cried out loud and strained her body toward him. This made Aganas wilder with desire. He was erect again, as he continued sucking her tongue, flicking her nipples, and finger fucking her.

Then Lucy came in short, multiple spurts as she cried for his name and arched her body in ecstasy. The orgasm came again, and again, until Aganas' hands were drenched in her love juices.

When her orgasms finally subsided and she lay there seemingly sated, Aganas spread her legs and held them up as he fucked her hard, grunting in pleasure as his ramrod penis came out of her slick pussy in fast, strong thrusts.

His body glistened with his taut, muscular arms as he humped her vigorously, and her body wriggled like a rag doll. The beast in him was let loose. Then Lucy screamed in elation as she came in one titanic orgasm anew, while Aganas slammed his groin against her and ground his penis to her pussy in climax. They stayed locked to each other's love organs until their breathing became normal.

It was already more than three hours that Aganas was gone. His friends would surely be looking for him.

"I wish I could embrace and play with my son," he wistfully said.

Lucy clung to him tight. "Promise me you'll come again and bring us both together," she pleaded.

"Kiss Aga for me," Aganas said. "I promise, I'll come for you both."

The village men were waiting impatiently for him by the roadside when he went back with the supplies. "It would be dusk soon, let's get going." He ignored their grim faces and led the group up the mountain trail for the hike home.

The next day, Aganas had decided to inform his parents of his plans. They were seated on the floor, around the stone hearth. They were waiting for coffee to boil as the crackling flame from the firewood danced in the early morning silence.

"Ama, Ina, I have a son," he stated boldly.

"Angaway is pregnant?" There was pure gladness in her mother's voice, while his father was smiling ear to ear.

"No, Ina, it's not Angaway, it's Lucy."

His words dropped like a bomb. No one spoke for a few minutes. Then his father was towering over him, ready to strike.

"You went back to that girl, against our wishes?" he asked Aganas ominously.

"Please sit down, Ama. I never went back after you have taken me away from her forcibly."

Aganas held both of his mother's hands and continued, "Lucy became pregnant before I left her and abandoned her. Don't you see that this is the will of Kabuniyan?" he eyed his mother, his eyes pleading for understanding.

"I've done everything you have asked me, but still here I am unhappy and childless." He was in tears then, not ashamed to show his parents how much he loved Lucy.

"I would never be happy if I don't have Lucy and my son with me." His mother was crying too as he kissed her hand and begged for understanding.

He turned to his ama and reminded him, "Haven't I followed all the village customs as you wanted? Haven't I?"

There was no response from his parents.

"Isn't it time I followed my heart, too?"

"But she's not a villager. She won't understand our customs and traditions."

"She will eventually, Ama. Our blood is running through my son's veins. His mother would surely want her son to grow among his blood relatives."

His father did not respond and stormed out of the house. Aganas and his mother were both speechless with grief.

"Go, tend the crop in the fields. I'll talk to your father," his mother kissed him tenderly on the cheek.

Aganas went listlessly in the fields and watered the rice seedlings. If Ama wouldn't agree, he would surely declare a tribal war to get my son and shun Lucy, Aganas thought.

He could not imagine life without his new found family. How he would like to teach his son to use the bolo and the spear to hunt for wild pigs. How he would wake up every morning with Lucy next to him.

He closed his eyes and prayed to

Kabuniyan to let his ama finally accept his family into their world.

When he reached home that evening, his parents were talking earnestly about village customs. In the village of Angway, customs and traditions were of utmost importance to the folks. These were their unwritten laws, which everyone respected and obeyed.

"Come here son," his father's eyes were clouded.

Aganas joined them, his heart thundering in his chest.

"Have you seen your son?"

Aganas nodded.

"Alright, go fetch them, but you must see to it that they follow and respect our customs."

Aganas was aglow with happiness.

"Let's see the grandson soon." It was obvious Aganas' father was proud of his grandson.

The following morning, Aganas started early for the trek to town. Every fiber of his soul was singing in happiness. Thank you Kabuniyan for listening to my prayers, he shouted to his unseen God.

His happiness was shortlived, however, because he was rejected outright by Lucy's parents.

"What's this uncivilized native doing here?" Lucy's father was angry. His daughter was almost killed by these savages, and this man is now asking for her daughter's hand?

"With due respect," Aganas uttered. "I apologize for my father's recklessness, but we are not uncivilized. Things are not stolen from any of our houses, unlike in this town. We may not wear the fancy clothes that you wear, but we are honest and sincere."

Lucy went to stand by Aganas' side and she held his hand as her father bowed his head in realization of the truth of Aganas' words. They have been robbed several times.

"I would be elated if you give us your blessings, Pa and Ma," Lucy said. "Even if you don't, I will have to go home, where my heart leads me."

Lucy turned to Aganas and told him to wait while she packed. Just then Aga came hopping from his room. He ran toward Aganas and cheerily uttered. "We have a visitor, what's your name?"

Aganas carried him then, and his heart was overflowing with joy. "I'm Aganas, and you?"

"I'm Aga," he replied, giggling. "We have similar names," he giggled.

"I am your father, son," Aganas wanted so much to blurt these words, but he stopped himself in time. There would be lots of time to do that later.

Lucy came out of her room with two big bags.

Lucy's mother stopped her, "Are you sure of this?'

"You know me, ma. I'm a brat, but Aganas changed me, and now we have a son. His parents – whom you call savages – gave their blessing. Can't you give yours, too?" she made them realize their unfair judgment.

Lucy's father knew that Aga's native grandparents and the village folk would not hesitate to mount an attack again if they wanted Lucy's son. Why create another reason for a tribal war when they could grab this opportunity to coexist in peace and harmony.

"Okay, we're granting you our permission, but you should vow to make your family happy," Lucy's dad acquiesced.

Aganas broke into a smile and he tickled Aga as he squealed with unbridled laughter.

Aganas took both the hand of Lucy's parents and said warmly, "You don't have to ask. Thank you very much. We'll come and fetch you tomorrow for the wedding."

And Aganas lifted Aga on his shoulders as Lucy held his arm, and they waved happily on their way "home" to forever.

11 LINE FROM HEAVEN PART 1

I stared at him shyly from under my lashes. He stood there, naked, in all his glory. I looked away uncomfortably.

"Let's talk tomorrow," I said tremulously and bade goodbye to Amir. I was still not yet ready for what he would like to happen.

I met Amir, one rainy day, when I was feeling lonely and depressed. My first impression of him was that he had a great command of the English language, considering the fact that he was Indian.

"Hi mystique lady, I'm Niceman."

"Hi, Niceman."

"So, how are you? Lonely too, I guess?" he queried.

"Hmmmm, not really," I said. I just wanted to do something to ease my melancholic mood.

"Okay, let's just talk then. What do you do?" he started.

I was just there to pass the time away and

did not have any intention of staying for long.

"I work with sick people," I replied, not wanting to reveal more. "What about you?"

"I work with a multinational company."

I was surprised with how open he was. "That's interesting; may I know what you do?" I asked wondering how he could reveal such information to a person he had just met, while I was wary to disclose too personal information.

"I attend to the management of a multinational company's Intellectual Property Rights," he said. Then, he went on to describe his work. Throughout our conversation, he had demonstrated wit and intellect and an undeniable sense of humor that the hours passed by in a blur. His command of English was superb, and he was open and genuinely interested in me.

"You're reluctant to open up, mystique lady, but my heart tells me you're different and special. I feel you are someone I could trust," he said emphatically. "I have never felt this way before."

I stared at his words on the monitor and felt a slight quiver in my chest. Was I feeling the same way too? Or was I just feeling lonely? I replied: "You're pulling my leg, of course. Anyway, I have to go; there are chores to be done."

"Wait, can we talk again tomorrow same time?" he asked.

I played with my keypads, before typing: "I'm not sure. I'll try," I countered. "Bye," and added a smiley with my message.

I was just passing the time away, and was

not really an online junkie. I did not wait for him to reply before I logged out from my Yahoo Messenger.

I was wondering if what Niceman told me were all true. The Internet is full of people who hide behind user names and aliases to hide their true identity. I was not even sure if Niceman was indeed a he or a she. Why did it matter? I would not talk to him anymore anyway. That was what I got from joining the "room" for Lonely Hearts category, just for the heck of it.

I was restless, so I search for some entertainment news to while more time away. I read about so and so actress getting a divorce from so and so actor, and I got more depressed.

I could not get Niceman out my mind, no matter how I tried. I was eager to log in to my chat the following day to talk to him anew.

And I had thought I would never talk to him again.

As soon as I entered the chat room, I saw his yellow icon.

"Hello mystique lady, glad you're here. What about on PM?" He suggested.

We shifted to private messaging and he pounced at me immediately. "May I know your true identity, mystique lady?"

"C'mon, you don't expect me to reveal it, do you?" I added a grinning smiley.

"Well, even if I have not seen you, I'll reveal mine," he responded.

"Really, okay, so who are you?"

"I'm Amir Gupta, and as I have previously mentioned, I work for a multinational company."

Then we went on to talk about fixed marriages in India, infanticide, global warming, and many others. I learned a lot from Amir about India. It was one of the countries that fascinated me most. After 4 hours of non-stop talking, we still wanted to go on, but I bade goodbye, afraid that I might get caught in a trap of my own doing, so I signed out even if I wanted to go on and on.

From then on, we talked whenever we could squeeze the time. Every weekend, we chatted until the wee hours of dawn, and I got more and more involved with a faceless man I had met through the Internet. I had finally disclosed my name and my profession. "I'm a nurse by profession, but I am on leave for personal reasons," I revealed to him.

I learned that he was living alone. I learned also that his mother was Irish and his father was from New Delhi. He was 23 and was 7 years younger than I was.

One weekend, he requested that we talk through video chat. I was reluctant because although he knew my basic information, I was still scared of identifying myself before a man; I had barely met a few months ago.

My curiosity got the better of me, however, because I wanted to see his face as well. What did he look like? I have learned how to admire his intellect and humor.

My hands trembled with excitement as I set up the camera. Was he what I imagined him to be? Without seeing him, I felt I had known him for years already. Perhaps because I learned all about him from the hours and hours we spent with one another?

During weekdays, we greeted each other in the morning, talked before we slept, and then we stayed logged on the whole day during Saturdays and Sundays, while we talked and do whatever we had to do, but never logging out.

My eyes focused on the screen as the camera flickered and his face came into focus.

The eyes came first, and I stared at two beautiful, deep-set eyes with very long lashes; he almost seemed feminine. My chest fluttered. Then, the nose and lips came into view. I gasped as I stared into the face of the most handsome man I had ever seen. He looked like an Indian Bollywood actor!

My eyes were glued to the monitor, when his voice came over my headset.

"You're stunning," he whispered.

I unconsciously ran my fingers through my hair and stammered, "You look dashing too." I had meant to say, "You're every woman's dream man," but I managed to control my tongue and smiled at the thought.

"What are you smiling at?" he chided me. "Why didn't we do this earlier?" he lamented.

I peered at him shyly from my laptop and made a face. "I don't do this normally; this is the first time, but don't fret, we can do it now every day."

During the succeeding nights, we were like two, infatuated teenagers eager and thrilled to be together. We started calling up and texting each other through our mobile phones and sending emails to one another.

After several days of our virtual meeting, he

said, "I want to make love to you."

I felt my body become flush. I was speechless. I felt the same emotion too and wanted to feel the heat of his body against my own, but how could one make love through the Internet?

I looked at the cam and shrugged my shoulders. By the look on my face, he knew I wanted it too. He stepped out of his shorts and prodded me to do the same. I stared at his semi-nude sinewy body and my pussy started to get moist. It was almost a year that I had no man since Mark walked out of my life.

"Hey, what are you doing?" I said hoarsely.

"Take off your blouse, please," his voice was hot with passion.

But I still was not able to, until he stood there naked with his rock-hard manhood proudly pointing upwards in worship. I gasped as he held his dick and held it up for me to see. And that was the time said, "Let's talk tomorrow," and bade goodbye to Amir. I was still not yet ready for what he would like to happen.

That was why I had responded that way to seeing him nude.

I received an email right after I signed off:

My Darling,

Hey, don't say it made you feel cheap. Come on Honey, I did not take it like that. You are beautiful. In my eyes you will always be.

Okay, I agree I should take more care in how I act. I'm sorry I made you feel cheap by my action but that was not my intention. Why would I ever want to make you feel like that when I know you are not that kind of person?

Please remember we both cannot be perfect in everything we do and say. Especially since we are both so sensitive toward each other.

Now stop thinking like that and have a stress-free day. Have a bright, colorful, and sparkling day.

Always remember, there is nothing that will change my love for you

Love you,

Amir

The next day, when we talked, he was somewhat distant.

"Is something wrong?" I asked.

"I've never behaved like I did yesterday, except with you," he confessed, as he eyed me on the boob tube. "When I see you, I can't help but yearn for your touch."

We went on talking until we came to the point again that we were supposed to hold each other and make love. Then he was pleading again for me to undress, so he could see me. I felt aroused as he started undressing and I stared at his sexy body with his manhood upright and paying homage to me.

"I want to hold you and make love to you," he said yearningly.

He began fondling his dick.

"I want you to hold me here," he whispered into my ear phone I felt hot watching him, wishing I could feel his throbbing penis inside my moist vagina.

"Tell me what you want to do with me," he crooned into the camera. "Close your eyes and let go, let's make love."

I closed my eyes and listened to his voice.

"Yes, that's it."

His voice was soothing and I was hot all over my body. I wanted him to fuck me, but I still couldn't bring myself to undress before him.

"Now, imagine me touching your breast," My breath came in gasps as I listened to him prodding me. "I am undressing you now, removing your blouse...go on remove them for me," he urged but my eyes flashed opened and shook my head in disagreement.

He was frustrated, "okay, okay, no worries close your eyes, Hon." His voice was soothing. "Go on."

I closed my eyes again, and he continued, "My hands are now inside your blouse. I'm rolling your nipple between my fingertips," he whispered hoarsely. "Oh, they're firm and warm in my fingers."

"Stop," I almost shouted, as I opened my eyes.

"What's the matter Hon?" he asked in his deep, husky voice.

"I can't go on, please give me more time," I pleaded. My body was ablaze but my mind was reluctant.

His hands dropped from his engorged dick and sat down near the monitor. "Okay, relax. Take a deep breath."

"I'll say goodbye for now," I stated, avoiding his eyes.

And I logged out.

The following morning, I received an email from Amir.

My Dearest Jess,

Sorry for making you uncomfortable yesterday. You might get the wrong impression that I am sex-starved. I love you so much; I wanted to make love to you. I hope you understand that. I wish we could finally meet and quench our longing for each other. I hope God will grant my wish, and I hope it is your wish too.

You are reluctant because of the age gap, but there are twenty-four hours in a day, how much of that time can be spent having sex? Chocolate ice cream every day and one will tire of it. Best to have it once in a while, look forward to it, much more enjoyable, in anticipation, part of foreplay.

There are other things, like companionship, understanding, someone who cares, who will be there for better or for worse. I guess we're all searching.

There was this movie I saw when I was young called Young Frankenstein, black and white, comedy, with this funny guy Marty Feldman. He had these huge popping out of his head kind of eyes, really funny. He was the assistant of the scientist, Gene Wilder, who created the monster. Marty is to steal a brain from the lab and bring it so that the monster can be brought to life. Off goes Marty. In the lab he finds these large jars with brains in them. The first one is marked A. NORMAL, the next one is marked B. NORMAL. Marty is confused which one to take. Then he sees one marked ABNORMAL and decides this must be the correct one.

I can't always be certain when you'll read the letters, Jess. If you're awake by the time I send, then night, if asleep, then morning. I think you're right about one thing, at 23 I must be past infatuation.

Nevertheless, I want to make love to you Hon, just like in those compositions, like it hurts I want to so bad. I want to do it slowly, every part of you, hold you close, our naked bodies entwined...I want to taste you. With my tongue and lips—teeth, lightly, not hard—I want your breasts in my mouth. I want to run my tongue over and around your nipples, bite them lightly, and hear you moan. I want your mouth, your lips, your tongue, on me— encircling and enclosing my phallus, my tongue in your petals, your womanhood, probing, tasting, teasing your clitoris with my tongue. Making it erect and hard....tasting your wetness...the scent of you. I want to enter you from behind, holding your hips while driving into you...my manhood throbbing and sheathed by your womanhood—hot molten and wet— thrusting back and forth against each other...your cheeks slapping against my hips...I want to look into your eyes when I hold your thighs apart and mount you, penetrating your wet petals when I'm deep inside you, your thighs clasping my hips...driving, thrusting in urgent desperate need...our groins aching...wanting more...and more...my tongue in your mouth and yours in mine...I want to feel your nails digging into my back. I want to hear your cry...I want to feel your arms tightening around me...like you're never going to let go....

I can't help writing this...forgive me if it offends you...I just want to make love to you so badly Jess.

I'm signing off.

Love you,

Amir

P.S. Thanks for Wet Pants and for the laugh, Daisy. Thinking of you.....A.

I wiped a teardrop that has fallen on my keypads. Was this love or just lust? I felt the same longing as he did. I knew it was then becoming more than an online affair; that it has progressed much more. What would happen next?

My Dear Amir,

That was hot...lol...I feel the same way too. Sometimes I question myself, how could, a supposed to be, level-headed person say she loves someone she has not even met yet? On your part, will you still "love me" when you smell my sweaty body after a hard day's work? Will you still say "you love me" when you see me in the rigors of everyday living? It is so easy to say "I love you," but it will have to be proven.... "Actions speak louder than words." I can go on and on...but I think you've got the picture.

May you have a stress-free day; I apologize if I have hurt you; it was inadvert. I just want to be honest with you. Honesty is one of the bases of a good relationship.

Take good care of yourself for me. I care for you.

Love you,

Jess

Amir called me up in the evening. My heart

went into hyper-drive hearing his low baritone. I was familiar with his voice, with his perfect English and slight Indian accent.

"So how's my princess," he teased me.

"I'm too old to be a princess," I shot back at him becoming conscious of the age gap.

We were thousands of miles away from each other but he sounded like he was only in the next room.

The other day's event was completely forgotten. We teased each other as we recounted what happened during the day. My heart was singing. After having my heart badly broken at 20, there I was falling in love again, with a younger man, whom I haven't met yet personally.

It happened naturally once more; he became horny afterwards and prodded me to have sex on the phone, but I refused again, telling him, we should wait until we see each other in person. How could you make love using a telephone?

He was so frustrated that he blurted, "I think you don't love me."

I explained to him that I was not used to that type of sexual encounter and that I didn't know how to do it. After about four hours, he finally calmed down.

"Would miss you, Hon. Love you," he said sadly, when parting time came.

I felt a stab of pain in my chest as I realized I would miss him too, every second that would not be together. What he was not able to express on the phone, he wrote it:

My dear Jess,

Well, tell me what you think.

One Sunday Night
Sleeping next to you, I can hear your gentle breathing. Your back is turned away from me while you sleep. I put my arm around you and snuggle up against your back. You slowly awake opening your eyes and turn on your back looking at me, smiling. I kiss you lightly on your lips and you part them with a sigh accepting my gently probing tongue. I prop myself up on one shoulder cupping your breast in my hand and caressing, squeezing through the flimsy cotton cloth. We kiss more deeply making soft sounds. My hand goes downward caressing across your belly and feeling the curve of your womanly child-bearing hips. I cover your pubis and feel its warmth emanating. I pull your nightie up and you raise your hips so that I may get it over. You half sit up to allow me to raise it over your head discarding it across the bed. The dim light of the moon coming through the window bathes your naked body, your breasts so inviting. You lay back on the pillow...I cup your breast and fondle them...pinching your nipples lightly with my fingers and thumb, then taking them in my mouth, hungrily sucking on your nipples.

I sit up pulling off my vest and shorts. You run your hands over my chest and ribs all over my body, my back, kissing me everywhere. You put both your arms around my neck, kissing me deeply. Your hand moves down finding my hard pulsating phallus; you encircle it in your palm stroking its length moving your hand up and down I have my hand over your mound of Venus, rubbing and feeling your thatch of hair, parting the lips of your vagina. I gently use my fingers exploring your womanhood and we start kissing again. Our breathing gets quicker...I bend down now to your mound of Venus, the beautiful scent of you filling me. I insert my tongue as deep within you as I can and you moan, thrusting your hips at me. You want more...thrusting again and moaning, calling my name. I run my tongue in and out, in and out of your vagina, your mound soft, warm, and moist. You take my engorged penis full in your mouth using your tongue, sucking, moving the length of it in and out, in and out of your mouth. We are now lying in opposite directions on the bed. I am buried between your legs.??

I cannot control myself any longer...I am impatient tonight...I stop, and picking you up I sit on the edge of the bed and place you on my lap, your warm moist petals receiving my inflamed shaft, your bent legs alongside my hips on the bed. I cup your cheeks squeezing them hard and start moving you up and down on me. Pressing you against me, you are thrusting hard with your hips tonight. Our bodies are covered in sweat now; it is a hot and humid night. We are practically lunging against each other crying out for release, crying out our names...but wanting more, up and down clutching each other...kissing wildly...with panting breath, gasping and driving harder and harder into each other, faster and faster, in and out...in and out...until at last we reach a crescendo. With a final cry, we climax, our essence mixing together in one last shuddering gasp.

I can barely speak, I whisper, I love you

Jess.

Lying in each other's arms in the afterglow, we smile into each other's eyes knowing that tomorrow we have to get back to the rigors of daily living, but we have each other and that's a blessing.

(I didn't mean to hurt you these last couple of days. It was thoughtless and foolish of me.)

Love you,

Amir

After I read his mail, I could feel all the nerves in my body craving for fulfillment.

When we got to talk at YM during the evening, we exchanged sweet nothings and I expressed how I wanted him as well, but I simply could not get myself to make love his way.

I told him we had to see each other. I started to plan about how to meet. Would I go to him, or would he come to me? I expressed my dream of seeing India, especially the Shimla, and we talked about meeting at Pune because it was a more peaceful place. After we talked, he sent me an email, as well.

Dearest Jess,

When you came into my life, I was on the verge of packing it all in—on YM. I did not want to go on with my life anymore at the time. I had no reason to. This is not self-pity. I am telling you where I was mentally and emotionally. I had become cold and did not feel anything—not even for myself. I am responsible for the predicament I am in because of my actions in the past—doing exactly what I pleased whenever I please—.I can't help that now.

I used to come at night before going to bed—

for a lark as you can see from most of my conversations—but then I met you and I started feeling that maybe there is some hope after all, a reason for going on. That is what you gave me because I fell in love with you, and I started feeling again.

You keep mentioning about your age and so on—even today. I am this and I am that...I am older and so on...in the morning I look like this...it is all so trivial to me. You really do not know what you mean to me...I love you...I live my life for you...I want to be with you Jess.

Come to Pune, Honey, if you can and I will come there.

You think I want to leave India because I criticize it—or do I criticize it because I love it as well. There are so many wonderful things about India, too.

It does not matter to me where as long as I can be with you.

Through your institution, I am sure you must know some people in Pune who can advise you—if you do decide to come.

I will come to Pune and be with you. You just tell me when and I will come. From my side, there is no problem. I can come whenever you want me to. Please try if you can because I want to be with you sooner rather than later, to always be with you.

This is not sounding like Lochinvar saving his damsel in distress but Lochinvar in distress calling out to his Damsel.

I love you Honey more than you will ever know,

Amir

I was crying as I read and read Amir's

letter, over and over. Was this genuine love? When I separated with my boyfriend about 9 years ago, I vowed to myself I would never fall in love again, that I would never marry, but there I was falling in love for Amir. Perhaps, this has been the love I had wished all my life.

12 LINES FROM HEAVEN PART 2

My relationship with Amir was getting serious, but the truth still remained that I was thousands of miles away from him—unless, I would finally decide to visit Pune on a business trip. I had learned from my readings, and from Amir's information, that Pune is one of the perfect havens in India for tourists.

The following night when we talked on the phone, I requested that we take things slowly and take some time apart first. He was angry initially, but calm down when I explained that it would benefit us both, if we could prove that we had, indeed, fallen in love with each other, even after the cool-off period.

I was the older person, but it seemed my emotion was clouding my judgment. How could I think about going to India to meet a person, whom I just met through the Internet?

He was teary eyed when we ended our conversation.

"It would be good for both of us because we would know if what we feel is true and lasting," my voice trembled.

"I'm sure of myself," he insisted. "But, fine, I'll give you time to think about it," his voice faltered. "I'll wait when you're ready. Just give me a call, text, email...whatever."

I was lachrymose too when I finally put the phone down. What would happen in the next few days? Surely, the rainbows from the sky would appear so that God could tell me if I truly loved Amir, to risk my home, my family, and everything I had.

Dearest Jess,

Perhaps your experience with your previous boyfriend made you so sensitive to every little thing as I have no doubt that you loved him heart and soul, but the reciprocation was not what you expected. That is my feeling; I am not saying I am right. I am saying that you were hurt that the love you gave did not turn out like the love you received. I repeat this is only my feeling.

I love you my darling and I wish that I can truly kiss away the pain just like in that song by Enrique. I hope you understand what I mean. I love you and won't hurt you or put you through any pain. But you must not live in the past. I wanted to hold you and explain that pain is part of life, not just love. There is pain in LIFE. But we have to choose whether we want to stay in pain, or whether we want to stay in the joys that life brings. The joys of life are worth any pain, but to stay with the pain is a choice that leads to negativity, you know. I love you, and will always will. I'm willing to wait till forever.

Love you,
Amir
Dearest Amir,

You know, you are right about saying it is either you love a person or you don't. But you see, love is like a seed that has to be nurtured. Both parties should MAKE AN EFFORT to sustain love and make it grow deeper.

It does not just grow and prosper. It is like a seed. When there is not enough water and sunshine, it will eventually die. That is love in real life. I have loved my ex-bf like I never did anyone—loved him to death. I was ready to die for him, but his constant neglect, pain, and hurt during our relationship had now made me scared to death to enter into a commitment.

Rome was not built in a day. It took a lot of time to build that incredible city; likewise with love, it is built by our actions, not by our words. It is through our actions that we validate what we say. If we speak the word, but our actions belie them, then the action would be a better proof of what we truly feel than what comes out of our mouth.

I will always be here for you. I just have to slow down and take everything in stride, follow your lead, or I will end up hurting myself. I hope you understand. I thought we would lie low for a while? And you don't have to say ILY all the time.

Always,
Jess
Dearest Jess,

Yes, love needs to be nurtured I agree, and it is never a one-way street. There are so many people in this world who have loved and lost— why do they love and lose Jess?

My belief is that they never did find true love in the first place. That is why they cling on to the belief that what they had was true love as it was the closest they got to it. It is really, really, really rare, and those who do find it are blessed—two souls who come together as one and cannot survive without the other after that—as it seems like a part of their soul has gone. That for me is true love. I don't know if it will be like that for me. I will only know once I am with you, just like you said, we will know when we are together, then only. Please do not go into too much analysis on this. Just take it as written; if I am not clear somewhere, ask before coming to your own conclusions. Just like everyone else, I am not perfect, maybe that is why we have to nurture it the way you explained.

Love you my darling,

Amir

I stared into the monitor. It was weird; we were not talking to each other through chat or via phone, but we were still communicating through our emails. I was unable to stop myself from replying.

I had to try to fulfill what I had intended to do in the first place—at least. I decided not to reply to his latest email. My heart was in agony, but I tried hard to endure.

My Darling Jess,

I am still here. You're really trying to drive me away. I'm very unreasonable, very difficult to drive away once I make up my mind about something.

Jess let's keep things simple. Let me remind you of our quote, the one you said to make our quote.

I love you, trust you, and believe in you; otherwise, I would be a hypocrite to tell you that I love you unconditionally. You have been through life and so have I. Nobody is perfect, but I know that you are someone who tries the best you can. I am far from perfect too— physically and in behavior—like I said please remember our quote.

Last night, I was a little hurt when you said how many times are you going to say ILY, but then I let it go. I'm okay now.

I have to tell you something, please understand. I know you have some doubts and suspicions about my intentions, but in your heart I know you love me. That is why I am saying this. I want to go there. When I am able to go and be with you, I will come on my own steam. God forbid I do not manage to get my life back in order again; please understand what I am saying, and why.

I will leave everything that is familiar to me to be with you. There's a WOW for you. I love you Jess. There I go again saying I love you, too many ILUs huh? But I am positive I will succeed because I like to look at the brighter side of life, even when things are not going too well. Just read what I have written. There is no innuendo. No hidden meaning.

I was not shattered with what you have said in your letter. Unconditional means no conditions Jess—no conditions. It means accepting your love the way she is, and that is what I was perhaps looking for all my life.

I say perhaps because you have rightly said that I do not know what it is like living with someone on a daily basis other than family members. What I do know is that I have never reacted like this to any woman, even when you don't want to ring me up, and last night when you sort of snapped "how many times are you going to say ILY," I reacted, like I was feeling hurt. That has never happened to me; before, it would not bother me.

All I want from you is the quote, and I will give you the same—and also patience and understanding. That is what I want from you, and you know what, these things that I want are much more valuable than any material possessions and also much more difficult to come by.

Love you,

Amir

My Dearest Jess,

I'm sorry I cannot do as you wish. How can I distance myself from you? What can I do?

Honey, can you really define love. Can anybody? Can anyone ever say or express it in words or actions completely. Humankind has been trying to since time immemorial.

If one even tries, one will end up with an endless number, infinite.

Love just happens to people. One cannot go in search of it. That is why I thought that it could never happen to me.

You came into my life in the least expected way. I just know I love you. I don't analyze it at all. I love you; that's all I know. My heart says so.

I have to go to bed now.

Nothing will ever change how I feel for you, nothing will do that.

I love you my darling always,

Amir

My Darling Jess,

Even if you keep ignoring me, please allow me to express my emotions this way. I have told you so many times that I love you. I love YOU.

I promised you honey and I will keep my promise because I love you, unconditionally. It is rare what we have and I will never go back on my promise to you. I love you and want to share my life with you.

There will be ups and downs at times, now and when we are together, but we will overcome as our love will see us through.

I love you my darling and nothing will change that,

Amir

He was so persistent, so patient, even without getting any replies, he kept writing. It had been almost a month that I didn't reply to his emails. How I wanted to. It was Calvary for me denying myself of the joy we could have had. I had missed him terribly. Soon, work will beckon and I might not have the chance anymore to spend long hours with him. I finally wrote him back.

My Dear Amir,

I miss you and I love you too, I can't explain why. I love you so much, it hurts. Little things mean a lot; things that should be spontaneously done, coming from within.

Yes, you are right, every relationship is unique and different from each other. I just have to trust my instinct and follow my heart because my heart says I love you.

Jess

My Darling Jess,

Thanks a thousand times for finally replying. Yahooo!!! I love you and miss you. You don't know how much because you can't see me. I want to be with you right now. God, how I long to hold you in my arms. You're so shy to do it on cam, so please allow me to do it this way.

Alone in my bed at night, awake and thinking of you in the darkness I imagine us meeting for the first time.

We are both a little nervous and tentative in our words, in our eyes, and in our smiles. We meet in a quiet hotel room with the air conditioning humming in the background, sitting across each other unsure as to how to proceed. Feeling each other out with our words and our eyes, time ticks away.

I know I have to make the first move. I get up and sit next to you on the couch, close. You turn a little to face me and I see your quick smile, a little nervous. I take your hand in mine, draw you to me, and gently kiss your lips my arm going around your waist. Your eyes are liquid pools of black, you haven't closed them, still a little wary. I gently pry open your lips with my tongue and now with a sigh you open your mouth accepting my kiss. I feel your body relax and lean against mine, your arms go around my neck kissing me in return, your eyes close and everything is fine. Our tongues slowly twisting, we kiss and the urgency comes flooding into both of us. The long wait is over and the yearning for each other takes over. Taking my hand from your waist, I cover your breast, squeeze and fondle them over the cloth of your blouse. Your hand goes to my crotch and you start rubbing me. I am already hard and rigid. You squeeze my penis and I grunt with pleasure. Kissing, rubbing, and fondling each other, we slide off the couch onto the carpeted floor. We kick off our shoes. I start to unbutton your blouse and you unbuckle my belt. We are now smiling and laughing, the nervousness all gone. We know this is meant to be and the feeling is wonderful.

I pull off your blouse, remove your bra, and throw them over the couch your naked soft voluptuous breasts swing free. I take them in my hands fondling and squeezing, pinching and rubbing your nipples with my fingers. Caressing, I take one of your breasts in my mouth hungrily sucking, rolling my tongue over the erect nipple, kissing and licking first one breast and nipple and then the other, so hungry, your beautiful breasts, my woman's beautiful breasts.

Your hands are busy at my crotch. You tug off my belt and quickly unzip and open my pants, pulling them off you throw them aside, my undies follow and my phallus springs up pulsating with the pleasure of your touch. You

*start massaging it and rubbing it. I unbutton
and unzip your skirt, and discarding them I
pull down your lace panties over your knees
and ankles and off. I quickly get rid of the rest
of my clothing. We are naked and grasping for
each other, clinging to one another, kissing,
hungry to touch and feel every part, sucking,
licking, and tasting. Our hands, mouths, lips all
over each other's bodies, we gasp, moan, cry,
and call each other's names, entwined naked
on the floor.*

*You climb on top of me and start kissing me.
From my face and my lips, you slowly move
down to my nipples, kissing and licking them
with your tongue, then to my belly. Kissing and
caressing, you reach my phallus and take it
into your mouth. I moan and reach down taking
a handful of your soft black hair looking down
at you consuming me. You continue playing
with me. With your tongue, you lick the
tumescent head of my penis, teasing, running
your tongue up and down its length repeatedly.
You come to the top and a drop of my essence
appears at the head of my phallus, and you
taste me, and take me into your mouth again
sucking and licking and teasing until I am
writhing on the floor grunting with pleasure.
You straddle my hips, and guiding me into, you
start riding my member. I hold onto your hips
and squeeze your buttocks, caress your
breasts while you go up and down impaling
yourself on my manhood, riding and riding. I
stop you and push you over onto your back.*

*I want to taste you and smell the musky
odor of your petals. I go between your legs,
crouching over you. I take your thighs and*

spread them; your triangle of hair slightly wet with your juices drives me wild. I cover it with my mouth kissing and kissing. My tongue darts into your passage. I run my tongue along the groove of your vagina repeatedly, up and down. Feeling your clitoris, I start licking it, stroke after stroke after stroke. Running my tongue over it again and again. Darting my tongue into you and tonguing you with long strokes, I keep on and on licking and sucking the core of you, your essence, tasting your juices, extracting all its quiddity until you are grabbing me by the hair and pressing me hard against your womanhood, spreading your thighs wider. Your legs over my shoulders with your heels digging into my back, I bury between your legs. The musky scent of you driving me to consume you more and more, quicker, faster, my mouth, my tongue darting, licking, probing, and teasing. Your thighs quiver and I go on and on and on at the core of your womanhood.

When I know that you are ready and I am ready, I stand up and pull you up as well. Pushing you toward the couch, I bend you over the padded arm. You push your buttocks out at me, turning around, smiling and laughing at me, teasing and rubbing your soft beautiful buttocks against my hard penis. I press against you caressing and squeezing the sweet mounds of your lovely buttocks, feeling its roundness. I bend down and kiss both cheeks, and your muskiness fills me again driving me to dart my tongue into your petals again from under you. I hold your thighs and plunge my tongue into you kissing and licking greedily. My phallus is tumescent, completely engorged and throbbing; I am aching for you to release me. Standing up, I shove hard against you and the hungry petals of your hot wet vagina consume my manhood. I start grinding against you with my hips, hammer and tongs into your depths. You keep on and on thrusting your buttocks at me, absorbing every forceful thrust of my hips. Your petals, suction on my pulsating penis. Like a piston, we move against each other, in rhythm. My phallus disappearing into the soft folds of you and your buttocks thrusting against my hips wanting more, pumping and slapping, my hips and your buttocks. It feels wonderful my darling, your petals around my penis enclosing and releasing. Our breathing gets ragged, gasping, sweating, our bodies wet with perspiration.

Clasping your hips in my hands, I frenziedly shove my hard hot penis deeper and deeper into your hot wet vagina. You goad me on harder, harder, pushing your buttocks out more urgently to receive the rapidly increasing tempo of my thrusting hips wanting more and more, the tempo increasing faster and faster, in and out, until with a final cry calling our names, we reach the top of the crest, peaking together like crashing waves. In rapid jerks, my semen spurts into the waves of your release, our very beings quivering with the union.

I carry you in my arms, lay you down on the bed, and lie beside you. We hold each other close and kiss softly, smiling and laughing in the afterglow of our lovemaking, satiated and fulfilled in body, mind, and soul. Words are no longer necessary.

(I love you my darling Jess, I will not hurt you in any way, I promise.)

I love you my darling and will be with you always,

Amir

P.S. I want to make love to you Jess (not have sex with you). Can you understand this? Love you. A.

I stared at my laptop monitor, my body hot with desire and yearning, an ache that emanated all the recesses in my body, especially the moist patch between my thighs. I lay down and touched the labia of my aching vagina.

Oh, how I longed to make that scene come true. I closed my eyes and the words in his email came flooding in, turning them into something real, but my hands were not accustomed to caress my body. I had touched myself before but I stopped before I could reach orgasm. That moment, I needed sexual gratification badly.

I emailed Amir back, requesting him to please come online. His reply was instant, like he was just waiting for my reply. His icon was already yellow when I logged on. We hurriedly switched to private messaging.

"Hon, how are you?" I asked, not knowing how to tell him how much I wanted him to make love to me and satiate the blazing fire of passion within me.

"I'm fine hon," he replied breathlessly; his face was suffused with passion. I just knew it.

"I want to make love to you badly hon," he said hoarsely.

"Me too, hon," I didn't care anymore how; I

just wanted to gratify the burning need I had within me. "What will I do?" I asked. I was like a naïve schoolgirl.

"Just close your eyes hon, and concentrate on what I'll be saying," he instructed.

I closed my eyes and listened to Amir's soothing voice.

"Now, take deep breaths, yes, relax, relax..." I listened to him as his voice went on.

"We're in a room; we are staring at each other, shy at first. Then I come to you." Behind my eyelids, I could almost feel him.

"I hold your hand, and we smiled at one another," he paused. "Then I started kissing you, my tongue darting into your mouth to pry it open. Hmmmm, you lips are so soft and sweet. My tongue searches for your tongue and wrestled with it."

I wet my lips with my tongue.

"While, I'm savoring and sucking your tongue, my hands are caressing your breasts through your blouse. Please caress them for me," he whispered into my earphone. "Don't open your eyes, just caress them and imagine me doing it," he continued.

My nipples tingled as I ran my hands through them, and they stood at attention through my flimsy blouse.

"I am kissing your neck now," he continued. "My fingers are slowly unbuttoning your blouse. Please unbutton them for me," he prodded me gently.

I hesitated only for a moment, then I feverishly managed to let go of my blouse. It fell to the floor with a final thud.

"You're removing my shirt as well, aching to

touch my bare skin. Then I freed your tits from your bra and cuddled them close to my face as I alternately kissed and fondled them. Do this for me please hon."

I felt my breath quickened, as I fondled my breast alternately. I was on fire, as I imagined his lips playing with my nipples.

"Then I rained kisses on every inch of your skin as my lips descended into your moist pussy."

I gasped as the thrill and lust for his lips in my vagina overcame me.

"You managed to get me out of my pants as well, as I slipped your panty and caressed your pussy with my hands. You're also fondling my penis as I explore your pussy too. We cling to each other, as we kiss and fondled and caressed each other's bodies."

I was wantonly fondling my vagina and then my breast, wanting to reach fulfillment. I was so aroused even right after I read his email, that I had lost all inhibitions. All I craved for was sexual fulfillment.

"Now, open your eyes," he encouraged me.

I opened my eyes, and there he was naked in all his splendor. His dick was so big, and hard, I felt my pussy aching for it badly. That was when I became fully aware that I was naked too and had spread wide my legs to fondle my vagina.

I tried to close my thighs, but he said, there was nothing more to hide. "Let's make love tonight," he stated matter-of-factly.

"Look at me now," he said huskily. "See, what you can do to me?" He caressed his dick with his hands, going up and down his shaft.

"I'm imagining you doing this to me," he said.

I was gasping from want to hold his dick and fondle it.

"I'm kissing and sucking your clit now," he urged me to caress and use my fingers on my clit.

I ran my fingers gently but firmly over my clit, rubbing and fingering it as his voice hypnotized me pleasurably. I felt my orgasm straining to surface. The fingers of my left hand were playing with my breasts, while my right hand was down in my clit increasing the tempo of my movements.

"I can't wait to fuck you, hon. Do you want me to fuck you now?" he said hungrily.

"Yes, yes, please hon," I cried as I felt my body tensing. I want to feel his pulsating penis enclosed in my warm and moist vagina.

"I'm straddling you now," he was panting heavily, and it intensified my arousal because I felt that he was really there making love to me.

I stared at his enormous erection and my body was aflame. How I would like to have him pounding that delicious penis into my hungry pussy.

He was holding it a few inches from the cam like he would come out from it and fuck me like crazy.

"Spread your legs hon, and imagine your fingers as my dick. Now insert three or two and as I thrust forward mimic my movement. Allow your fingers to go in and out of your love tunnel," he said.

"Now, I'm penetrating you, and I could feel your delicious pussy welcoming my manhood.

Oh, it feels so good, hon. Hmmmm."

He started thrusting through his fingers and I finger-fucked myself too. He was groaning in pleasure, as I moan in the throes of my incoming orgasm.

We were whispering endearments to one another as we imagined ourselves locked into each other.

"Go faster and harder please," I begged him, and his fingers went up and down his dick with increasing tempo, as I writhed and matched his tempo with my fingers.

"You're so sweet Jess, hon...I love you...hmmmm....hmmmmm...your pussy is so tight and juicy.... Spread wide your legs for me hon...that's it...hmmmm...I am going in and out of your pussy in deep strokes now, pumping harder and quicker...hmmmm....hmmmm...I'm nearing climax now hon...what about you?"

I didn't have to answer Amir's query because I was moaning in ecstasy as my climax brought me to a Nirvana I had never been before—I heard him groaning in pleasure and saw him arching his back as he came too, his semen squirting from his engorged penis. My orgasm kept coming that I had to insert my fingers several times and caress my vagina, imagining his dick still inside me, before the orgasms ceased. It was a heavenly experience!

It was my first sex online, and I was completely satiated, and overjoyed that it was with Amir.

13 LINES FROM HEAVEN PART 3

After my first online sex with Amir, I became less and less shy. I even danced for him before we made love, in certain occasions. Amir expressed his desire for us to finally meet in person. It was an online affair with him in India and I in Hong Kong, and my fears intensified of what might happen when we would actually be together in person.

Although we talked daily through webcam chat, we still wrote long emails to each other.

My Darling Jess,

First, I have to ask you about marriage as you have explained to me about your customs there.

Where my beliefs of love and marriage are concerned, one should only marry for love and if it is true love then I believe it will last no matter what.

And also, it is a two-way street—the love you give is the love you receive. If it is not that way and turns out only one way, then it is not true love.

That is why some marriages do not work out, relationships as well.

On death, I believe that every birth is a death so live your life.

And every death is the birth of another form of existence. We continue to exist in one form of matter or the other as part of the whole. Am I confusing you?

Love is rare Jess; that is why so many beautiful stories are told and movies made on the subject.

Yes, I do believe that we met the way we did for a reason.

We will know for sure if our love is true when we are together, and I want you to know that the way I feel for you even though I have not met you is something I have never felt for anyone...any woman.

Will you get irritated and impatient after a while, with my—sometimes—childish behavior?

Jokes aside, all I want from you is that you love me in spite of myself.

But will we live together forever? I would of course like us to live together forever. Till then, I guess it is your call as to what arrangement would be best for us.

I'm sending some symbols, but God knows maybe after sending, they change due to something. Anyway it was a female sign plus a male sign then equals love and music. You got the meaning right. That is what I wanted to tell you how I feel about our relationship...how I feel about you, about us.

What the future holds for us, we will know

when we will know. I am looking forward to it. It will be an adventure of discovery...of each other...of our love. It excites me.

Love you,

Amir

My Dearest Amir,

We were thinking of the same thing, if this is love, then not any event, anything or anyone can ruin it...no matter how big the storm that might assail it.

You must be very picky of your women because how can one explain that you have never fallen in love?

My face lights up whenever I receive your letters and my steps quicken. I think of you when I sleep alone in bed and imagine holding your face and tracing its contours.... I think of you as being part of my future...one of the great reasons why I wake up every morning, recharged and ready. But sometimes reality bites and I nurture second thoughts of how wise my decision is...I have been tremendously hurt and would not want to undergo the same Calvary again. Yes, you keep assuring me that you won't hurt me, and I try to focus and hold this thought in my mind at doubtful moments like these.

Am I the only woman you communicate with online? Doubts and doubts.

I know eventually, these moments will pass, if I can feel and see that you are genuinely sincere.

I do hope you could be as steadfast as an oak tree, against the whiplashes that would still come—a test of the love that we, so profess. I'm signing off now. Take good care of

yourself for me.
  LOVE YOU,
  Jess
  My Darling Jess,
  I have a feeling that you think there is someone online that I might have had something going with—is that it?
  Let me tell you I had exchanged a few emails with one or two women, but they were just pleasantries and then after I met you I no longer allowed any emails. I hope this answers your question. Just remember I am very introverted and it takes me a while to get to first base, so to speak. So, no, there is no one I have had any kind of relationship online with.
  Jess I love you so much.
  The reason for the way I addressed you is that I was afraid that knowing my past, it might make things different...like I was afraid I might lose you. Now I know I won't and I'm not afraid anymore.
  You have given me something very precious my love...something that money just cannot buy, and that is more precious that any material thing. I love you my darling Jess.
  I love you I love you I love you I love you I love you I love you I love you I love you I love you I love you I love you I love you I love you I love you I love you I love you...
  Does this indicate that I am crazy about you or just plain crazy, huh?
  No, not plain crazy...just crazy about you.
  Love you my darling,
  Amir
  P.S. There is only you Jess. I love you.
  I did not reply to his email because I was so

tired coming from my first night duty. The following day I slept most of the day and got ready again for work the following evening. How I missed Amir, but I was simply exhausted I was not able to force my eyes open to chat with him. Before I went to work again, I opened my mail while getting ready for work.

My Darling Jess,

Where are you, my love? I want to make love to you. You are very special to me Jess. You are the one I love. My one and only love. Don't ask me how I know, I do. Believe in me. I love you.

I believe love is the one thing that transcends everything. It is patience, forgiveness, care, giving, understanding, without any boundaries. That is why it is so rare to find someone who loves you just the way one is, without conditions. That is when one knows that one is truly loved.

We have come quite a way from when we first met. We have been open with each other about ourselves and our families, personal things that we would not just tell anyone. It has brought us closer together. There have been some ups and downs I agree but we have got past them. We have seen each other on cam in our homes, you eating tuna sandwich and cookies and me with my boiled egg...hehehe...the little little things.

Please wait for me. I'll be coming soon.

I love you my darling. Can't you see how much I do?

I LOVE YOU,

Amir

My Dearest Amir,

I'm sorry for not being able to come online yesterday. Work was so toxic; I hit the sack as soon as I arrived home. I was only able to read your email. Sorry for not sending even a short reply. I was half asleep while reading your letter and was asleep already before I could even turn off the computer...funny, but true.

I missed you so much hon, but I have to go to work. I have slept through the day and hadn't even eaten lunch. I hope you can come here sooner. I can't wait to be with you and feel your warmth and make love to you all day long....

GTG, work is calling, love you so much, hon.

Missing you,

Jess

Amir and I finally chatted after a week when the work rotation schedule was changed. I was on duty 2 to 10 pm, which left us time in the morning and the late evening to chat.

When we finally chatted that evening, we flirted and then made online love with all the lights on. I wore a negligee, no longer shy of flaunting my voluptuous body to Amir. It took me a few months to finally give in to his request for online sex, but when I did, it seems I couldn't get enough of it.

We stared hungrily at each other across the webcam. He was already naked and hard, waiting eagerly for me. I put on some slow music and danced seductively for him, revealing my body inch by inch. I could hear his heavy breathing through my headphones.

"Yes, honey, fondle your breasts while stripping. Do it for me," he hissed passionately into my ears.

He was caressing his manhood slowly and staring at my gyrating body fixedly. I dropped my negligee on the floor as the music came to a stop. I had nothing underneath it.

He gasped and said: "Darling Jess, come to me."

I pressed my luscious breasts into the monitor as he fondled his penis and pressed it too. We both groaned with passion.

"I'm going down on you now," I whispered huskily. "I'm caressing your dick, and then sucking and licking its crown."

He moaned, "Go on sweetie, get it into your mouth."

I was licking two of my fingers, as I pinched and fondled my nipples. He was standing right in front of the camera and he was also slowly caressing his rock-hard penis as he stared at me playing with myself.

"I'm getting you full in my mouth now, sliding my mouth up and down your engorged shaft," I whispered into his ears.

"I grabbed your hair and guide you up and down my phallus. It feels so good, hon," he whispered back.

He increased the tempo of his fingers' movement on his penis.

"I suck your dick, as I fondle your balls," I went on. "I am sucking and licking, enjoying the taste of your manhood in my mouth.

"Kneel for me, my love," he commanded me lustily.

I knelt and displayed proudly my rear to the cam. I couldn't imagine myself a few months back doing this, but Amir has taught me well.

I heard him panting heavily.

"That's right honey, what lovely buttocks you have. I have my dick poised to enter you from behind. I can't hold on any longer," he groaned. "I'm thrusting my red-hot dick into your moist vagina now. You taste so good honey, hmmmm, hmmmm."

I fondled my clit and my labia as he was talking and I urged him to go deeper as I inserted two of my fingers inside my wet and eager vagina.

"I am thrusting now into your tight and slick pussy...hmmmm...how warm and loved I feel. Honey, you're so sweet. I am increasing my tempo now." I peered between my legs into the monitor and he was stroking his penis faster, and faster, as I finger fucked myself.

I turned around and urged him, "Can you straddle me, please?"

He sighed eagerly as I lay supine on the floor. I stared from the floor at the cam and spread my legs wide as I beckoned him. He stood above me with his big, angry penis and my love tunnel was so wet for it.

"Fuck me hard honey," I begged him, my voice quivering with excitement.

"I'm straddling you now," he said, towering above me. "I'm ramming you hard with my dick. Hmmmm, you're so tight and juicy honey. Ahhhh...Now and then, I drop to suck your breasts. Hmmmm."

I felt hot all over. Every nerve fiber in my body was aching for him. I inserted three fingers of my right hand into my vagina as my left played with my tits.

"I'm increasing the tempo now, going faster

and harder, ramming my penis into your warm vagina. Hmmm, you're an ambrosia sweetie...love you," he panted as he masturbated, as well.

I was busy with my fingers too, matching his movements, as we "fucked" and reached orgasms simultaneously. Then we collapsed on the floor and whispered sweet nothings to one another.

The following morning, I received this email from Amir.

My Darling,

Thanks for last night. It was incredible. I love you and miss you again. You don't know how much. I have my tickets ready now. I didn't tell you the exact date because I was still not sure yet if it would push through. Thank God, I'll be there in 2 days.

I will come as promised. Take good care, see you soon.

As ever,
Love you my darling,
Mwah
Amir

I stared at the monitor in surprise and excitement. He was finally coming, my heart rejoiced. My beloved Amir was finally coming for me. I was not able to concentrate on anything that day. I was too thrilled to focus, so I filed for a week of absence from work, citing personal reasons.

Those two days of waiting were interminable for me. Each minute was unending; I couldn't wait for Amir and me to finally be together. Doubts clouded my mind: Would he still love me when he sees how plain-looking I was? Would he still want to marry me after he comes to know me more? These questions were weakening my resolve to meet him, but...

"I'm on my way to the airport now my darling. I'll be there at 9 p.m. Tuesday, June 12, Air India flight no. A450. Miss you again. I can't wait to hold you in my arms. A few more hours and I'll be there. Be there at the airport," he said.

Then later: "I'm boarding the plane now, sweetie. I would call you again when we land," he stated.

I barely could reply back in my anxiety and excitement. I prepared the small apartment I was renting. I spruced it up with some romantic ambiance; I added a mirror opposite my queen-sized bed and some artsy bedside light that exuded a blue color. I bought a new negligee and several pairs of sexy undies.

The moment of truth was at hand. It was time to go to the airport. I took a bath longer as I tried to assuage my fiery body. It was already ablaze with passion, trembling at the promise of eventual gratification in Amir's arms.

I wore a simple blue pantsuit that fitted well with my voluptuous frame. I wore very little make-up, pink lipstick, some blush-on, and a light eyeliner. I stared at myself in the mirror; I was plain-looking, not the breathtaking beauties that turned heads, but I prayed in my heart that Amir loved me for who I was.

Traffic was heavy and I was glad I started earlier from home. The airport was teeming with people, as well. I proceeded to the waiting area and bought some snacks, as I had an hour more to wait. There were butterflies in my stomach, and my hands trembled as I slowly sipped my coke.

Then the announcement came that Amir's flight has landed. I stood up after 30 minutes and looked down on the arriving passengers with their bulky pieces of luggage. Would he look exactly like he did on cam? Was the color of his hair black? I was going into a panic. Yes, it was black. I took deep breaths to calm my nerves.

I scanned the passengers, one by one, my heart in my throat. There was a dark-haired man but he was bearded and Amir was not. An elderly man with Amir's built stopped and looked up, my heart fluttered. He looked away, no, the man is too old to be Amir. Perhaps, he was actually old? Cameras can sometimes be deceitful. What would I do then? God, my pulses were racing, as I continued watching everyone coming out from the arrival area.

No one matched Amir, and everyone has already gone. Where was he? Maybe he was not able to board his plane? I tried calling him up but his cell phone was off. My excitement turned into worry. Where was Amir?

I looked down broodingly, at the now empty, arrival area. I felt dejected. He didn't have the guts to come after all. I started to turn away, when a man slowly came down the ramp. His strides were determined but slow, like he was savoring the moment. He stood tall and lean with his face slightly hidden by his cap. Then he looked up and our eyes met, and I knew it was Amir.

I covered the distance in a flash and ran to him eagerly, my pulses raced and my heart singing with joy. Amir has finally arrived!

I stopped a few feet away from him and was at a loss whether to run into his arms or to introduce myself first formally. He looked exactly as he did on cam, only taller than what I expected: perfectly chiseled nose, full, sensual lips, and deep brown eyes, with black heavy lashes. He looked like a Greek God, so handsome and so strong. It was so easy talking and interacting with him online, but now that he was right in front of me, I was tongue-tied and didn't know what to do.

Amir smiled warmly, when he noticed my hesitation and beckoned me to his arms. I ran to him then and felt the jolt of electricity as the warmth of our bodies merged in one sweet embrace. The feeling was heaven; I felt joy, warmth, and security in his arms. "Namaste, meri pyaar" (Hello my love), he crooned in my ears.

Then, we were heading home, our hands linked together in felicity. He was telling me why he came out last. "I was anxious that you would not like what you see, so I stayed and relaxed a bit," he said laughing. "But now, I noticed, you're more anxious than I am," he laughed again.

The sound of his laughter was music to my

ears. The taxi driver kept glancing at us at from his front mirror. We were just holding hands, but Amir's feet was already secretly rubbing against my own, sending quivers of anticipated pleasure coursing through my spine. I can feel my crotch becoming wet.

I looked down at Amir's crotch and he had a visible erection straining to be set free. We were lucky my neighborhood was not so populated so people come and go without being seen. When we alighted, we ran inside like two excited kids.

As soon as the door closed, we melded into each other's arms, our lips furious and hungry for each other. We tore at each other's clothes and let lose all those months of online sex and imagined encounters. We were not able to reach the bedroom. He pulled my blouse free, while he sucked my tongue and devoured my mouth. I reached out for his slacks and freed his tumescent, glistening penis.

He groaned like a tiger and slammed me into the wall. His lips descended on my right breast as his hands were feverishly getting me out of my pants and undies. As soon as my pants dropped down, I pulled him to me, aching for his dick, urging him to take me right then and there.

He was wild now, panting heavily and red in the face as he thrust his dick into me and the force reverberated through the wooden partition of my living room. His dick slid smoothly into my already moist petals and I clung to him in exquisite delight. It felt so good.

I had one of my legs around him and he was lifting me partially as I had my arms around his neck. He rammed his dick again, and we both cried in pleasure. It was even sweeter than what I imagined. The sensual pleasure was so dizzying, I felt I could faint any moment.

Then he lifted me by holding my two buttocks; I was totally in his mercy. The fire that was ablaze in my groin was growing into an uncontrollable conflagration. He carried me up and down his dick, slamming against my pussy as I strained to grind it into his enormous manhood.

We were moving to the tempo of our urgent need for release. We were sweating, panting, clawing at each other and he was banging me like there was no tomorrow. The walls rattled as he pounded me relentlessly, the ultimate pleasurable sensation of his dick going in and out of my tight vagina was beyond description. I screamed and cried as my orgasm rolled in a thunderous explosion. I trembled in ecstasy as he continued pounding his steel-hard dick into my dripping love tunnel.

I came again when he continued fucking me, getting everything that I could offer. Then with one final shudder, he groaned like a wild animal and locked his groin into mine as I felt his semen spurt warmly into my satiated pussy.

He kissed me on the lips lingeringly as our heavy breathing started to subside. He carried me into the bed where we curled and fell asleep, naked, and in each other's warm embrace.

I awakened from a dream where I was running after Amir and calling out his name but he did not hear me. I was sobbing when I came to and disoriented of where I was. Then I felt Amir's warm, naked body pressed to mine and all my apprehensions disappeared.

I looked at his face in repose and realized how handsome he was. I traced his lips with my fingers and he stirred and snuggled closer to my breasts. He was undoubtedly exhausted from his more than 10-hour travel. I slowly disengaged myself, but he woke up, startled, and pulled me back into the circle of his arms.

I thought he would go back to sleep but he didn't. He started kissing me, kissing every inch of my skin, down into my breasts. I felt the familiar stirrings down my crotch and all over my body. Amir suck my nipples alternately as his hands were gently massaging my labia with tantalizing pressure.

I spread my legs and he went farther down my thighs, down to my eager, yearning petals. It was wet already as his tongue licked my labia up and down, with darting, titillating strokes. I slung my legs on both his shoulders as he lifted my hips to devour my womanhood.

His tongue then settled in the area around my clit. It darted around my most erogenous zone without coming in contact with my clitoris. He inserted two of his fingers into my vagina and began applying pressure to my G-spot. I was writhing in pleasure and trying to get my mound of ecstasy into his tongue until I cried for him to suck me there.

He did then, and I exploded into an incredible clitoral orgasm that left me arching my back and screaming his name in pure delight. He didn't cum as I did, but mounted me instead and fucked me in quick short strokes. He increased the tempo as he dug his "scrumptious" dick deeper and deeper into my pussy. It was nirvana!

I came again, and again, and again. I trembled with utter fulfillment as I sucked at his neck as the pleasure flooded my body like a succession of delicious tidal waves. And then he came too in one, long squirt. We collapsed against each other as we lay there satiated yet again, and extremely happy.

Little did we know that we needed all the happiness that we could treasure because soon a monstrous problem would assail our relationship. Had I known, I would have not asked him to come at all.

I snuggled closer to Amir's embrace as he lovingly stroked my fulfilled and totally loved body. It was the happiest moment of my life.

14 LINES FROM HEAVEN PART 4

Amir and I stayed in my rented apartment all week and just made crazy, wanton love like there was no tomorrow. In between our passionate love-making, we talked about getting married.

"We would have to ask the blessings of my parents," I informed Amir.

We went to see my parents the following week. They were not pleased with my decision. They were civil to Amir but mom pulled me aside and said:

"Please don't do this sweetie, we don't approve of it. Marry our own kind, and we'll die happy."

"Mom, what do you mean our own kind?" I asked, angry.

"He's from another country. His beliefs are

different from ours."

"Mom, please don't say that. I love Amir and I want to get married soon. Please give us your blessings."

We left mom and dad without their blessings. I was devastated. The two most important persons in my life had refused to accept the person I loved.

Amir had an arm around me, but he was silent, aware that my parents didn't like him. I cried all the way back to my apartment as Amir tried to calm me down.

That night as I was sitting by the bed, ready to cry again, he prodded me to lie down, and to close my eyes and relax.

I lay down with tears on my face. He kissed my tears away and showered my face with light, flurry kisses. My muscles relaxed as his tongue and mouth continued to rain kisses on my neck. His tongue darted now and then to lick my skin.

I felt my arousal starting again. We still hadn't gotten enough of each other. It would take years perhaps, before we do.

Amir kissed my shoulders and nibbled my ears as his lips planted soft kisses on the surrounding areas. I shivered as the embers of fire of passion started to smolder inside me.

He continued down my chest, kneading my shoulders with her hands, while gently darting his tongue to lick my skin. He stood up and came back with an ice cube in his mouth. Then he traced the contours of my breasts with it. I gasped as the pure sensation the ice cube created on my skin, enervated my senses. When the icy tip touched my nipples, I went wild with want. My nipples stood at attention savoring the delightful sensation. I ached to have that pleasure between my thighs.

Amir's hands were busy as well, touching erogenous zones I never imagined I had: the back of my ears, my navel, the inside of my thighs, and the soft area on my back. He finally proceeded down my crotch when he saw me lifting my hips in anticipation. The gelid touch on my labia was too much to bear. I screamed wantonly and gyrated my crotch towards his mouth as he went round and round my labia with the ice cube, while his thumb pinched and fondled my clit.

I was going to cum in a moment. He left the melting ice cube on top of my pubis and inserted his tongue inside my eager vagina. I arched my back as my arousal reached its peak. Then he switched positions; his mouth went to my clit, while two of his fingers went into my dripping vagina. His tongue twirled my clit, licked it and sucked it, while his fingers went in and out of my pussy, making squelching delicious sounds.

"I'm coming..." I cried in joy, and Amir increased his tempo, until I climaxed and shuddered in utter ecstasy underneath his expert ministrations.

I ground my hips on his face as my orgasm came and drenched his fingers and face in my love juices.

His penis was red, angry, and throbbing for gratification then. It was my turn to pleasure him, and I intended to give him a spectacular blow job.

I followed his lead and took an ice cube in my mouth. I started tracing the contours of his face with the ice cube, while the fingers of my two hands were busy fondling his dick and nipples.

Amir moaned as I went down his neck and stopped near his nipples. I learned previously from him during our chats, that his nipples were one of his erotic zones. I secure the icy object between my lips and used it to tease and arouse him. I went round and round his two nipples, touching their tips every now and then.

His nipples became hard as marbles and his dick grew to unbelievable proportions. It was so huge; I felt my pussy becoming moist again with a crazy hunger for his dick.

The cube has melted and I got another one to trace his thighs as he towered over me, shivering in anticipated felicity. I took him in my mouth then and nibbled and licked the tip of his rock-hard penis. My right hand massaged the base of his dick, while my left, held his balls and caressed them like they were two cuddly puppies.

I sucked his crown, stopping to blow small kisses to his distended dick. I felt he was nearing climax, and I wanted him inside me, as I was again ablaze with desire in spite of having climaxed earlier.

I had read somewhere that if you want a man to prolong his erection, use ice. So, I stuck an ice cube in between my lips and went down on him, running the cold cube up and down his trembling shaft.

He became harder as he strained and

moaned in pleasure while I fondled and played with his manhood using the ice cube. When I knew he was ready, I straddled him and felt my slick, moist pussy, parting in joy to welcome his huge erection.

Amir panted in pleasure as his dick got buried inside my tight love tunnel. My vaginal muscles were squeezing his manhood, as I started moving up and down, savoring the sweet friction coming from our groins. He held me on my waist with both hands, and slammed me towards his waiting, throbbing penis.

I rotated my ass and ground my pussy against his crotch as I slid up and down him, my clitoris hot with the constant pressure. Amir reached up for my two breasts as I dipped down to catch his gaping, soft lips to suck at them. It was Nirvana!

He uttered a guttural cry, and in an instant he was atop me crushing my lips as he rammed his dick wantonly into my pussy. We were both nearing orgasms and we moved to the silent music of our passion and lust.

My head was jerking like those of a rag doll as he rammed his delectable manhood into the deepest sensitive area of my pussy. The sensation made me mad with pleasure; I was screaming and writing underneath his powerful strokes. He went faster and harder as we panted and clung to each other, our bodies glistening with sweat and unbridled passion.

Then everything broke loose, I shuddered and let go and climaxed as multiple sensations flooded my whole body; he still kept pumping until I felt myself floating in cloud nine for the sheer ecstasy of sexual fulfillment. We finally locked our groins together, savoring the indescribable sensation as the love juices flowed freely through our thighs and legs.

We stayed entwined in each other's embrace until our breathing subsided. He planted a kiss on my forehead, and I knew that I'd die if we got separated. My heart was singing with its new confidence in the strength of our love.

For the rest of the day, we decided to tour Disneyland like two small kids enjoying their rides for the first time. We posed with Cinderella and Alice in Wonderland, and ran around the place laughing with glee. That night, after sharing a light, delectable sushi dish, we made love again, slowly, prolonging the foreplay and hungrily exploring each other's erotic areas before fucking like mad.

I snuggled to Amir's warm, muscular naked body, ecstatic that I didn't have to imagine making love to him, like what we did online, before we finally met in person.

I was really with him in my own bed. I woke up in the middle of the night and was startled to notice Amir's side of the bed empty. I opened the bath but he was not there. My heart did a double flip. Scared, I ran to the kitchen. I found him at the terrace smoking a cigarette.

"Is there any problem, hon?" I asked, worried.

"I've been thinking, hon," he hugged me close to him. "Let's go to India. Let's get married and live there. I love you and I couldn't bear to be without you. Would you come with me?"

I was speechless. I stared at him fixedly and saw that he was serious. His eyes were clouded with unshed tears. I said yes and smothered him with kisses, as we held on to each other amidst our joy.

I wrote a long letter to mom and dad, explaining that Amir and I had decided to get married in India, and would they please grant us their blessings.

Sadly, there was only a curt reply: "If you insist on what you want, and you choose that man, over us, your parents who took care of you since birth, then you go without our blessings."

I was devastated. My happiness would have been completed had they agreed. I was already of age and I knew I was deciding correctly. Amir was my life now, my everything.

We started preparations for our travel to India. I was on a fiancé VISA so it was relatively easy to obtain my documents. I left the apartment to a trusted friend and packed only the necessary belongings I needed for a new life with Amir. I was ready to cross the 7 seas for him.

Amir and I made love during our last night in Hong Kong. We made sensual love in the bathtub, with our bodies wet and slippery. He lovingly soaped my pussy, carefully, working the lather under the folds of my labia and into my clitoris. I was seated at the edge of the tub, my thighs spread wide for him, while he was partially submerged in the tub as he lathered my vagina.

His head was positioned opposite my breasts and he shifted now and then to suck my nipples or my mouth, while I held his head and caressed his hair. It was leisure and I was enjoying it.

After lathering, he carefully rinsed my pussy, tenderly caressing each fold, especially the clit area, as he washed off the lather. It was a sensual act that made me moist and ready for his dick.

We both submerged ourselves in the lukewarm water. We kissed and explored each other's bodies as we basked in each touch and sensation. I slid into his lap and wound my legs around his hips as we continued kissing and our tongues grappled wanting more from each other.

The water splashed around us as our passion got the better of us and we feverishly rubbed our wet bodies against each other. He lifted me from my backside and knelt from behind me. The water was just below our knees, but he managed to slide his engorged penis into my ready pussy.

I pushed back as he held my waist and thrust forward. I was on all fours, and I could feel all the crevices of my tight vagina enveloping his huge penis as it deliciously enters – in and out – my pussy. My doggy position had even made me tighter, and Amir was enjoying it too.

His face was suffused with passion as he drove his ram-rod manhood into me, shuddering with the instinctive tightening of my vaginal muscles. We were riding in our love horse and we galloped faster and faster, slamming into each other, the sound we were making was insane. And then he arched his back and pushed his dick deep into me, as I pushed back against him to accept him, in an explosion of mind-boggling sensations.

Whenever we made love, he always pleased me first before he did himself, even in ordinary things we did every day. I was able to see how much he loved me, and there was a warm glow in my soul because I loved him back just as well.

Amir and I traveled to Delhi in a Jet India flight, and the 10-hour flight with Amir was one of the most memorable trips I had ever experienced. We had the chance to just talk and I listened to additional revelations about himself that made me love him more.

It was funny also because whenever our bodies came in contact with each other, the sparks fly and we got aroused.

"We're on a plane," I laughed at him, when he winked at me and indicated his crotch. I saw his visible bulging erection underneath his jeans.

He winked at me impishly again. "C'mon hon, what do you want me to do?"

He didn't reply, but I could see that he was in actual pain with his enormous erection. I pretended to sleep on his lap and he draped his jacket over my upper body. He turned off the small light opposite us and we pretended to fall asleep.

I released his penis from its confines and it happily sprang forward, eager to be loved. With my head covered, I suck his penis and licked his shaft until he gave a little groan and ejected his sperm into a waiting wet wipes I held in my hands.

The other passengers might smell Amir's semen but I was ready for it. After carefully wiping him with the scented wet wipes, I sealed them all in an air tight plastic container, which I had bought for emergencies like this one.

I looked around if someone noticed but no one bothered. Amir smiled broadly at me and whispered, "Do you want me to eat you?"

I was aroused and the idea heightened it, but we may not get lucky the second time around, so I declined. "No honey, you can eat me all you want when we arrive in India," I smiled seductively at him.

"I can't wait to do that, hon."

My first impression, on board, was that India was an incredibly beautiful country, with its plain, mountains and colorful costumes. On land, Delhi was hot and humid, but I felt that I was finally home.

Amir taught me simple greetings like putting your hands together, as in a prayer, making a slight bow, and saying "Namaste."

Amir lived with his sister and her family. His sister was lovely, a blend of the east and west features that made her face exotic. She and her family greeted as warmly as we arrived on her doorstep.

The house was modest: 4 small cozy rooms,

an intricately decorated living room, a gleaming kitchen and a spacious, verdant backyard. I always wanted big backyards.

Amir had called ahead of time and by the time we arrived, my room was ready. He was not supposed to sleep in the same room as I was; her sister still believed that people should get married before they shared a bed, and that they made it perfectly clear to us.

In India, it was customary that the girl gave a dowry before marriage, but Amir detested that custom, and he specifically stated this during one of our dinner conversations. His sister didn't approve of it as well, most probably because of their Western upbringing, so there was no problem about me not giving a dowry.

During the night, I ached for Amir. He slept at the cot in the living room, while I slept alone in the guest room, and it was like a century that we had not been in each other's arms. I was sure Amir was feeling the same way too. I was able to sleep only when it was nearing dawn.

The following day, we made preparations for our wedding. Amir asked me if I would like to be wedded the Hindu or Christian way. I said it didn't matter as long as I was with him. But it would be good wearing one of the colorful saris.

Amir's sister, Kajol, accompanied me to buy my bridal sari. I chose a fiery red color with a bit of white lining and an intricate feathery design. I had to agree with Kajol that I looked stunning in it. She also said that I would have to have mehndi (henna) to adorn my feet and hands.

The preparation was so exciting with all the exotic ornaments that I would be wearing. I even had my nose pierced to make my wedding outfit a truly Hindu marriage. Our mangalsutra (wedding necklaces) and garlands were ready too. The Kumkum (red paste) applied to our forehead would declare that we were married.

Our Hindu wedding day came, I was walking on clouds as relatives and friends of Amir arrived. Except for a few elders, they were happy for Amir and me. Amir's parents were already gone, so it was his elder sister and husband who acted as our parents.

Amir was dashing in his pink-colored wedding costume. The air was festive and it seemed all surreal for me, like I was living out one of my fantasies. The mangalashtak (wedding poem) was composed by Amir and it was lovely; it made me cry when they finally sang it.

"I know I love you because I can't stop thinking of you.

I know I love you because when you are not there I feel empty.

I know I love you because I feel you are a part of me.

I know I love you because you took my heart and I let you.

I know I love you because I love you..."

The priest declared we were married and singing and dancing erupted to enjoy the bond that I knew would last forever.

We proceeded to Shimla as Amir's relatives, and mine too, now that we were married, celebrated the occasion. We were like two thrilled kids on our way to our first trip to Disneyland. After a quick change of clothes, we hopped into Amir's old car and sped away as fast as we can.

When we reached the outskirts of Delhi, Amir could not contain himself; he stopped the car and kissed me full on the lips. His manhood was already throbbing with desire.

"Hon, we can't make love here. It's been too long, but I want our first night as husband and wife to be special," I held his handsome face in my hands.

"Okay, hon," he looked at me passionately, "Be ready when we get there," he winked at me and drove on.

It was summer and the road to Shimla was dusty, winding, and precarious, but when we arrived there at the top, the spectacular view of the surrounding landscape seemed to be taken out of a Van Gogh painting. Nearby verdant mountain ranges rolled by from view, the mist-shrouded peaks of the Himalayan Mountains shimmered in the distance. The air was unadultcrated, calming my nerves and soul. It was a heavenly place! I could live there all my life together with my beloved Amir.

Amir and I went straight to the guest house though as my need for him could no longer be contained. We barely made it inside, when we clawed at each other's clothes to touch our naked skins. It was only more than a week, but it was like forever.

He carried me to bed and traced the contours of my body with his fingers. When his fingers touched my nipples, I sat upright

179

and fondled his already engorged penis. He groaned and pushed me to the bed, prodding me to lie down.

He spread my legs and entered me with a frenzied cry of fulfillment. I moaned as he thrust with all his might, fucking me with all the passion that has been stored for the past few days. I crossed my leg over his back as he rammed his rock-hard dick into my warm and wet pussy. I felt my orgasm rearing its head as I joined him in his feverish tempo of going in and out of my love tunnel.

He was groaning in pleasure as each of his mighty thrusts penetrated deep into the delicious folds of my tight vagina. We were sweating now, our bodies glistening with the joy of our union, but we kept on straining to reach Nirvana.

A warm, pleasurable, sweet sensation started to emanate from my vagina spreading to all my extremities as I lifted my ass to grind my pussy into his huge, angry dick. Then with one hard thrust, he rammed his penis into my pussy and roared like a lion, as we climaxed together, locking our groins, as his semen and my juices flowed like a dam from our gigantic orgasm.

We didn't need foreplay because the foreplay were the days we hadn't spent together. Every moment of those days have made us crave for each other, making us ripe and ready for our first night as a married couple.

We fell asleep for a while after making love. I awakened with a feeling of disorientation. The wedding preparation had me sleeping less, and I needed sleep. I felt a pleasant sensation coming from my groin. I looked down and saw my husband's head between my thighs.

"Hello Mrs. Jessica Gupta," he smiled at me impishly, "May I have something to eat?"

I started to get up, but he pushed me down. "This is more than sufficient for me, ma'am," he whispered and then he bent again and continued exploring my pussy with his tongue. I closed my eyes and relaxed against the warm, soft sheets. "That's right, honey, relax and let me love you. I love you so much," he stated fervently.

He licked and sucked my clit until I cried out. Then he ran his tongue down my toes and sucked my toes. He went up again my vagina, running his tongue along my labia, teasing my opening with the tip of his tongue. I writhed in ecstasy, as his tongue went back to my clit and tweaked it relentlessly until I arched my back and cried his name.

He continued sucking my clit, increasing the gentle pressure until he knew I was ready. Then he offered me his dick as he turned me upside down in one sweep of his powerful arm. I was sucking his penis, as he was giving me more pleasure in my vagina. I ran my tongue along his shaft and suck him as my mouth went up and down his penis. He groaned in delight as he continued to lick and suck my clit.

His penis became as big as a horse's with his arousal, and I wanted it to be inside me again as I was nearing climax. With great effort, he tore himself away from me and came behind me, spoon fashion to fuck me from behind, by lifting one of my legs.

The position made me even tighter and as he inserted his dick into my extremely juicy pussy, I begged him to give it all to me. He played with my breasts with one of her hands, while the other hand was holding one of my thighs as he fucked me hard and in quick deep strokes from behind.

I went wild with delight. My vagina became tighter but since it was moist, it made the friction so delicious and indescribable. I cried out for more and more until all hell broke loose as the getaway collapsed and tons and tons of earthly pleasures wracked our bodies and we collapsed in the bed, exhausted but truly gratified in mind, body, and soul.

My first day as Ms. Amir Gupta was a day I would never forget for as long as I live. I felt in my heart that Amir and I would grow old together, still loving each other as we had vowed, we would.

Finally, I had found true happiness at the end of the rainbow.

15 FLIGHT IN PARADISE PART 1

He stood there: tall, lean, and the most handsome man Amy had ever met. His blue eyes were deep seated, and his aquiline nose complemented all his facial features. His blonde, short-cropped hair curled at his ears, giving him a boyish look. He was one of the Airmen from the U.S. bases nearby, and it was the first time he had bought something from Amy's sari-sari store (i.e., small retail stores) and diner.

"Five pesos of these please," he said, pointing to the jar of Halls candy.

Amy's hands were trembling when she handed him the candies. Her pert nose and small lips trembled as her hands came in contact with his. He did not notice though because he was preoccupied with something Amy was not aware of. Well, she thought, it did not matter. She didn't know him anyway.

The next time he came to buy something,

he was with some of his friends. Amy knew one of them: Tom, who often passed by the store before going home. Tom lived alone in an apartment down the street.

"Hi, Amy, what's up?" Tom waved at her.

"Nothing new," Amy replied, smiling.

"Oh, I've got company now in the apartment," Tom motioned the Airman Amy met the other day.

"This is Dave. He just came in from Thailand."

"Hi, Dave. Welcome to the Philippines." Amy wanted to extend her hand, but she knew they were clammy, so she just nodded her head in Dave's direction.

"Thank you," he said.

That was all.

When they left, Amy was angry at herself. She was 19, but she was acting like a teenager having her first crush. I would have to forget him, she scolded herself.

The next days that ensued however made it difficult for her to do so because Dave and Tom drop by the store to drink cola or buy something before they proceed home. That went on for several weeks.

It was one rainy day when Dave ran for cover in their store.

"Could I stay here for a while," he asked.

"Sure, you'll get drenched, if you don't," Amy smiled at him.

"By the way, I'm Dave."

"Yeah, I know. We were introduced before."

"Oh, I didn't quite get your name," he was apologetic.

"I'm Amy." She extended her hand.

Every day, she eagerly waited for him to come from work. Sometimes he rode in Tom's car; at times he walked. It was two blocks away from the main route where passenger jeepneys plied their route.

Amy and Dave got to make small talk about trivial things like the locations of tourists' spots in the city, the name of Filipino dishes, the weather, and similar topics. Amy was elated spending a few minutes talking to him about any topic. The "Hi" and "Hellos" became longer conversations, until they were talking about international issues like the European market and the U.S. elections.

Amy's hobby was to read books, newspapers, magazines, novels, short stories, and everything she could get her hands into. She also graduated cum laude from her Medical Technology course and was tending their store while reviewing for the board exam.

"Wow, I wouldn't have guessed you have a powerhouse brain in that small frame," Dave commented one time when he and Amy had a debate on the dangers of uncensored TV viewing on children.

There were times, during weekends, that Dave drank beer so he could stay longer to talk with Amy. Dave was fascinated by Amy's intellect and sharp mind. He obviously enjoyed his conversations with Amy because he stayed longer and longer as the days dragged by.

Amy was a picture of joy and contentment. Her plain face radiated with an innate beauty that only being in love could bring. Amy slowly turned into a lovely woman before Dave's eyes.

While Amy was attracted to Dave, at first, for his handsome features, she was drawn to him as days passed by because of his sincerity, goodness, and sensitivity.

One time, when they were animatedly talking, Dave's hand happened to rest on Amy's. Their eyes locked and they held on to each other's hands, and the tempo of their breathing quickened. The next thing they knew they were kissing. They only stopped when someone entered the store.

"Can I have your number?" Dave asked Amy, the emotions he felt were mirrored in his voice.

Amy gave her number without hesitation. She was thrilled knowing that Dave wanted to take their relationship to the next level. She turned hot whenever she remembered Dave's kiss. It was a passionate, wet kiss that had awakened her dormant sexual desires.

They kissed whenever they had the chance, away from prying eyes. Sometimes, they kissed behind the curtains or in the shadows of the night when there were few customers.

Dave was increasingly becoming demanding. At first, he just explored Amy's sweet, young lips, sucking on her tongue and lower lips, but the following day, his hands caressed Amy's breasts. Amy, surprised, pushed him back; she was still a virgin in spite of her age, and she was still naïve and inexperienced about sex. She had read various books on the topic, but it was totally different when you were on the spot.

Dave, however, didn't release her but held

on to her and prodded her to relax with her tongue and mouth. But Amy pushed him aside because there were still a few people in the store.

"Can we meet outside?" Dave's eyes were begging. Amy could notice his erection beneath his jeans.

"Where will we go?" she asked, afraid to commit.

"What about in the park? Or let's watch a movie?"

They agreed to meet Sunday afternoon at the city park. Amy couldn't wait for the appointed day to come. She touched her lips and she already yearned for Dave's kisses. Her face went hot when she remembered how his hand strayed to caress her breast beneath her thin blouse.

That Sunday afternoon in the park, they brought some snacks and found a secluded corner where they spread their picnic blanket and talked about current international topics. As dusk approached, one by one the families left with their children and only the lovers were left in the shadows of the lampposts. The park has a curfew at 9 p.m., and during the two-hour period before the curfew, couples took advantage of this time to neck and pet.

Amy was excited and nervous at the same time. She felt her whole body aching for Dave's touch. She felt guilty that she was feeling those sexual yearnings.

Time flew fast and soon it was evening. While they were talking, Dave had been caressing secretly her hand, her thighs, and her legs. So when evening came, her body was on fire. Just as soon as the people within view of them left, Dave was all over Amy, kissing her lips, her neck, and her ears while fondling Amy's tits underneath her blouse.

Dave was hyperventilating with lust and desire for Amy. He wanted to slow down because he knew she was still a virgin by the way she responded to his caresses. Her sweet lips were soft and pliant under his own, and her tongue was inexperienced, not knowing what to do; he had to coax her with his own and whisper encouragements when their lips parted.

"Let's go to my apartment," he whispered hoarsely into Amy's ear.

But Amy shook her head. Her body was aflame with desire, but she has still a tiny portion of her brain functioning. She had heard endless stories about many Airmen getting girls pregnant and leaving them tearful and brokenhearted. They don't even try to help the girl with the kid's expenses, especially if the kids inherited more of the mother's features.

Amy wanted Dave's company, not because of the sex but because he could interact with her mentally. Dave felt the same way too, but he had been celibate since the time he arrived in the city; he was fearful too of having casual sex with girls in the pubs and bars because of the dangers of sexual promiscuity.

For the days that he and Amy talked, he was slowly drawn to her. She was shy but she was smart, kind, fun to be with, and beautiful inside, which makes her charming in the outside as well. His day became incomplete when he was not able to see her.

The kiss they had for the first time provoked feelings from him that he thought would never surface again, a feeling of pleasure and great desire to delve deeper – soul and mind – into her being.

Amy was breathless with desire as well; she wanted the kisses to go on and wanted the clamoring need in her crotch be fulfilled, but she didn't want to take chances. She would surely be another easy conquest for Dave once she gave in, a conquest just like the other girls who were easily forgotten.

But Amy wanted Dave to go on with the pleasurable things he was doing. He was still sucking her tongue and nibbling her lower lip every now and then while he caressed and fondled her breasts.

Amy could feel the heat of Dave's erection through his jeans. He was almost on top of her. Then Dave's hand crept inside her blouse. She shuddered as Dave's fingers came in contact with her bare nipples. The sensation jolted her to an even more sensational pleasure when his fingers twirled and fondled both of her nipples alternately.

One hand crept inside her skirt into her crotch and started caressing her vagina underneath her undies. Amy moaned with pleasure, her body aflame with desire. Dave's lips were still hot on hers, biting lightly, sucking, licking, and exploring the soft areas of her mouth, while his hands were busy fondling her down. Amy signed and gave in to the delightful sensations; she did not know it was this much pleasure. She wanted him to go on and on.

Dave held her hand and guided it to his crotch; he had a huge erection, and it was straining to be freed from under his jeans.

Just then, there were approaching voices and a cough from afar, and panting heavily, they torn themselves apart and pretended to talk. A group of teenagers settled right beside them and unpacked their music gears; they seemed to be spending some jamming with their friends. They were unmindful of them and Amy thought how rude they were.

"I have to go home now," she requested Dave. "They might need me at the store."

Dave did not speak while they drove back.

"Can you please come to my apartment? Or somewhere private?" he begged Amy.

Amy held her ground though. She had seen countless girls in their area losing their virginity and being left behind after they became pregnant; she had promised herself she would not allow that to happen to her.

Dave texted her the following day, asking how she was. "I'm fine," Amy replied with a one-liner.

She was afraid to go out again with Dave because her body was responding to Dave so willingly; she was at the verge of giving in and of just enjoying making love with him. The consequences would be fatal however; she would be branded, and most Filipino men would not consider her as good wife material – a loose woman, because she was no longer a virgin. There were still old-fashioned men in their perception about marriage and relationships.

Due to Amy's fear, she avoided going out with Dave to the secluded places. Her body was no longer under her control but under Dave's command. For the few times that they were left alone in the store, Dave's kisses were like opium, pleasurable and enticing. He always made her breathless and heady with desire. Amy wanted to bask in Dave's arms forever.

It was after two months when Dave announced he was being stationed in Japan. Amy was devastated. The time that she had dreaded has finally arrived; Dave was leaving, and whether he would return or not was a question that there was no answer to.

Amy cried when Dave visited her to say goodbye.

"What we had is special," Dave held her hand and locked his eyes with hers. "I'll never forget you. I won't promise anything, but I know that you'll always have a special place in my heart."

Amy allowed herself to be enclosed in his warm embrace. She could feel the warm heat of desire emanating from his body.

"Could you stay with me for the night before I leave?" Dave begged her.

Amy knew what would happen if she did, and she refused.

"It's better this way, Dave," and he understood what she meant.

The succeeding days were terrible for Amy. She suddenly became an insomniac, spending sleepless nights on bed. She knew she had to move on; Dave was only assigned to the Philippines on TDY (i.e., temporary duty) and may not return anymore. He did not leave any number or address that she could contact, and that had implications that Amy understood.

Studying for the boards became tedious as her mind wandered to Dave very often, but it was a fruitful refuge for her because she tried her utmost to study.

Days passed by and slowly Amy recovered from the loss of Dave. She had also successfully passed the board exams and was applying for work in various institutions.

That was the time she met Mark Castro. Mark was working as a technologist at the base hospital. He had the next-boy look that every girl wanted, was medium built, swarthy-skinned, and fun to be with. Amy found out that Mark has also the same intellectual pursuits that she had. He was also an intelligent conversationalist, like Dave.

They went out several times before Mark attempted to kiss her. Amy was excited at first, but when their lips met, there was a bland taste to the kiss; she felt no excitement like what she had felt for Dave. When Mark attempted to touch her further, she pushed him away.

From then on, she only went with Mark when she was sure there was not a chance he would become intimate with her. Soon, she was forced to reveal to Mark that she considered him only as a friend. And if he wanted for them to stay together, then he had to accept her hand in friendship. Mark had no alternative but to do so. They became the best of friends eventually, getting together whenever they can and keeping no secrets from each other.

Mark discouraged her from entertaining any American GI. "You'll be reminded of Dave," he said.

It was the wet season again and Amy remembered the first time she met Dave. It was the same season when she was introduced to Dave by Tom. Tom was still assigned at the U.S. Air Base, but there were no messages from Dave so she dared not ask him how Dave was.

So, it was a shock when she arrived at the store from work to see a familiar face drinking a can of cola in one of the tables. Amy was speechless and unable to move. She just stood there staring at Dave as if she had seen a ghost. Perhaps she was seeing a mirage because she had dreamt of him every night to go back to her meaningless life once again.

"Hi, how're you doin'?" Dave spoke first.

"Er...I'm fine, thanks," she stammered.

"I arrived the other day."

Amy nodded; her heart was beating so fast she was afraid she might have a heart attack.

"May I speak with you in private?"

Amy led him to the adjoining living room of their house and offered him a seat. She sat far away from him, awkward and uncomfortable.

"When I left, I tried to forget you, but I wasn't able to," he shook his head and looked down. "I waited patiently for this day to come, and this time, I won't let that chance slip away again."

Amy looked at him and her heart hammered in her chest as the old longing and desires came flooding back like it was just yesterday. How she wanted to touch his face and kiss his lips.... How she wanted to rush into his muscular arms and cuddle in his warmth.

Dave went closer to her and knelt. From his pocket, he brought out a dazzling diamond ring and said, "Amy, I love you. Will you marry me?" his face lighting up with felicity.

Amy was shocked and unbelieving. Did she hear it right? Was Dave asking her to marry him?

"Will you marry me, Amy?" he repeated; there were tears in his eyes.

"I...I...."

That's when Amy's realization crystallized. She loved Dave too – loved him enough not to be able to love anyone since he left.

Dave held both of her hands and kissed them.

"Yes, yes...I love you too," Amy whispered tearfully. "But we will first have to inform my parents."

Dave kissed her then, a tender, lingering kiss that stoked the growing ember that was awakened in Amy's body. They kissed again, sucking each other's tongue and lips, exploring the soft spots inside their mouths, making soft sucking noises. Their bodies were ablaze in an instant.

Amy knew that their yearning for each other during the long months that they were not together had to achieve gratification. Dave would not dare ask her. She had to be the one to say it. She wanted Dave badly as well. Her whole mind, body, and soul were clamoring for fulfillment.

"Can we go somewhere private?" she asked, her voice hoarse with passion.

Dave did not wait for another word. He pulled Amy to her feet and hurriedly flagged a taxi after Amy informed the maid that they were going somewhere.

Dave chose an unobtrusive, modest hotel where the taxi could deliver customers right to the doorstep of the unit. They tried hard to contain their feelings inside the cab, but once the door of the unit closed, they tore each other's clothes hurriedly while their mouths and tongue wrestled with each other.

Dave pinned Amy to the wall as he kissed her and exposed Amy's naked body to his touch. Amy touched his erect penis and he groaned wildly, as she caressed his dick gently with her hands. He was so big, Amy thought, her pussy turning moist and eager to accept his penis. She heard from the other girls that the first wouldn't hurt as much as long as the man knows what to do. But she no longer cared for that; all she wanted was for Dave to continue what he was doing.

He was now rubbing her tits and her labia simultaneously. Ah, such indescribable pleasure, Amy thought. Then Dave was down on her, touching the tip of her labia with the tip of his tongue. Amy moaned and spread her legs wider. It was the first time she experienced cunnilingus and it made her crazy, her pussy wanting more.

Dave took her thighs and placed them on each of his shoulders, allowing Amy's crotch to be fully exposed to his ministrations. Amy was lying flat on her back, her thighs on Dave's shoulders, while the upper half of her body was on the bed. Dave was kneeling on the floor just beside the edge of the bed.

Dave used his tongue to lap Amy's feet and thighs. His tongue played with Amy's labia while his thumb tweaked her clit. She was making soft, purring noises that fueled Dave's desire. Dave knew that he had to take his time because Amy was a virgin. He wanted to make her first experience memorable and delightful.

Dave alternately fondled, sucked, and tweaked Amy's clit and vagina. He flipped his tongue repeatedly on her clit as one finger was being inserted slowly into her pussy. Then he swapped positions again; his tongue went to her vagina as his fingers went to her clit.

He ran his tongue up and down her labia, slowly opening the folds so that his tongue could lick the inside folds. His fingers went round and round, then up and down her clit as she raised her hips to meet his mouth. His tempo increased and she held his head, as her moans grew louder.

One of his fingers now was inserted inside

her pussy and the pace of his tongue became quicker, as it played with her reddened clit.

"Please take me," Amy begged as her desire consumed her body with need.

"Not yet, baby," he whispered.

Dave finger fucked Amy until she cried and shuddered as her orgasm went on and on. She was all wet. She thought that was all there was to it, but it was not. Dave was at it again but this time, he allowed Amy to perform fellatio as well. Amy learned fast enough. She had read books about it, but she never thought it was not as easy as they used to be described in books.

She caressed his balls and ran her tongue along his throbbing shaft. "You have to be gentle with your tongue and hands," she remembered the book saying. How she had longed to do this to Dave. She felt his relentless tongue arousing her again, and she returned the favor by adoring Dave's penis with her tongue. She sucked it and took him all into her mouth as her head bobbed up and down. They were now lying on bed facing opposite directions. As Dave used his tongue to give immeasurable delight, Amy also returned the favor. She was dripping wet again and was ready for another explosive climax.

Dave then straddled her, lifting one foot to each of his shoulders. He placed a pillow under Amy's buttock and slowly allowed the tip of his penis into Amy's vagina.

"It will hurt a bit," he said.

"Please fuck me now," Amy cried. "Please...." Her body was ablaze with desire, and all she wanted was to fulfill the craving deep inside her vagina.

Still Dave went in slowly, rotating his hips, stopping now and then to allow her vagina to adjust to his penis. He was almost halfway in when Amy groaned as if in pain. Dave pulled his penis out and sucked her clit again until Amy prodded him to enter her again.

Her pussy was really tight but it was so wet that Dave could no longer contain his passion. He thrust deeper as his mouth went down now to suck her breast and to kiss her lips. Amy was straining to achieve her biggest orgasm, as the sensations from her clit, G-spot, and vagina were all reaching their crescendo.

Dave had his dick ensconced in Amy's vagina already. Her pussy was so tight that she could feel each corner of her pussy filled out and the immense pleasure that every pulsating capillary of his dick created. Dave felt the exquisite tightness too and he was so aroused he started going in and out slowly, savoring the tightness and slickness of Amy's vagina.

Amy felt fullness and slight pain when he went in and out, but the pleasure was more intense. She crossed her legs over Dave's back as her need of fulfillment increased until she cried out to him to go faster and quicker.

Dave did as she desired and he fucked her hard and long, going in and out of her pussy in fast, delicious strokes as Amy writhed and moaned under him. She is so good, he thought as he felt Amy climax, her vagina gripping his penis in a sweet embrace. He thrust even harder, going in and out as his body glistened with his sweat. His body grew taut and he locked his groin to hers as Amy continued to climax again and again while he came in one gigantic burst of ecstasy.

After 15 days, they got married in the church in a simple ceremony attended only by relatives and friends. During the span of 15 days, they made love three times a day and anywhere when they had found privacy. They were compatible not only mentally but also sexually. Not many people were like that, and Amy was thankful he found her perfect partner in Dave. Amy wanted to call her fate a singing nightingale that sang at the right time for two people in love.

16 FLIGHT IN PARADISE PART 2

After Amy and Dave got married in a simple church wedding, they decided to go to Baguio City for their honeymoon. Baguio City was the summer capital of the Philippines because it served as a refuge when the summer temperature in the low lands was at its hottest.

The spectacular views of verdant, rolling hills and mist-covered mountain peaks provided tranquility and refuge to those who wanted respite from the bustling metropolitan life. During summer, a variety of flowers gave their loveliest bloom, and the scent of pine trees often refreshed visitors.

Amy and Dave did not go out immediately though. The first thing that they did was to make slow, gentle love on the warm tub. They undressed themselves slowly while kissing and necking. Dave caressed Amy's vagina underneath her undies, deliberately not removing the thin clothing that separated his hand from Amy's most precious opening.

He fondled her clit underneath her panty while playfully biting her nipples under the folds of her blouse. Amy, too, massaged his erection under his pants. His penis was as hard as rock already and was straining to be released from the folds of his pants, but Amy did not give him that luxury; she continued caressing his dick not bothering to free it.

They kissed and necked until they could not hold their passions any longer. Dave removed Amy's blouse first, unbuttoning it slowly and kissing each exposed area with care and love. Their bodies were burning with desire, but they wanted to please each other until they could not hold on any longer.

Dave kissed her shoulders and then removed her bra using his teeth to pull off her straps. The bra fell down to the floor. Then he rained kisses on her neck and shoulders until he reached her breasts. He nestled his head in her luscious breasts and said jokingly, "How do you want me to treat your delicious ripe melons, your highness?"

"Oh please, devour them as you want. Don't spare any piece."

And that was what Dave did. First, he ran his tongue all over her breast, one after another, not touching her nipples. When her nipples were standing upright, straining for attention, that was the time he nibbled and took them into his mouth, as Amy sighed and moaned delightedly.

Dave twirling and sucking her nipples and

his hand caressing her clit beneath her panties drove her wild with desire. She fumbled for Dave's zipper and finally freed his huge, erect manhood. She still was awed at how big Dave was. After the first time that they made love, she had experienced a slight splattering of blood and a dull pain in her vagina. The incomparable ecstasy that she achieved during their lovemaking was all new to her, and she wanted to bask in it – wanting to have it more often like it was an addictive drug.

Dave groaned when her fingers enclosed his dick, but he continued exploring her breasts, like they were delicious melons. He was forced to stop when Amy knelt before him and nuzzled his penis into her mouth. He let go of Amy's breast and clutched her head as he stood with his back rigid with the pleasures of fellatio.

Amy ran her tongue through the opening of Dave's penis. She then fondled her balls with her right hand and massaged his shaft with her left fingers. Dave was moaning softly. Amy was a quick learner. He had various encounters before with other women before they got married, and Amy's touch was different; she could arouse him within seconds just by her touch.

Her tongue then encircled the crown of his penis in gentle but firm strokes, lapping his crown like it were some delicious ice cream. Amy took her time adoring his penis, running her tongue up and down its length, until Dave begged her to take it into her mouth.

He held her head as Amy took his dick

gently into her mouth. It was so huge she almost choked. But Dave taught her how to do it properly. "Ease it into the sides of your mouth, careful not to let any teeth into it," he had urged her, the first time they did fellatio.

She started moving her mouth in and out of Dave's dick with his guidance. She sucked tenderly as her mouth went out and blew into its head as she went in again. Her right fingers caressed the base of his dick and followed her mouth as she went in and out, her head bobbing wildly as Dave increased the tempo using his hand to guide her head. His muscles were taut as a violin string, ready to break at any moment.

Then he gave a guttural cry as his semen spurted into Amy's mouth. Amy stared at the sticky liquid coming out of Dave as he ejaculated into her breasts. She took the cue and cupped his penis with her two luscious breasts as he thrust in and out, squirting the last of his juices. Amy licked the tip of his penis as the tip came through between her two breasts.

"Honey, I love you," Dave held her tight against his warm body.

Amy was aroused more than ever but Dave's penis was already limp. She did not have to say anything though because he already knew what to do. He carried her to the king-sized bed and continued with his previous ministrations.

Her nipples were taut and enjoying his attention, but her pussy was yearning for his tongue too. It was already moist when he finally tasted her juices. He licked her labia, running his tongue up and down her lips and kissing now and then her inner thighs. Amy relaxed and savored every pleasure Dave's lips gave her. When his tongue flicked her clitoris, she lifted her pussy to his head, pleading for more.

Dave focused then on her clit, alternately sucking and caressing it until it was swollen with desire. Amy was murmuring his name, urging him not to stop, grinding her pubis into his face, wanting more and more. He ran his tongue around her clit, down her pussy, inserting his tongue into her vagina and tasting her sweet juices. Then he went back to her clitoris again, licking it continuously, increasing the tempo.

Amy wanted more as she spread her legs widely so Dave could reach her innermost erotic zone, her G-spot. He inserted two of his fingers into the ridge-like portion inside her vagina and massaged it continuously until he felt the contraction of her muscles.

Her moans and cries of delight aroused him again, and his dick was tumescent once again, ready for the expected pleasures Amy could offer.

He pulled Amy into his lap and thrust his penis into her pussy as she went down on him. They were face to face; Amy's legs were across his back as he knelt and fucked her hard and fast. They were French kissing also as Amy went up and down, enjoying the exquisite sensation produced by the friction of her tight pussy with his huge, long dick. Dave alternately sucked at her nipples and her mouth as he hugged her tight into his sweating, muscular body.

They went on fucking hard, their bodies moving wildly against each other as they both strained to achieve their climaxes. The sound of Amy's pussy slamming into his dick made them even wilder as they moved frenziedly to a humongous orgasm that made them cry with unbridled delight as they clung to each other and kissed until the gigantic waves of pleasure subsided.

They went to sleep afterwards, making love again after their energy was replenished after a sumptuous meal of rice, veggies, and chicken. They stayed naked after taking a bath together in the shower, soaping their bodies gently and exploring and discovering more erogenous zones in their bodies.

They made love again on the couch in the living room, with Dave standing up on the floor and Amy on all fours at the couch so he could easily enter her from behind. They made love on the floor near the fireplace while they drank wine and talked about their first meeting and the days when Amy had clung on to her virginity.

Dave revealed to Amy how he had tried to forget her when he went back to the States.

"I dated every girl I met, hoping I would forget you, but it was useless," he said.

Amy laughed when he told her how he masturbated thinking of her. "I was a fool not realizing immediately that I was in love with you," he disclosed.

They were on each other's bodies again, experimenting with new positions and unique methods to please themselves.

Amy wanted to stay on top the third day they were in the hotel. They just went out for food and some air, but most of the time, they stayed inside the hotel, pottering about naked, tweaking each other's bodies and teasing each other until they ended up making love again.

Amy straddled him and rotated her hips as she pressed against his angry penis. Dave's face was beet red with his arousal, as he slammed her pussy against his groin. Amy stooped down, now and then, to kiss him and nibble his lips. Then he lifted her up and turned her around, exposing her clitoris for his hands to fondle. Her thighs were on top of his as she went up and down her juicy pussy, engulfing tightly his dick as it came down.

Dave reached out for her clitoris and his fingers caressed it now and then as their arousal heightened. The movement introduced another new sensation to Amy. This became one of her favorite positions because it made Dave's dick penetrate deeply and allowed her or Dave to fondle her clit. Her clit had always introduced her to new sensational pleasures she never knew were possible.

When Dave touched her clit again as she was moving up and down, she came in short but multiple bursts of pure delight.

They slept soundly afterwards entwined in each other's warm embrace, the flames in their bodies temporarily assuaged, ready to burn again once they awakened.

It was only on the seventh day that they were able to tour the city a little while longer before they went back hurriedly to the hotel to make love again. They seemed not to get enough of each other. The city's tourists' spots were exciting to see, but they were more excited being together and exploring each other's erotic zones than wandering and admiring the amazing spots in the city. It was their honeymoon anyway, to which they both reminded themselves.

It was unbelievable, but they made love at least seven times a day – and that was the least. How could anyone get enough of each other? Amy thought. Dave was an attractive and sexy man and was superb in bed. How could anyone desire to be out instead? She wanted to be fucked every hour by Dave, her beloved Dave.

It felt good waking up in the middle of the night and feeling Dave's sinewy body against her own. He was muscular, almost 6 feet, and could make love all night long without showing any sign of fatigue. He was an animal in bed, rousing her to indescribable pleasures she never imagined existed.

Their honeymoon was nearing its end, but it did not matter to Amy because she knew that she would be with Dave forever.

After their honeymoon, they went back home and started their new lives as Mr. and Mrs. Dave Smith. They rented a modest apartment near the Air Base. He reported to work at 8AM to 5PM, while Amy was still looking for work. She applied at the base hospital and was waiting for some news.

After Dave's work, she had everything ready for him: from his warm bath, to his scrumptious meal, to his body massage, which always ended up with them hungrily devouring each other and making love like there was no tomorrow.

Dave even bought a waterbed so they could utilize it to fulfill their sexual cravings. The first time they made love in the waterbed was funny because Amy kept falling, unable to just relax and allow the bed to conform to her position.

When Dave straddled her and fucked her hard, the bed moved with them, increasing the friction and the sensations. They rolled around the waterbed with their groins locked up and their lips glued to each other as Dave humped hard, grunting with each penetration, enjoying Amy's slick and tight vagina.

They savored each day and treasured each other greatly that they had no major disagreements. During the times that they debated about something, Dave always gave in, "Okay, you can work, but please don't work at night." Amy was accepted for hospital work and the day when she would work at night would surely come, so after a day or two, she gave in to Dave. "Hon, I won't be accepting work anymore. I don't want to make you unhappy." So Amy stayed at home and did the household chores, and tried to make Dave happy.

One time Dave came home a little bit late. He smelled of alcohol. Amy said nothing but cooked dinner for him and tried to strike a conversation with him. He spoke in monosyllables and he seemed preoccupied.

"Hon, is something troubling you?" Amy asked him.

"It's nothing, hon. Don't be bothered."

On the following days however, he became more and more unreachable.

"Hon, please tell me if you're angry with me," she said plaintively.

"I'm not angry," he said tersely.

As days passed, he retreated deeper into his cell. He went home late more and more, and whenever Amy spoke to him, he answered briefly and uncaringly.

Amy cried and asked him to speak to her what was troubling him. "Was there another woman?" Dave did not answer, and Amy cried herself to sleep that night.

The following night, Dave did not go home at all. When he did, it was to tell her that he was moving out of the apartment. Amy clung to him crying.

She asked him what she had done wrong. "You didn't do anything wrong, Amy. Go and find yourself a worthier man than I am," he replied. "I'll send you a monthly stipend and the divorce papers for you to sign," he added indifferently.

Amy wanted to scream in pain. "What happened, Dave? I thought you loved me. Please tell me what went wrong?"

Her question was unanswered as Dave left her clinging to the balustrade for dear life. She was devastated. What had gone wrong? She had thought she had everything. Did she fail as a wife? She crawled in bed and cried her heart out. She was devastated. Why live when you didn't have something to live for? she thought. She wanted to forget everything and just disappear into oblivion.

The next days that ensued were intolerable for Amy. She stayed cooped up in the apartment, not wanting to go out. At times she went outside to buy booze to drown herself from the pain. Her body and soul ached for Dave. For how long, she knew it could last forever. Her hero had taken flight from their paradise. She waited for the divorce papers as Dave stated, but it never came, and Amy was grateful for it.

She came to a realization that she did not want Dave to think that he was everything to her. She had to be brave and show him that even without him, she could survive. She had to overcome her depression. It was easy to say so, but it took Amy almost a month to be able to control her tears whenever she thought of Dave. She knew it could take forever for her to get over Dave, but for then, at least she could control her tears.

She re-applied for work and started working just as soon as her application was approved. Her hospital duty kept her from wallowing in her despair. She did not entertain any suitors though. Dave was nowhere to be seen. One day when her mom and some relatives visited, she told them Dave was at work, or somewhere else, and they never suspected.

Amy wondered if Dave left the country. Perhaps with another woman. The healing gash in her heart opened again and she clutched her chest as the thought of Dave with another woman made her cry in pain. The pain was almost physical; she could literally feel the knife plunged deep into her heart.

It was one lazy Sunday afternoon that she saw Dave again. She was shocked to see him so thin and pale compared to when they were together. Her heart went out to him and she cried in the corner of the supermarket. Was his woman not taking care of him? She hid herself and decided to follow him to see how his woman looked like.

David went straight to the base hospital. His girl must be working here, Amy thought. She followed him inside and saw him entering the oncology unit. She waited for him outside for a full thirty minutes before he finally came out. She was hidden behind the post near them, and they didn't see her. They were talking in low tones unheard by others a few distances away. But Amy could hear everything.

"Don't forget your schedule. We'll have to increase your treatment," the man, who was obviously a doctor, reminded him.

"Do I need anyone to watch over me? Because I don't have anyone," Amy heard Dave reply.

"Aren't you married?" the doctor asked. Amy heard no reply from Dave. "Perhaps, we can inform your family in the States?"

Dave's voice came out angry and had increased a pitch higher. "Please don't do that, doc; I don't want to be a burden to anyone."

Amy's heart was painfully beating in her chest as realization suddenly dawned on her.

Was that why he went away? Was that why he made her believe he had another woman? She wanted to confront him then, but she had to be sure first. As soon as Dave left, she rushed inside and looked for the doctor.

The doctor was reluctant at first to reveal any bit of information, but when she showed him her ID and some house bills proving to him that she was indeed Dave's wife, he relented. Amy also informed him about their situation, of how Dave left without any plausible reason. When the doctor understood the circumstances, he revealed that Dave had stage 2 cancer of the colon.

Amy remembered how Dave sometimes complained of abdominal pain, but they didn't focus on it because they were too busy making love.

The doctor instructed Amy to be there on his next treatment. "Let's allow him to tell you himself."

Dave's next schedule was after three days. Amy was to enter at the middle of the consultation. And she did. Dave was speechless with shock and anger.

"What brought you here?" His raging voice echoed in the silence of the room. He stared at the doctor angrily. "I could sue you for this."

"Please listen to me, Dave. By not telling me the truth, you're actually being selfish." Amy was in tears. "Look at me. Don't you see the pain and unhappiness that I went through? Haven't we vowed to love each other in sickness or in health? Let's stay together and be happy for whatever time God has given us."

Dave's face softened but his body was still

rigid with anger.

"I don't think you know how serious my condition is," he retorted.

"Well, I don't care how serious it is as long as we're together. Can't you see, Dave? I am not happy without you."

Tears fell down on Dave's face as well, and she ran into his arms and they clung to each other, their souls, bodies, and minds united into a bundle of joy and love. "I love you," they whispered to one another as they kissed, unmindful of the doctor who was teary-eyed as well.

That night, back in their apartment, Amy made gentle love to Dave. She lovingly sponged his body with lukewarm water, kissing every inch of the pale skin, lovingly massaging his weakened muscles and caressing his bony back. Dave was leaner, but he was still strong and he humped her while Amy welcomed the awakening of her desires once more, when Dave adored her pussy with his warm, teasing tongue and fingers until she came again and again, each one more satisfying than the previous.

"How I missed you, babe. Thank you for coming into my life," Dave whispered breathlessly into her ear.

Amy monitored Dave's medicine and treatment. She was not a nurse, but she too worked in a hospital setting, so she was not ignorant. Dave was given an indefinite leave so he just stayed home resting. He had started a memoir and Amy was still not mentally prepared to think about the future. She had to enjoy the "now" with Dave before everything becomes too late.

She took a leave of absence too, and they decided to visit Baguio again. The City of Pines was as beautiful as ever. Flowers were in bloom and the air was crisp and cool; it was a perfect environment for Dave. They visited Wright Park, where one had an amazing view of the mines around it. They strolled around Burnham Park and rejuvenated themselves amidst the city's tranquil ambiance.

"Are you not scared?" he asked Amy once they were seated on the stone bench overlooking the lake.

"Not really. I'm so happy right now," Amy smiled joyfully to him. "I trust our relationship will last forever." And she kissed him full in the lips, seeking his tongue and sucking on it.

"I remember something. How come you haven't sent the divorce papers before?" Amy asked.

"Because I couldn't bring myself to. You don't know the lonely nights I have spent wishing you were there with me. Hoping you would appear out of nowhere and kidnap me and force me to come home," he replied.

"You should have come home hurriedly, hon, and find me pining for you as well."

"Let's go back to the hotel and make love," Dave intoned excitedly, his penis already erect and eager.

Back at the hotel, they romped and rolled on the bed, breathless with desire. Amy was afraid Dave would experience the pain again, so she was the one who made love to Dave. She adored his body, caressing, gently massaging his dick and staying on top, thrusting her yearning pussy into his distended and equally yearning dick until they locked their groins together and both climaxed, their bodies melding into each, desperate for each other.

After their vacation, they visited the doctor as scheduled, and the doctor was amazed at how Dave had gained more weight and had a sunnier disposition.

"Your positive behavior has hastened your recovery," the doctor said. "If you proceed this way, you could go into remission."

Dave and Amy were so happy; they stayed awake most of the night and talked about their plans for the future. We'll have a dozen of kids and we'll buy a house on the hilltop with a fascinating view of the city."

"Yes, we'll do all that, hon," Amy touched his lips with her finger. "As long as you have faith in us and in our love."

"I love you," Dave said and kissed Amy back.

Dave's remission stayed. The doctor said it was a miracle. A miracle that only love can do. After 6 months, Amy got pregnant with a baby boy. Dave was exultant; there was nothing he could ask more. They both realized that indeed love could conquer everything.

17 FLIGHT IN PARADISE PART 3

The advent of Amy and Dave's baby boy turned their lives into a rewarding, fruitful life. They have become genuinely happy.

When they visited the oncologist, Dr. Brown, he said that he was optimistic of Dave's prognosis.

"It's good you came to consult earlier. A few months more would have worsened the disease, where cure would no longer be feasible."

"You are responding properly to your medications. Congratulations."

Amy and Dave celebrated the good news by watching a movie after leaving the baby with a baby-sitter. Then they strolled around the park, breathing the cool, refreshing air, their arms linked together and relishing the priceless moment.

They arrived home, their hearts full of warmth and love. Dave kissed her softly on the lips, making suckling noises as he sucked her tongue, trying to draw the sweetness from it. During the previous days, they made perfunctory lovemaking, afraid that Dave's remission might discontinue.

The doctor assured them though that it was safe to have sex. So, with their baby with the baby-sitter, they had all the time in the world.

They started kissing gently; the unique taste of Amy's tongue aroused Dave as always, increasing the yearning ache in his phallus. Amy's head reeled as the old sensations resurfaced and made her breathless with desire.

She released Dave's engorged penis from his pants, and it sprang readily to her touch. She massaged David's shaft with her fingers, applying a firm but gentle pressure. David caught his breath momentarily but continued in playing with Amy's nipples while kissing her.

Dave undressed Amy, piece by piece, discovering yet more erogenous zones in her body. He rained kisses on each inch of her skin, which sent shivers up her spine. His hand flew to her pubis, caressing her vagina incessantly and tweaking her clit with a delicious tempo that made her raise her hips.

Amy continued fondling Dave's dick, as they stood there in the middle of the living room, aflame with passion, necking and petting like newlyweds on their first honeymoon. Indeed, it felt like their first honeymoon because Dave had not been in tiptop form in the past months.

Dave unhurriedly lay Amy on the carpeted floor and slipped the final shred of clothing she had. Amy's body was petite in frame, with her small but firm breasts and perfectly chiseled muscles. He then lifted her legs onto his shoulder and knelt. He nestled his humongous erection beside Amy's craving vagina and bent to kiss her lips.

As he kissed her, he entered her in short quick strokes, moving leisurely and relishing the tightness of Amy's pussy. One of Amy's held one of her breast and the other one was tapping and rubbing her clit, as Dave humped her. His movements turned into frenzied thrusts as his arousal increased and he rammed his ravenous dick into Amy's slick vagina. Amy's ass slapped against Dave's groin as he pulled her towards him, as he invaded her pussy, going in and out of it in delicious strokes.

Soon, they were both straining to achieve their orgasms, their moans of delight coupled with the squishing sounds coming from the succulent union of his dick and her pussy. With a final cry of joy, Amy writhed and rotated her hips as she savored the extremely delightful pleasures that inundated her whole being. She was still climaxing when Dave grunted with pleasure as his semen squirted into the air. They clung to each other, sweating and breathless, as they continued to bask in the joys of sexual pleasure.

They slept in each other's embrace, gratified and happy, only to wake up again to partake to the sensual pleasures of copulation. They transferred to the bed this time, with Amy sitting against Dave's face, her pussy pressed into his lips as he suckled and licked its folds with his tongue. Dave lay on the bed toying with his own dick, whereas Amy was facing the other direction while sitting on his face. This provided Dave the freedom to play with Amy's pussy more freely and deeply.

Dave tongued Amy's clit while inserting his thumb into the ridged portion inside her pubis called the G-spot. Amy gasped as the combined sensation of his thumb and tongue turned her body into a wild conflagration of desire.

When Dave felt Amy was nearing orgasm, he pinned her down into the floor and straddled her like a madman. He fucked her hard and long, thrusting his rock-hard dick into her wet pussy. Dave went in and out of Amy's delectable pussy with his tumescent phallus incessantly and continued increasing the rhythm as they cavorted and clawed at each other's naked bodies, until they were spent.

Enclosed in Dave's warm arms that evening, Amy remembered her first meeting with Dave. He was the silent type who never said anything but just stared with his blue eyes and blonde hair. While the other U.S. airmen were boisterous, he was not. This characteristic is what attracted Amy to Dave. She pined for him, not knowing that Dave felt the same as well.

"Do you want us to live in Cheyenne?" Dave asked Amy.

"Is your duty done here?"

"No, I was just thinking...."

"I like it better here," Amy informed him.

"Okay, if that's what you want," he said in acceptance, "then we will stay."

Dave got even better as the days passed. His previously sunken cheeks were now rosy and filled up with flesh. He was back to his old body: lean but muscled.

Amy thought her Calvary was over; she had a doting husband, an adorable baby, and a simple but fulfilling life. She had never been happier before. One day, however, the new storm arrived in the form of a letter.

"Love, remember what I told you before about Jeff?" Dave asked Amy.

"Jeff who?"

"My son, remember?"

Amy's heart did a double flip. "Oh...yeah," was all Amy could say. Dave told her about his son Jeff, whom he sired when he was still in his teens.

"He's coming next week," Dave's words felt like heavy raindrops on Amy's heart. She felt despondent, and she did not know why.

The next week came soon enough, and they fetched Jeff from the airport. Amy's forebodings proved to be true because together with Jeff was his hot and sexy mom.

Amy caught her breath when a lovely, tall brunette walked toward them with Jeff in tow.

"Hi, Dave, this must be Amy," she turned to

her and flashed a great, charming smile. "I'm Lucy," she extended a long velvety hand.

"Oh, I thought George was the one coming. How've you been?" Dave moved to shake her hand, but she hugged him tightly.

Amy did not want to think about it but she noticed the naughty glint in Lucy's eyes. There was a stab of pain in her heart.

There was Jeff, who looked up shyly at them. He was more endearing in person, with his blue eyes, same as his dad's, and his brilliant smile.

"This is Jeff," Lucy tugged the 6-year-old's hand.

"This is your dad and Amy," Lucy introduced us. "You've seen them in pictures, right?"

Jeff looked up, half-smiling, and nodded. Dave scooped him up proudly. "I've missed you, tiger. What's up?" Dave asked Jeff.

Lucy was so beautiful. How did Dave let go of her? Amy asked herself. She wanted to ask Dave the question then, but said instead, "The car is waiting. Let's go."

At home, Dave and Lucy updated each other about news from Cheyenne, with Jeff playing close by, and Amy felt like an outsider. Dave called her by his side, but she excused herself saying she wanted to check on Joshua. Joshua was barely a year old, but he could turn his crib upside down.

Dave and Lucy's laughter echoed in the house. It should be a happy moment for Amy, but she could not let go of the feeling of anxiety.

Joshua was fast asleep, his small, stocky

feet up on his pillow. He was smiling in his sleep, unaware that his mom was uneasy and troubled.

Amy went back to the living room and found them looking at some pictures she had diligently made into an album. They were sitting shoulder to shoulder, their heads close to each other, and Amy felt a twinge of doubt at the rear of her head.

What was the matter with her? Was she so insecure to be thinking there was more to it after all those years? But Amy's feeling did not subside. They looked good together, she thought.

She went over to them. "I patiently organized those pics," she hovered over them.

"You were able to put all those loose pictures into this great album, hon," Dave quipped.

"Yeah, this is cool," Lucy looked up and smiled at her, her sensual lips red with lipstick.

"Hey, tiger, what about helping me with lunch," Amy playfully punched Jeff's tummy.

"Do you have pasta?" the boy asked, his face brightening considerably.

"Well, we can cook pasta later if you help me," Amy offered him.

Hand in hand they marched to the kitchen as Jeff began to loosen up as he asked questions incessantly. Amy warmed up to the cute little boy, who had his father's thin lips, aquiline nose, and deep, blue eyes.

During lunch, Dave and Lucy were still engrossed in their conversation.

"Amy here wants to watch the Frontier

Days. Are they still as exciting as before?" Dave tried to draw Amy into the conversation.

"They are. You should settle in Wyoming, Amy," Lucy stated determinedly.

"I would surely visit Cheyenne, but I prefer it here."

They went on to talk excitedly about the Frontier Days during lunch, and Amy's niggling doubts faded in the distance.

That afternoon, Jeff played with Joshua. Amy could not help but love Jeff. He was a sweet, intelligent child, who was endlessly curious about almost anything around him. He kept asking questions about why the color of the room was white, why Joshua is unable to talk with him, and so on, and so forth. It kept Amy busy and entertained.

Dave played with his kids, playing horsey-horsey, while Amy and Lucy went around the backyard admiring Amy's orchids. They were in the process of blooming, and the array of budding colors lent a festive but tranquil ambiance to the place.

In the evening, Dave and Lucy got back to their reminiscing conversation once again.

"You were so handsome in your blue shirt I thought I was seeing a mirage," Amy heard Lucy piped happily, as she pottered in the kitchen.

The kids were asleep and every sound was amplified. She heard them go out to the patio and heard the chairs being pulled, and then silence ensued. Her heart heavily fluttered in her chest. Why were they silent? What were they doing? She tiptoed to the kitchen's window to peer outside.

Their heads were together. There were thundering hooves sounding through Amy's heart. Her knees went weak, and she could barely breathe. Then Dave roared with laughter, "You naughty girl, how did you know all that?"

Amy was startled and had almost tripped on the stool beside her. They had been looking at something held in Lucy's hand.

It must be an insect, because she heard Lucy say, "Dumbo, that's why they could ran fast," and they both laughed in glee. They were so happy together that Amy was wondering why they did not stay together.

Amy collapsed into the nearby stool, until her breathing became normal. What was the matter with her? Postpartum insecurities? But it had been months that passed already for postpartum blues. Perhaps, she was just threatened because it was the first time that a woman came into their lives: a stunning, intelligent woman at that.

When they finally settled for the night, Amy asked Dave, "It's apparent you have good chemistry with Lucy. How come you didn't marry her?"

Dave looked at Amy curiously, "You're not jealous, are you, love?" There was a beginning smile at the corners of his mouth.

"Of course not," Amy vehemently denied. "Why should I? She's your past. I was just curious."

"It's because what we really felt for each other was friendship. That one time we made it had been an accident when we were too drunk." He laughed. "You know, being young and imagining you could do anything in this world. Perhaps, we wanted to experiment too? She was my best friend even in preschool."

Dave sighed poignantly. "I miss them all back home, and it's great to have them here with us. I hope you'd welcome them warmly too."

He kissed Amy tenderly. "She's still my best friend, but I have you now, and I love you."

Amy's misgivings all flew out the window as Dave embraced her tightly and began undressing her.

"Wait, what were you two laughing about at the backyard?" she asked.

"Ah, the spider," Dave chuckled. "Lucy has a habit of catching spiders and counting how many legs they have."

Amy thought to herself what kind of a fool tortured herself with unwarranted suspicions of her husband's assumed infidelity. God, she was so insecure.

She sat atop Dave's chest and stooped to kiss him passionately on the lips. She realized she would die should Dave dare to look at other women in a romantic way. She wanted her man all to herself.

When they were in bed, Amy slid her crotch up and down Dave's, as she playfully bit and sucked his lower lip. Her earlier fears during the day, of losing Dave to another woman, had made her more passionate. She stood up on the bed and slowly disrobed, fondling herself at the same time, running her fingers on her breast and her pussy.

Dave's penis was already standing at attention underneath his pajamas. Amy had always this effect on him. Amy straddled Dave and started kissing him, drawing out his tongue to suck it and twirl it with her own. The sound of their wet, passionate kisses ignited their lust as they relished each other's mouth and fondled.

Dave massaged her breasts feverishly, his sexual desires taking over his body. He quickly pulled his pajamas out of the way to expose his throbbing, angry phallus. He pulled Amy onto his lap, down into his upturned, eagerly waiting dick. They both moaned in delight, as flesh met flesh and exquisite pleasures emanated from that contact.

They were facing each other, as Amy sat astride Dave's lap, who was half-kneeling and supporting her buttocks with his laps. They started moving slowly at first, Amy bobbing up and down and Dave thrusting forward as he lifted her up and down into his waiting dick. Now and then, Dave sucked Amy's nipples and lips, urging her to move faster.

"Love, move faster," he prodded her.

Amy rotated her hips as she impaled Dave's dick with her slick pussy. She could feel her orgasm building in her groin and from all areas of her body. The sensuous pleasure was driving her nuts as she increased her pace, sliding in and out, up and down of Dave's delicious shaft. She was nearing climax, and by Dave's labored and beet red face, he was too.

He suddenly shifted positions and pinned her on the bed, mounting her from above. Amy gasped as Dave shoved his hungry dick into the tight folds of her vagina. It felt so good that Amy cried in ecstasy. When Dave started pounding into her, she moaned and writhed, her eyes fluttering in pure delight. She could feel her pussy tightening on his dick and sucking it back inside as he pulled out with a squelching sound.

His dick became so enormous; Amy felt all the corners of her vagina being filled with Dave's throbbing manhood. The sensations emanating from the friction of their sexual organs were so intense; Amy stuttered as she prodded Dave to shove all of his dick into her willing pussy. With two arms planted firmly on each side of Amy, Dave drove his dick in and out of her pussy. They went on for several minutes, straining against each other, their crotches slapping against one another as their sweaty, high-strung bodies slammed together to satiate a special need deep within them.

Their sensuous movements quickened, and still quickened, as they raced to achieve orgasm. Amy clutched Dave's back and raised her hips as waves and waves of pleasure assailed her body. She trembled and cried as more waves came when Dave continued humping her. Then Dave trembled in joy as he grunted, held his dick, and squirted his own thick, creamy semen into Amy's pubis. He collapsed on top of Amy, kissing her, nibbling her lips, and telling her, "I love you."

The next day, they decided to visit the

nearby resort. Joshua and Jeff were already up, and Jeff was jumping up and down with excitement. "Dad, are we really going for a swim?"

"Yeah son, so bring your swimming trunks," Dave carried him and tossed him up into the air, catching him safely. Jeff squealed in joy.

Amy and Lucy were laughing too as they watched the priceless scene before them. Amy was dressed in pink tube top and khaki shorts. Lucy wore a navy blue sleeveless blouse and matching shorts. It was a blessing Dave was still on his sick leave from work, and this allowed him some time with his family.

They trooped to the car with the Joshua in a carrier. He was also crooning contentedly. They were a picture of a happy family.

They rented a deluxe cottage with a spotless kitchen, where they could cook; two spacious rooms with soft, comfortable sheets; and their own private swimming pool. Within the vicinity of the resort were public swimming pools where kids could play in the assortment of slides and rides. There was also an aviary where exotic birds were housed. Another tour bus was waiting for visitors who would like to go mall shopping.

They unpacked their things for an overnight stay, and Jeff immediately jumped into the water, splashing water as he repeatedly jumped into the pool.

"Don't go into the other side. That's waist deep," his dad cautioned him.

Amy changed into her bathing suit and

waded into the water with Joshua in hand. Joshua was afraid of the water at first, but when his initial fear subsided, he also started splashing water around him, saying "mama, mama."

Lucy came out with an eye-catching two-piece bikini. Amy saw Dave gasping in admiration. Her heart skipped a beat again. She had to admit that in that department, Lucy had won hands down. She was petite, had small breasts, and not as tall as Lucy.

"I can see you have been keeping in shape," Dave exclaimed.

"Uh-huh," Lucy dived perfectly into the deep portion of the pool. She went down with a big splash, showering Dave who was still standing by the pool. He shouted and dived as well, shouting at Lucy, "I'll race you to the opposite side."

Amy watched them as they raced back and forth, splashing water at one another and yelling in joy when Dave won the race. They were back to being children again and Amy was happy that they came for a short vacation.

They emerged from the pool energized and jovial.

"Your swimming skills are yet to improve," Dave said to Lucy as he approached Amy and kissed her.

"Shall I cook lunch, your highness?" he bowed before Amy.

"It's okay. I have prepared lunch beforehand." She smiled at him.

Lucy laughed out loud. "Does this guy bother you often, Amy?"

"Not really. Just every once in a while," she replied.

"Give him some work to do; he is as fit as a horse," and they all laughed as Dave made another bow. They spent the rest of the day swimming and teaching the kids how to swim. In the evening, when the kids were asleep already, they barbecued and roasted beside the pool, and drank some red wine. Amy listened as Dave and Lucy recalled their childhood days in Cheyenne: their first Christmas tree shopping, their first rodeo together, and their hilarious experiences when they were in high school.

They were precious memories, indeed, Amy thought, and she blurted, without thinking, "you would be perfect as a couple."

Her words hang heavy in the air; there was momentary silence, which Lucy broke, "Are you kidding me? Except for that night when we got drunk and experimented, I would never marry a man who treats me like a man," she sputtered amidst her laughter. "But I'm glad we got drunk that night because you gave me Jeff."

"Oh, you were very competitive, not wanting to lose on anything," Dave playfully threw dust at her.

"We're perfect as best friends. Don't worry, Amy. As long as you'd help me with Jeff's schooling, we won't be having any problems."

Amy felt a sweeping feeling of relief overcome her, making her soul at peace. At last all her doubts were erased.

"Thanks Lucy for coming back into our lives," she smiled at Lucy across the short distance.

They drank more wine and soon Dave grew tipsy.

"Move over, woman. I want to feel your warmth," he spread a big towel on the grass near the pool and motioned Amy to stay beside him.

Amy, who was tipsy too, went towards him, wavering in her steps. Dave pulled her towards him and kissed her hard on the mouth. Amy responded back, allowing all her worries and anxiety to fade away into oblivion with Dave's kiss.

"I want to make love to you here in the open," Dave firmly stated.

"Hey, love, let's go to our room. Lucy's here," Amy whispered amidst her drunkenness.

"Hey Lucy, you're my best friend, right? You won't mind if we make it out here? You can join us if you want to," he teased Lucy.

Before Amy could move, Dave stripped Amy of her bathing suit, exposing her slim, supple body. Lucy sat transfixed a few feet away, staring at them, feeling her hormones, responding naturally to the scene. She was becoming aroused herself.

Dave was now spreading Amy's thighs and burying his head in her crotch. Amy knew she was helpless once Dave was aroused like that. Besides, she was weak with drunkenness. She opened her thighs wide and placed each of them on Dave's opposite shoulders. She was wide open for his ferocious tongue. Dave wasted no time in running his tongue around her clitoris, tweaking the erogenous mound every now and then. Amy started to moan; she no longer cared whether Lucy was there or not.

Lucy was playing with herself, stroking her pussy with upward and downward movements. When she could not stand it any longer, she went to them, still playing with her nipples and labia, wanting to be gratified.

She knelt and kissed Amy's slightly opened mouth. Amy's eyes opened wide when her eyes met Lucy's, but she was so aroused she no longer cared about it. Amy closed her eyes as Lucy sucked her lower lip, and then her upper lip, and stroked her tits and nipples in slow pleasurable movements. With Dave concentrating on sucking and licking her clit, the dam of pleasure was ready to open. God, it was more than anything Amy had experienced. Pleasurable sensations came from multiple parts of her body; she was drowning in them, gasping for breath, crying for more as Dave and Lucy relentlessly continued with their ministrations. Then Dave knelt and pulled her ass down as he shoved his rock-hard penis into her waiting pussy.

Amy moaned loudly and writhed as Dave went in and out of her tight juicy hole. Lucy was nearing orgasm just watching them in their throes of pleasure. She offered Amy her pussy by sitting on her face, and Amy instinctively brought out her tongue to pleasure her as her body was wracked with thousands of pulsating nerve endings ready to burst with her climax.

Dave humped Amy, as Amy explored Lucy's vagina with her tongue while basking in unadulterated ecstasy as her climax exploded and let loose the tons and tons of pleasure points when Dave rammed his dick into her.

Lucy was climaxing, moaning and arching her back, as Amy licked her juices. Dave followed within minutes, letting loose a delighted groan, their delightful exclamations lost in the noise of the neighboring karaoke. They lingered fondling and stroking each other until they were satiated and spent.

The haunting melody was still coming from the next cottage, but for Amy, Dave, and Lucy, tomorrow would be another day.

18 FLIGHT IN PARADISE PART 4

After the grand time that Lucy and Jeff had with Amy and Dave, it was time for Lucy and Jeff to go back to the U.S.

"Keep in touch," Amy hugged Lucy warmly.

Amy hugged Jeff next and told him to send pictures and write e-mails.

"I will for sure. I'll ask Mom to help me," the 6-year-old said, teary-eyed. Then he turned to Joshua and embraced his half-sibling.

"Don't give headaches to Dad," Jeff murmured to the 1-year-old uncomprehending child.

Dave watched his elder son embrace his younger son, Joshua, and a lump formed in his throat. He went to them and clasped both of them in a warm embrace.

"Take good care of yourself, Champ," he commanded Jeff.

Then it was time for David to say goodbye to her ex-wife. Amy talked to the kids, as Dave hugged Lucy tight and kissed her cheeks.

An image of Lucy naked, grinding her pussy to her face, flashed in the mind of Amy. She shook her head to erase the memory; things happen when one was drunk, she thought, and it was a thing now of the past.

"Don't forget your exercise, sleepyhead. It keeps you sexy," Dave whispered huskily to Lucy. "You'll always be my best friend."

Lucy clung to him, crying, "I'll miss you. Come visit us too," she said amidst her tears.

Lucy beckoned Jeff, and they turned to go, waving to them, as they entered the embarking area.

After they left, Amy and Dave walked listlessly to their car. The vivacity of Lucy and the joviality of Jeff were sorely missing in the background. Were they too serious about their lives that they could no longer enjoy it?

Dave placed a protective shoulder around Amy, and together, they pushed Joshua's carriage towards their car.

That evening, Amy wanted to enliven Dave's mood, so after Joshua slept, she prepared a "show" for him. She sat him in a comfortable armchair and dimmed the light. She put on a slow, sensual music and came out wearing a sexy negligee.

Amy gyrated sensuously to the music, caressing her body as she danced. She swayed to the tempo, undulating her body suggestively and peeling off her clothing one by one. Her bra fell on the floor, exposing her firm tits to Dave. Dave's penis sprang into life, bulging beneath his undergarments. Amy cupped her breasts with her two hands and started kneading them as she danced to the music.

Then she discarded her lower undies while spreading her legs wide for Dave to see. The lips of her vagina were red with suffused blood that was waiting to be released. Dave's erection grew bigger, and he had to pull free from his undergarments as the tight clothing was causing him pain.

His penis broke free and rejoiced in its new freedom. Amy rotated her hips with the music, wetting her fingers with her saliva and inserting them into her vagina. She rubbed her nipples lightly and kept dancing.

Then she took a feather from her cap and traced the contours of her breast using the feather. This made her shiver with delight and made Dave touch his ramrod penis in anticipation of the promised slice of heaven. Amy ran the feather along her thighs and into her pussy. She gasped with pleasure as the titillating soft material came in contact with her clitoris. It was an incredible sensation as every nerve in her body was focused on the beginning ember of her sexual gratification.

The feather found its way to Amy's clit. She stood in front of Dave as she parted her labia and ran the feather up and down her mound of pleasure. She moaned softly as the feeling of delight mounted, and she ended up reclining on the floor, not wanting to stop the continuous caressing action coming from the feather.

Dave was at her side in a jiffy, taking hold

of the feather and stroking her engorged clit while kissing her opened mouth simultaneously. Amy moaned and grabbed Dave's penis as they shifted into a 69 position on the floor. Dave kept on playing with her clit using the feather while his tongue descended into her pussy. His tongue parted the lips of Amy's vagina. He inserted his tongue deep into her.

Amy, in turn, was sucking the crown of his dick and running her tongue up and down his phallus. His body grew rigid as Amy increased her pace, stroking the base of his penis with her fingers and sucking his crown in and out of her mouth.

Dave grew delirious with delight, as his tongue returned the pleasure, invading Amy's juicy pussy. His fingers found her anal opening, and he inserted one finger, tentatively driving it in. Amy gave a start; it was a new sensation that aroused her all the more. Dave's tongue then went to her clit, and he let go of the feather to insert a finger into her warm, welcoming pussy.

Amy moaned, "Ahhhh, yeah, yeah, that's it." She moved her hips up and down, rubbing her pussy against Dave's face.

"Do you want me to fuck you now?" Dave gasped with his arousal.

"Yes, oh yes, please," Amy begged.

When Dave finally penetrated her pussy from behind with his 9-inch dick, she cried out his name, thrusting backward to meet his manhood. "Yeah, harder, harder...oh God," she prodded him.

They moved in unison, thrusting their

groins against each other, enjoying the union of their erogenous zones, and then moved hurriedly to fulfill their passion.

Vacation time was over for Dave; he had to get back to work the following Monday. What made their days merrier was Joshua, who was growing to be an inquisitive and precocious child. When he first said "mama," Amy's joy was immense; she felt her heart burst with gladness.

Joshua made Dave's days lively too; when he came from work, they frolic on the floor like two tots. They were one happy family.

Dave learned that he would be stationed back in the U.S. He was to be assigned to the Minot Air Force Base in North Dakota. He, however, had a different plan; he wanted to get out of the Air Force. He was an architect by profession, but he wanted to be able to work with minimum stress. The doctor said stress could endanger his chances of a full recovery from his condition.

Amy was supportive of his decision. She loved Dave with all of her heart; she was willing to go with him anywhere. So, it was decided that they would go home to Cheyenne, Wyoming, where Dave's family resided.

It was a wintry December when they arrived in Cheyenne. Snow was wonderfully piling at the Walker's front porch when they arrived. Amy was anxious whether Dave's family would accept them with open arms, but her fears were ungrounded; his parents and two siblings, Derek and Sean, have been most welcoming.

Amy and Joshua had to adjust to the freezing temperatures too, which was totally different from the tropical climate they got used to in the Philippines.

"Hey, love, is everything okay?" Dave asked, concerned about Amy's brooding countenance.

"I'm fine, love. Just adjusting to the weather."

After Amy, Dave, and Joshua were rested, they had a welcome party the following night. Dave's parents, Karl and Melanie, were beaming with pride as they presented their first grandchild to the rest of the relatives. There was Dave's funny uncle, Matt, who was the star of the night, with his funny jokes, and there was Dave's cousin, Glen, who was the "beauty and brains" of the family. She was tall and had long, curly tresses that accentuated her Nordic features. She had also the curvaceous body of a sex siren: 36-24-36.

And yes, Dave's ex-wife, Lucy, and their son, Jeff, were there. Jeff was so happy to be with Joshua once again.

Amy mingled with them and was asked primarily about Joshua, and since it was a topic loved by Amy, she was not uncomfortable recounting Joshua's "firsts": his first words, first steps, and other activities.

The scrumptious dinner of roasted turkey, veggies, mashed potatoes, and homemade cookies was perfect for Amy. There was red wine going around while everyone sat in the living room near the colorfully lit Christmas tree.

Amy was like in a surreal world. The celebration of past Christmases in the Philippines with her family and Dave was simple. There were no tons of beautifully wrapped gifts under the Christmas tree, like what Dave's family had. There were several gifts for her, for Dave, and for Joshua displayed prominently, and she was grateful and happy for their acceptance, but she missed home.

When she and Dave retired for the night, they were too tired to make love. They slept entwined in each other's embrace. Dave had a contented smile on his face.

Amy and Dave went partying and visiting relatives on the next days that followed. Everyone loved Joshua. They spirited him away and played with him all day long. Dave had a wonderful family, and they made Amy and Joshua feel at home. Amy had nothing more to ask.

That night, they made love in deliberate, slow movements. Amy rode Dave, slowly sliding her moist vagina up and down of Dave's enraged penis. They went on for several minutes, basking in the joyful delight of Amy's gripping love hole and Dave's enormous phallus. The tightness but moistness of Amy's pussy provided Dave a slick entry that made a suctioning, delicious sound, like a foot being pulled from a field of mud.

They were not able to maintain their slow movements, however, because their mounting desire prompted them to increase their tempo as they thrust wantonly against each other; their gleaming, passion-ridden bodies were straining to achieve their orgasms at all costs.

Dave had to establish his business first: to find customers who would entrust him with their constructions. The business of finding a house to stay in was their first priority. His parents offered a place to stay, but Dave had always been independent and wanted to succeed through his own efforts.

After the Christmas celebrations, they moved to a rented modest house down the block. Dave wanted them to start the New Year in their own home. The house had two cozy bedrooms, a kitchen, a small living room, a bath, and an ample space for Amy's backyard garden. Amy had no complaints because for her it was sufficient for the three of them as long as she was with Dave.

The months that followed, however, had Dave traveling to distant cities more often to visit construction sites and similar venues to obtain a hands-on experience. Those were long lonely and cold nights that she had to endure.

They barely made love because whenever Dave came home, he was tired from the trip and Amy was also exhausted with the endless household chores and of taking care of Joshua, who had become super-active at age 2.

Romance had lost its luster as the challenge of daily living crept into their lives. They barely talked to one another. The upside of it was that as Dave became successful, they were able to purchase the house and other pieces of furniture to make them more comfortable.

One time, while Amy was doing her laundry, she fished out a piece of paper from Dave's pant pockets. Her heartbeat stopped, and her chest tightened as a lavish handwriting, apparently a woman's, appeared before her eyes.

"Let's meet again at Fresno's. I missed you." Her hands trembled, and she was too shocked to cry.

Perhaps this note was not for Dave but for someone else. Perhaps, it is not what it really means. Perhaps...perhaps...perhaps. But as Amy held on to the piece of paper, she knew it was real, and perhaps Dave wanted her to read it. She shook her head and assured herself that there must be an explanation to this. Why was she losing her trust on Dave? Dave would not do this to her after all that they have been through.

When Dave came home after two days, she treated him as she previously did. It was good there were a few days to psyche herself.

It was only when they were about to sleep that she brought it up.

"I saw this in your pocket while doing the laundry." Amy handed him the piece of paper.

"Oh," Dave's eyes avoided hers, "it was a note for Freddy from his wife." Freddy was an engineer from Colorado who had teamed up with Dave.

Why was it in HIS pocket? Amy wanted to ask.

Amy said, "You can tell me the truth, Dave. I can handle it."

"It's the truth, Amy," Dave insisted.

It was a lame excuse but Amy had to believe him. Was she so naïve to turn a blind eye to her intuition and believe his explanation? She had to; otherwise, she couldn't bear to think of the consequences. Was she willing to share Dave with another woman? Could he forget Dave should she decide to call their relationship "quits"? All these questions assailed her and she did not have any answers.

Dave wanted to make love that night, but she was not able to bring herself to. When Dave tried to kiss her, she said softly, "I'm tired," and then she turned her back to him.

Dave started to turn her around, but he stopped himself when he thought how tired she must truly be.

Life went back to its humdrum cycle. Dave was away more often, and Amy no longer waited for him in the evenings. After she was done with the household chores, she and Joshua played until he went to sleep. Then she was left alone. She could not even reach Dave, because he has specified that he did not want to accept calls unless it was an emergency.

Amy remembered the first time Dave left her; it was because he had been sick, and he did not want her to know. Perhaps, it was the same circumstances this time. The more Amy thought about it, the more it became possible.

Amy sipped her coffee thinking about her life with Dave. Would it be better for her to go home to the Philippines? She missed her parents and everything that was Filipino: the fried rice, the fish sauce, the hamburger at Jollibee, and the places they had frequented previously. They were so happy then.

At present, Dave was barely at home. When was the last time they made love? Then she remembered that it was her who refused to make love the other night. Confused, she cried herself to sleep that night.

She loved Dave and she knew he did too, so the only rational thing for her to do is to believe him. She decided to play along with his game, whatever it was.

When Dave came home that evening, she greeted him with a passionate kiss.

"Hey, what's up?" Dave kissed her back.

"Nothing. I had a craving for pasta so I prepared your favorite food, spaghetti with meatballs, and some tacos," she beamed at him.

"Oh... right," Dave replied happily, "I'm starving," and they consumed what was on the table, with Joshua eating some of his portion and playing with the rest.

"Love, I got a contract from HP," he disclosed proudly.

"That's great news," Amy beamed and kissed him.

Then the magic returned in an instant. All the days that Amy had been missing him were deleted in an instant, as he kissed her, sucking on her upper lip, twirling her tongue with his own. Then they were all over each other, frenziedly undressing and reaching with their tongues whatever portion of skin that was laid bare.

Amy's palms finally closed in on Dave's manhood. Ah, how I missed it, she thought. She massaged it lovingly with her fingers. Dave closed his eyes and surrendered himself to her delightful ministrations. Amy cupped his balls with her other hand and lightly played with them, running her fingers around them and squeezing them gently. Dave was softly moaning. His eyes were closed and he lay on his back enjoying the moment.

This was the old Dave that Amy knew, his beloved Dave who loved her as much as she loved him. She licked the drop of liquid that was on the tip of his penis. Dave raised his pelvis to meet her tongue. Amy ran her ravenous tongue down his shaft and up, and then down again, taking care to include the sensitive ridge between his penis and his scrotum.

Amy let her tongue glide smoothly up and down his phallus until he begged her to take him into her mouth. She gave in and sucked his crown first, her fingers massaging the base of his dick.

Dave was coaching her, prodding her to take more into her mouth. She sucked and licked him using her mouth and her tongue, giving him no respite until he grabbed a handful of her hair to prod her to go faster.

His erection was so huge; Amy momentarily gagged when Dave shoved his red engorged dick down her mouth. But she managed to slide his erection into the side of her cheeks, providing her the necessary friction and moistness to be able to suckle his penis effectively. Soon, Dave was thrusting his dick lustfully into Amy's delightful mouth.

Amy went up and down his tumescent phallus repeatedly, licking, blowing, and sucking until Dave gave a grunt and spewed his semen all over her face. She nestled his dick in the corners of her lips as she sucked its crown and massaged his balls.

When Dave was done delivering the last drop of his love juice into Amy's face, he spread her thighs and caressed her vagina.

"Close your eyes, love. It's my turn to make you happy."

Amy closed her eyes and felt Dave fondling her tits and pussy in firm gentle strokes. She was so wet that Dave's fingers slid in perfectly into her G-spot. His index and ring fingers started stroking the small area in an upward movement. His thumb was glued to his clitoris, rubbing it up and down as well.

His lips were on hers and he would stoop now and then to capture her nipples with his tongue and mouth. His left hand alternated from fondling each of her breasts. Amy felt a gigantic orgasm building from her G-spot and clitoris. Orgasm caused by clitoral stimulation was the most pleasurable sensation Amy experienced, but a proper stimulation of the G-spot yields a triple orgasm that was indescribable and Dave had done this at times that he wanted to be aroused once more.

Amy's hands groped for his penis and found him starting to have a hard-on. Dave continued the firm pressure on her G-spot, not letting off the tempo. The ridged-like area began to bulge and enlarge, indicating that Amy's arousal was peaking.

Dave increased more the intensity and the pressure as Amy was gasping for breath, moaning and crying wildly, while Dave's fingers went in and out of her tight pussy. His thumb was also persistently "strumming" her clit, until it was hard and ready to burst. When Amy climaxed, it was a gigantic tidal wave that rolled on and on, as Amy's body convulsed with the flow of exquisite, unnamed ecstasy that defied any pleasures the god could offer. She was moaning and wailing loudly, until Dave's mouth came down on hers, and she suckled his tongue as the waves of pleasure came, again and again, tossing her like a helpless rag doll in the height of sensual delight.

By then, Dave was erect once more. Amy's moans and cries of joy had aroused him more. He straddled her and thrust at her without mercy, driving his rock-hard erection into the deepest part of her pussy. Amy thought she was fully satiated, but when Dave started pounding her again, she screamed his name, as another huge orgasm flooded her body, making her clung to Dave, sucking his neck as he fucked her hard and long; he gave one deep thrust and released his juices into the warmth of Amy's skintight pussy. They collapsed against each other, their breaths ragged, their bodies awash with sweat, but completely satiated with their love for each other. They smiled and just held on to each other as their breathing subsided and their heartbeats were back to normal. They were too lazy to wash up, so they slept naked and once more united by the strength of their love for each other.

Dave woke up in the middle of the night and was afraid to stir, lest he would wake up Amy. He stared at her lovely face, the face of an innocent child. He was on the verge of destroying that trusting face forever. The note that Amy saw in his pocket was actually meant for him. How he hated himself afterwards for lying to Amy. But there was some grain of truth in it when he said that Freddy was involved.

The woman who wrote the note was someone he and Freddy met one time when they went to the bar for a drink. He was sexually starved as Amy was perpetually tired whenever he was home. He knew it was not a valid excuse, but when the booze worked on his brain and body, he could no longer prevent the woman's advances, and they ended up in a hotel bed.

Dave regretted it and tried to avoid the woman, but she was persistent, sending him the note that Amy read. Not knowing what to do, Dave ran to her best friend, Lucy, his ex-wife. It was Lucy who talked to the woman, making sure she understood that Dave was not interested in pursuing further their relationship.

Dave vowed to Lucy and himself that he would not allow it to happen again. He caressed Amy's hair as he realized that he loved her so much and would not want to hurt her. At times though, he remained silent because he was afraid he would hurt her more.

He kissed Amy's partly opened lips, and she stirred, murmuring unintelligible words. She was visibly contented, a smile curving in the corners of her mouth while she slept. Amy snuggled comfortably in the crook of his arms as he stroked her hair and went back to sleep too.

With Dave's name becoming known by valuable clients, they decided to put up a home office where Dave could monitor all his contracts from there. The office was not as spacious as Dave would like it to be, but it was organized and well designed by the architect himself.

He also created a business website, where he facilitated his services to his clients. He still traveled to the actual sites every now and then, but these trips were few, so he got to spend more time at home with Amy and Joshua.

Lucy and Jeff dropped by every now and then so the two brothers could bond together. Dave was the happiest as he watched the half-brothers care for each other. It was a priceless reward for him as a father to the two adorable boys.

Winter had passed and the sun peeked now and then from the horizon. They were at the backyard surveying the area.

"I could extend my office up to this corner, and you could plant your veggies in this area." Dave indicated with his fingers the adjoining piece of land they had purchased.

Lucy crackled with laughter. "Are you serious?" she asked Amy. "You're planting vegetables, not flowers?"

"Well, why not?" she retorted. "Then I would not have to buy my veggies."

"Right," Lucy agreed, still amused with Amy's practical sense.

"I like that idea," Dave interrupted their conversation. "That would make sure that my veggies are always fresh."

Then they trooped to Dave's office and browsed over his wonderful designs as they drank coffee and watched the boys romp on the floor.

19 MOMENTS IN TIME PART 1

He stood there like a Nordic god, perfectly sculptured and beautiful; his sinewy body rippled with his movements as he came towards her. His manhood stood erect in all of its glory, throbbing and rigid as a rock. Carla gasped as the yearning inside her crotch became almost unbearable. She wanted to have all of his tumescent shaft enclosed deep into the folds of her moist love tunnel.

He grabbed her not so gently and pushed her against the wall, his lips seeking her own to suck and explore with his tongue. Carla's hand instinctively went to his ramrod penis. His penis was about 7 inches long and was hard as rock; Carla could hardly enclosed it in her hands.

He shuddered as Carla's fingers ran up and down his shaft while he devoured her mouth and her nipples. Their movements were frenzied and wild as they sucked each other's tongue and lips and explored their bodies with their hands.

His index and ring fingers caressed Carla's labia as his thumb played with her clitoris repeatedly until she was begging him to fuck her hard and long. He lifted her ass in both of his muscular arms and was penetrating her when....

Carla woke up with a start and found out it was only a dream. It was so vivid her heart ached for her husband. She missed Mark, her deceased husband, tremendously, and the dreams were increasing in frequency. She was at her arousal peak and knew she had to masturbate again to achieve release. It has been more than a year that she did not have a man—fearful of getting hurt again. She did not like the idea of one-night stands, and she still had not found someone whom she wanted to have a serious relationship with.

Carla's pussy was on fire with need. She plopped herself back on the bed and closed her eyes. Her vagina was aching for its counterpart. She undressed and lay on the bed without the covers on. She closed her eyes and tried to recall her dream. With her right hand, she massaged the inside of her thighs in gentle but firm strokes, while her left kneaded her luscious breasts and nipples. Then she ran her fingers up and down her labia. She was already aroused because of her erotic dream.

Her pussy was already wet with her juices. She inserted two fingers inside her moist pussy and searched for the ridge of her G-spot on the upper portion. She applied firm strokes on her G-spot while finger fucking herself. This intensified her arousal. She tweaked her left and right nipples while sucking the back of her arm as her orgasm continued to peak.

Her thumb played alternately with her clit, and the titillating sensations coming from her clit, G-spot, breasts, and mouth made her cry with extreme ecstasy as her climax burst and enveloped her body in pleasurable convulsions. She continued playing with herself until all of her juices were exhausted and she curled up with her pillow, still naked and wet from her own juices. She went back to sleep and murmured contentedly, now and then, in her unconscious.

Carla Walker looked out from the window of her modest villa and took in the spectacular view of the rolling hills of Ibiza, Spain. Mark's death from a car accident in Wyoming seemed a distant past when she was awake, but in her dreams, he was a constant visitor, arousing emotions she had never felt before.

Slowly, Carla undressed and hurriedly took a cold shower. It was summer, and Ibiza was teeming with tourists basking in the sparkling, clear waters and dazzling beaches within the area. She decided to take a stroll in the beach and then go for some groceries.

Her union with Mark did not produce any offspring, and this made her sad because she would have had company if they had a child. Mark's savings and assets, however, had allowed her to live comfortably the way she wanted to, so she concentrated on her writing. She wrote short stories which she plans to compile and publish eventually.

She donned faded jeans, which clung beautifully to her 5'5" svelte frame, and a tube blouse, which exposed her creamy arms and bursting cleavage. She carried her sandals while walking the length of the beach and enjoyed the fine, soft sand against her bare feet.

Carla came to the less populated area of the beach and sat on one of the small rocks, with her feet immersed in the crystal-clear waters. There were topless women sunbathing and couples enjoying a swim from the distance. She was staring absentmindedly at the vast expanse of the blue water when a voice interrupted her solitude.

"A penny for your thoughts?"

She looked up to a pair of deep blue eyes, with a twinkle of mischief in them.

"I'm Helen," her voice was husky. She had extended a hand towards her; Carla had no recourse but to shake hands.

"I'm Carla."

Carla and Helen became inseparable for the next days that followed. They got along together well with Helen's outgoing, vibrant personality and Carla's silent and introvert nature. They were opposites and they balanced each other well. Even their looks were different but they looked good together. Helen was slim and muscular, while Carla was voluptuous and curvaceous; Helen had dark straight hair, while Carla had silky, long curls. They avoided asking personal questions from each other and just enjoyed their time being together.

"I have two tickets to the Seaside Beach Club. Do you wanna join me?" Helen excitedly beamed at Carla one evening.

"Seriously, you should be going with your husband," Carla stated matter-of-factly.

Helen stayed mum for a few minutes and then blurted out, "Well, I had one, but I am officially divorced as of last week," she declared without a hint of sarcasm.

"Oh, I'm sorry," Carla murmured.

"What about you?" Helen asked.

And Carla found herself confiding in a friend she just met a few weeks ago. The pain she felt with the memory of Mark, however, was just a dull ache, no longer tearing her soul apart. They were cozily seated on Carla's porch while dusk started to settle in.

"It must be difficult for you," Helen sighed. "Mine was a marriage for convenience, so there was nothing to be sorry for."

A tear fell on Carla's cheek—a tear of relief and joy that she had finally overcome her poignant memories of Mark.

Seeing her lachrymose, Helen rushed beside her and hugged her tight.

"I'm fine," Carla said, but Helen continued hugging her and caressing her hair. Carla gave in to the warmth and security of Helen's embrace. It felt good after more than a year that no one had hugged her that tight.

Then Helen was kissing her—her eyes, her nose, her neck, then her lips. Carla was taken aback; she was so shocked to respond. When Helen's mouth came down on her own, she felt her spine tingle. She pushed Helen away and struggled away from her. What was she doing?

Carla thought.

Carla ran to her room and did not open the door until Helen left the house. Then she went to the mirror and touched her lips. What was wrong with her? She liked what Helen did to her. Her lips tasted of sweet mint, her lips soft and gentle. She closed her eyes as the familiar stirrings of lust began to surface in her groin.

The following day, Helen called several times during the day, but she did accept her calls. She texted: "Hey, it was just a spur of the moment. I'm sorry. It won't happen again."

Helen also had gone to Carla's house twice but Carla refused to open the door.

The truth was that Carla was afraid of herself. Why did she like Helen's kiss? It was one of the sweetest kisses she had experienced, but she felt she was cheating on Mark, thinking about Helen.

On the third day, Carla gave in. She replied to Helen's text.

"I'm confused. Are you offering the hand of friendship or something more?" Carla asked.

"Friendship," Helen replied. "I'm sorry for the previous incident."

They got back together again doing their shopping, swimming, and partying together. There were awkward silences, but Helen always broke the silence by a silly joke or something.

Carla invited Helen for a swim in her outdoor pool. She decided to go topless, dropping her bra and exposing her big round breasts. Helen stared at her luscious breasts as Carla dived into the pool.

"It's warm, c'mon," she beckoned Helen.

Helen unstrapped her bra and joined her, making a big splash, as they raced towards the other side. They collapsed against each other on the pool side, laughing like two children out on their first swim. Helen had one hand on Carla's arm and her tits were just a few inches from her fingers. Helen could not help herself. She touched Carla's upright nipples and slowly traced the contours of her breast.

Carla was momentarily surprised and had started moving out of Helen's reach, but there was a growing sensation from her groin that wanted to be satiated. Helen reached out for her other breast, and she felt her pulses race. They were both reclining on the concrete side of the pool, but their discomfort seemed trivial against their desires.

Helen's lips was on Carla's, sucking her lower lip, and then her tongue was grappling with hers as she felt her body respond to the touch of another person, which she had longed for a long time. She was fondling Helen's small but firm breasts too, encircling the nipples with her thumb and index finger, brushing them with her fingers, and pulling them now and then.

Then the doorbell rang.

They looked at one another startled. Then the doorbell rang again, as they hurriedly hooked their bras and wore their robes.

Carla's parents had decided to spend three days with their daughter. The gnawing need for sexual fulfillment disappeared for Carla, as she toured her parents around Santa Eulalia and spent some time sunbathing and swimming in the amazing beaches in the area.

Carla decided that she and Helen should get a man instead of developing a relationship between them. She still did not feel comfortable imagining herself making out with Helen. Carla avoided Helen, spending the whole day with her parents. Her parents, who were in their late sixties, seemed to be on their honeymoon, and Carla wished that she would end up with a man like her dad, loving, faithful, and responsible.

When the 3-day vacation of Carla's parents ended, Carla felt a certain sadness.

"Sweetie, haven't found someone yet?" her mother asked her. "It's more than a year. You have to move on."

"I'm only 25, Mom," Carla smiled at her mother, "Don't worry. The next time you come, I'll introduce you to my man," she assured her.

In her mind, Carla had no idea how and where she would find her man; she didn't even go out often. She reminded herself to circulate more often, so she could meet the man of her dreams.

One evening, they were invited by some of Carla's neighbor to attend a closing party for summer visitors. It was the first for them both, so they were thrilled to go.

It was an erotic, somewhat wild party, with gorgeous women in two-piece swimsuits and hunky men in briefs cavorting sensuously to the festive music while everyone got drunk and intoxicated. There were shirtless men beating drums, while people in bathing suits swayed their bodies to the drums. The jovial spirit was infectious and soon enough, Carla and Helen found themselves one with the crowd as they danced and laughed the night away.

They were so drunk; they decided to check in at a nearby hotel.

"Did you see the male dancer? His penis was visible through his briefs," Carla laughed. "That would be one huge erection."

Helen roared with laughter. "We have to get laid. I'm hornyyyy."

They collapsed on the couch in glee, holding their tummies, as they talked about the dancers who had their lust surfacing in the open.

"Apparently, we can't go out and look for a one-night stand," Helen said, "I'm horny, you're horny, why don't we masturbate each other instead of doing it alone?"

Carla thought, why not? She did intend to masturbate tonight.

Helen saw her hesitation and was beside her in an instant. "Hey, let's just try. If it doesn't work, then we'll stop." Her words slurred in drunkenness.

When Carla did not reply, Helen began to undress her. She started unbuttoning Carla's blouse in slow deliberate movements. She kissed every inch of flesh that was being exposed by her trembling fingers. She didn't tell Carla but she had also been masturbating instead of going on one-night stands just to be sexually gratified. So, she was more than excited to do this.

Carla was standing rigidly, her hands at her sides, not knowing how to react to Helen's advances. Helen knew exactly what to do. After removing Carla's blouse, she kissed her skin all over again before unhooking Carla's bra.

Carla's body began to relax as Helen kneaded her flesh and kissed the areas around her nipples. Her nipples were standing at attention, eager to receive Helen's ministrations. Carla closed her eyes as Helen's mouth descended into her nipples, and Carla had to hold on to her because she was dizzy with desire.

When Helen led her to the bed, she was breathless with excitement. It was the first time she has had sexual intimacy with a woman. While sucking her nipples, Helen's fingers were caressing her vagina beneath her undies.

"Just lie down and relax," Helen kept whispering in Carla's ears, as she touched her in places she knew she herself wanted to be touched.

Helen's fingers explored Carla's vagina until they were moist with her juices. Then she removed all her restrictive clothing. She knelt at the edge of the bed and pulled Carla down to the edge. She bent down and slung each of Carla's thighs on each of her shoulders, exposing Carla's pussy fully to her face.

This was Helen's favorite position with her husband during cunnilingus, and she wanted

Carla to enjoy the full satisfaction of the act.

Helen's tongue did not go straight for the clit and the vagina, but rained kisses on Carla's thighs and pubis while rubbing gently her labia. She flicked her tongue repeatedly around Carla's clitoris until she begged her to suck her clit. Carla's clit was red and already enlarged with her arousal. Her eyes were closed and her body responded to Helen's touch like a taut violin waiting for its master.

Finally, Helen gave in to Carla's pleas and started sucking her clit in gentle suckling motion of her lips, her tongue darting every now and then to lick the tip. Helen's one hand was fondling Carla's tits while her tongue and lips concentrated on her clit. She knew the gentle but firm pressure has to be maintained for a longer period for a woman to truly achieve orgasm.

Carla was lifting her buttocks now, grinding it towards Helen's face, crying in pleasure as the sensations heightened. Helen did not let go; she knew that although Carla seemed to be enjoying it, she was not yet in the throes of her orgasm. A woman usually goes nuts—eyes rolling, shudders and cries when coming—so she kept sucking Carla's clit, pulling it now and then and then running her tongue up and down its engorged head.

When she knew Carla was ready, she inserted her fingers into her slick pussy. Carla clutched her hair and cried out loud in extreme delight. Helen deliciously thrust in and out with her fingers in Carla's quivering and hungry pussy. Her pussy tightened around her fingers, ready to devour them. She inserted three fingers, rotating them and wiggling them as she thrust them inside, while she lapped and sucked her clit.

There was a loud moan from Carla, and she was moving her head sideways and producing guttural, animal-like sounds. But Helen went faster with her movements. As a woman, she knew what could please Carla most and she concentrated on these areas simultaneously: her clitoris, her breasts, and her vagina.

Carla felt like a dam of unimaginable pleasure was ready to burst. She opened her legs wider and leaned on the pillows as she held Helen's head and moved her hips to match Helen's increasingly dizzying pillars of sensations. She clawed on the bed sheets, gyrated her hips wantonly, and cried Helen's name when the gigantic dam broke loose and waves of pleasures, one after the other, washed her body into a sea of exquisite sensations. Helen did not stop; she kept at it until Carla finally stopped shuddering and writhing in pleasure. She climbed on top of Carla and kissed her, exploring the softest portions of her mouth.

Carla had never been so satiated before; it was a different but totally fulfilling experience. Who says women cannot live without dicks? she thought. It was her turn to return the favor to Helen.

Just as Helen made love to her, she did it likewise, pleasuring Helen with the same sensations she had accorded her. Then they lay there naked, entwined in each other's embrace, kissing softly, tasting each other's sweet tongues.

"Let's buy some vibrator next time," Helen laughingly suggested.

Carla threw a pillow at her, "Ha, ha, ha, that's turning me on again," she laughed.

"A big dildo…" and they fell on each other again, discovering other sensitive areas they have not discovered earlier. They explored and pleasured each other the rest of the night, touching, licking, sucking, and fondling each other's bodies until they achieved pleasures unknown to them before.

After her sexual encounter with Helen, Carla decided to find a man, someone, as long as it's a male whom she could date, instead of developing further her relationship with Helen. She went to a single's bar and sat silently, sipping her martini. She was dressed in a long-sleeved but fitting blouse over faded jeans. She wore little makeup, just a shade of pink on her lips and a light blush-on.

She wanted to appear casual, and not desperate. The other night, she woke up from an erotic dream again, and she had to shower to drive the desires away. Her sensual dreams were increasing in frequency, and she knew she had to masturbate eventually to ease her longing for another man's touch.

Carla's alluring beauty attracted soon enough a dark-haired tall man, who approached her boldly. He had dark deep-set eyes with curly lashes and a golden tan that spoke of hours under the sun.

"Hi, you seem to be alone. May I join you? I'm Ken."

"Sure, have a seat."

"I'm new to this place," he revealed. "It

would be fun touring the place with someone."

"Well," Carla hesitated.

"You are not under obligation to say yes, of course."

"No, I'll check my schedule and will let you know," she replied. He was fast, she thought. Within a minute of introducing himself, he already had a tour guide.

She learned that Ken was from Greece and he was there alone on a holiday. He was 35 but seemed mature well beyond his years. He worked as a bank manager in Athens, and he disclosed that he was planning to put up his own bank eventually.

Carla told Ken only the common facts about herself. She was still not comfortable disclosing the contents of your soul to a one-day acquaintance. As they talked and drank wine, the distance between them drew closer and closer. Soon, Ken was rubbing his thighs against hers under the table. Every time he moves to reach out for something, he purposely rubbed her arm or hands on Carla's breast. Carla was tipsy and she wanted what Ken was doing.

"Let's dance," Ken pulled her to her feet, and they were in the middle of the dance floor. It was a slow dance, and the couple beside were kissing and openly necking.

Carla instinctively jerked away when she felt Ken's erection beneath his pants, straining to connect to her body. How long have she been without a man? she thought, and her pussy started to throb achingly. Ken pulled her back into the circle of his arms and unobtrusively pointed his growing erection towards Carla's crotch.

They move slowly to the music, their faces a few inches from each other. Carla could feel her arousal deepening. She wanted to get laid even with this stranger. She wanted to feel his throbbing dick inside her pussy. Was she that desperate? She wanted to prove to herself that men are still her preference, and not women.

There was nothing wrong with being gay, right? She asked herself, but she had to know. She was turned on by Ken, so she had not changed, even with her sweet encounter with Helen. She was so happy; she reached out and kissed Ken on the lips. Ken grabbed her back and kissed her back, drawing her tongue into his mouth. By then, Ken's arousal was embarrassingly evident through his pants. The lights were subdued so it was invisible in the shadows.

More people were arriving at the club, and it was growing nosier and crowded.

"Should we go somewhere more private?" Ken suggested. He held Carla's hand and they waded through the throng of people. Their bodies were ablaze with lust and passion, wanting to be gratified.

The cold air outside blasted through Carla's face, making her come to her senses. Was she prepared for a one-night stand with Ken? She didn't even know his surname. Was it better that way? Could he make love to Ken I-don't-know? Or would she rather make it with Helen? There was also her option of masturbating. She wanted to get fucked properly that night though, with a real dick inside her warm pussy.

Ken hailed a cab, and they sped towards Ken's rented villa. It was at the outskirts of the city and it was difficult to contain themselves inside the cab. They contented themselves with fondling their private parts under the cover of their clothing.

They were not able to reach the bedroom before they literally attack each other. With the wine on Carla's head, she was free of her inhibitions, nearly reaping off Ken's clothing from his muscular frame. Ken was already freeing his enormous dick from his pants and pinning Carla to the wall; he thrust with all his might, as the wooden walls rattled. Carla panties were not even removed but just pushed aside to accommodate Ken's sexual fury.

The entry of Ken's delicious dick into her pussy made Carla groan out loud with pleasure. She was tight, but her already wet pussy welcomed Ken's dick with enthusiasm as it enclosed his penis with warmth and tightness, making Ken grunt in ecstasy. He was wild in lust, his face suffused with the raging hormones of sexual desire.

Ken tore her panty off and lifted one of Carla's thigh, as he continued fucking her in a standing position. Carla clung to his neck, kissing him and sighing with pleasure as Ken's movement became faster and harder, thrusting his rock-hard penis in and out of her juicy pussy.

Then Carla came; it has been a year since she had a man's penis inside her, and just the sight of it had made her so horny she would have climaxed instantly. Ken's dick did more than that.

"I'm cummminnggg," she shouted in glee, as tons and tons of juices trickled down their conjoined groins, "Oh, god, god...."

After a few more powerful thrusts, Ken rammed her hard on the wall and groaned and withdrew his penis, milking it as his semen squirted up in the air.

Carla disengaged herself happily and turned to come face to face with Helen's beautiful picture staring at her from the upper portion of the wall.

20 MOMENTS IN TIME PART 2

Naked and sexually satiated with her encounter with Ken, Carla remained staring at Helen's stunning picture on the wall.

Ken's naked body brushed hers, "Oh, that's Helen, my ex-wife," he stated matter-of-factly. "She's lovely, isn't she?"

Carla was shocked and speechless about the discovery that the Helen she made love to was the same person staring back at her from the wall. She realized that she made love to both Helen and Ken in different occasions. What the hell was wrong with her? She had been a recluse for more than a year, and there she was doing one-night stands with people she barely knew.

Ken and Helen? God, who would have thought they were related? She cringed inwardly. Perhaps they would even make a sexual threesome one day. She shook her head at the wild thought. Was she out of her mind? What would Helen say if she learns she had sex with her ex-husband? Carla considered Helen to be a special friend, but she never bothered to ask the whereabouts of her ex-husband, just as she did not want Helen to ask about her past.

But why did Ken still have Helen's picture on his wall if they were divorced?

Carla hurriedly dressed and started to leave.

"Hey, sexy, not so fast," Ken came out of the bathroom with a towel draped over his torso. He dropped the towel and pulled her to him while undoing her blouse's buttons. He was grinding his beginning erection into her crotch.

Carla struggled away from him. "I have to go. I have an appointment today," she said against his lips.

"We need to do this properly," he murmured to Carla's ear as she inserted his fingers into her opened blouse and fondled her breast. "We were so drunk last night and had been in such a rush that we omitted foreplay."

Carla had not been with a man more than a year ago, and being fucked last night by Ken with his enormous, pulsating dick was a pleasurable experience she would like to reenact. More than anything else, she wanted his dick deep inside her pussy again.

She had entirely forgotten about Helen, as Ken's fingers closed on the mound of Venus in her pubis.

Ken undressed her again and sat her at the counter top, spreading her legs wide and exposing her vagina widely to him. He kissed her full on the lips, inserting his tongue into her soft palate, drawing her tongue out and grappling with it.

The fingers of his left hand were caressing her tits, while his right were deftly running up and down her vagina. Carla lifted her buttocks as Ken's mouth descended to her pussy. His tongue was persistent, flicking his clit relentlessly until she was moaning delightedly, wanting more. In Carla's subconscious, she was comparing Helen's gentle sweet tongue exploring the same spot where Ken's tongue was, and she felt more aroused.

His tongue explored her vaginal opening and clit thoroughly as Carla held his head grinding her pussy to his face. When Ken knew she was ready, he stood up and slung her legs on his shoulders, pulling her close to him. He pointed his ramrod penis to her vagina and entered her, grunting with pleasure as his dick was covered with her sweet folds.

Carla was leaning backwards with each hand planted on her sides, supporting her body. She was sliding back and forth as her groin and Ken's met together in an explosion of extreme sensual pleasures. Ken's head was turned towards the heaven, his eyes wild with passion, as he thrust his dick in and out of Carla's tight love tunnel. The aching longing in Carla's insides grew, as Ken thrust his dick into her slick vagina over and over. She was on the verge of her orgasm. Before she reached her climax, however, Ken carried her to the bed and once more went down on her.

Her pussy was juicy as he tasted her, eating her over again, sucking her clit, making her writhe and cry in sheer enjoyment. Then he flipped her on her back and mounted her from behind; their skin slapped against each other as he fucked her harder and deeper. Her delighted moans prodded him to thrust frenziedly, and more powerfully, as they clung to each other, moving to the music of their own passion.

They came together, locking and grinding their groins, as they called each other's name, and their juices mixed happily in orgasmic pleasure.

They took a nap, naked, in each other's arms and then made love again, doing all positions just like newlyweds on a honeymoon. Carla knew she would miss Ken after this encounter. It was surely a one-night stand for him, and for her, what else could it be as well?

After Carla's sexual adventure with Ken, she went home exhausted but sexually gratified and happy. She spent the following day pottering around her house, rearranging decors here and there, and then finally settling down on her laptop to continue her short story.

"No, you don't," Sheila stepped boldly in front of her captor and challenged him.

"And why not?"

"Because you're not human."

"Come here, sweetie, and touch my arm. Feel how softer they are than yours?"

"Not on your life."

Carla stopped typing and stared at the

screen of her laptop. Would she insert a sex scene? Ken's sweating arms pinning her to the wall flashed through her mind, as her senses awakened. "Oh, no, not again," she shook her head in denial. It was just yesterday, but she felt her pussy quivering in desire. She had survived for so long without a man, but now she seemed insatiable, longing for sexual satisfaction each day. She stopped typing and hurried to the shower to assuage her physical need.

Helen called her up the next day, asking where she was the other day; she had been trying to contact her but her cell phone had been turned off.

"I went shopping," Carla said, and my cell phone was low on battery."

"Can I come over?"

Carla knew what that meant: Helen was horny, and she needed release. Helen was Ken's ex-wife, and now that she knew it, what would be the best thing to do? For Ken, it was a one-night stand for sure, but for Helen... Helen truly cared for her as a person. What would Helen do if she came to know that Ken fucked her? She was confused and did not know what to do. Her consolation was that her action was unintentional.

"Hello, Carl, can I come over?" Helen repeated her question.

"Not today," she heard herself saying. "I've work to do."

After lunch, when Carla went back to continue writing, the doorbell rang. She ignored it on the first buzz, thinking how Helen had always been a persistent person.

But since it kept buzzing, she gave up and stood to open the door; she had prepared an unfriendly remark for Helen.

When the door opened, she was totally shocked to see Ken, dashing and fresh looking in his blue sweatshirt, beaming at her from the doorway.

"Hello. I'm sorry. I came unannounced," his eyes sparkled with mirth, "but I came to return this."

He handed to her a pair of eyeglasses. "I thought you might need them."

Carla had worn them just to protect her eyes from the wind; that was why she had completely forgotten about them.

"Errr...There's... no need, really," she stammered. She was so taken aback; she was still gathering her wits. "How did you come to know of my address?"

"It's a long story," he replied. "Can I come in? I'll tell you about it."

"But I'm alone...."

Ken had a glint of disbelief in his eyes, saying, "After all that had happened between us?"

Carla felt the absurdity of what she was saying. She made love to this man without even knowing who he was, and now she was suddenly being shy?

She opened the door and allowed him to come in. She felt the sexual stirrings in her crotch but ignored it. She was sober, and that made her clear-minded.

They sat silently, looking at each other uncertainly. They were perfectly sober now, without the influence of alcohol, unlike the other day when they were drunk and horny and had wanted to get laid.

"I never asked your surname," they chimed in simultaneously.

They both laughed, and Ken stood up and extended his hand to Carla, "I'm Kenneth Armstrong, presently connected with HP."

"I'm Carla Walker, presently writing my first book," she said impishly. "Well, I hope someone would publish it once it's done."

Ken settled more comfortably in his chair, as he met Carla's eyes boldly. Ken's red, angry penis flashed through Carla's mind. She felt her pussy quiver achingly, but she said instead, "Do you want anything to drink?" and added with a laugh, "not alcohol this time."

Ken looked at her curiously. "A soda please."

Did she hate the experience? Ken thought. Although he was drunk, he had enjoyed it extensively. That was why he came over; he wanted to continue their acquaintance.

"So how did you get my address?" Carla asked.

"If you want something badly, nothing can stop you.... I got it from the yellow pages."

Of course, Carla thought; she was not under a witness protection plan, so her address was there for public consumption.

After the initial awkwardness, they began to relax and converse easily. He was a sane person after all, Carla concluded. Ken was sizing her up as well, not being able to associate this well-mannered, prim and proper lady to the tigress in bed, who made wild, wanton love to him the other night. He felt a certain aching in his groin.

Carla waited for him to open up about his ex-wife Helen, but he only talked about how he decided to spend summer in Ibiza. "It's good to relax for a while; you know... get your face wet, and have some wild sex with a sexy stranger...." Ken stopped talking in mid-sentence. "I mean...."

"It's okay," Carla filled the silence. "I had the same wish too that day."

"Are you regretting it? I hope not," Ken asked anxiously. He wanted their relationship to advance to the next level.

"No," then a pause. "No, of course not. But we were crazy then, don't you think so?" she asked broodingly.

"Not really, drunk perhaps, but even without the booze, I would have invited you anyhow."

Carla laughed, relieved that they were talking about it sensibly.

Then out of the blue, she asked, "What about your ex-wife?" Carla still did not have the courage to reveal to him that she and his wife are in a relationship.

"We divorced last month," he said, refusing to divulge further information.

Carla wanted him to say more but he changed the topic. "Hey, let's go out for dinner. My treat."

"Perhaps next time," Carla refused.

"Tomorrow?"

Carla remained silent. Ken held an undeniable charm that was difficult to ignore, but she was thinking of Helen. Would she be willing to give her up for Ken?

"The day after?" Ken insisted, "Any time you're free. There's this bistro by the beach others are raring about."

"I'm not sure yet."

"I'll call back tomorrow to check then." Ken left perplexed and confused.

An hour after Ken left, Helen arrived with a naughty smile on her face.

"You seem to have swallowed a canary," Carla teased Helen.

"I have some goodies with me," Helen kissed Carla full on the lips.

Helen's bag yielded two 9 inches, strap-on dildos, and a double-ended dildo.

"You're crazy," Carla excitedly ran her fingers up and down the silicon dildo, feeling its firmness, imagining Ken's angry, red penis.

And she still did not tell Helen about Ken.

They cooked dinner together, Parrillada de Pescado—mixed grill of fish—a dish they had tasted in one of the restaurants in town. They then asked the cook how they could prepare the dish at home. Afterwards, they had sangria beside the pool, relishing the Spanish wine with apple.

Carla had learned to love her quiet evenings with Helen. There were no hurried movements, just slow, leisurely pace that made her relaxed and happy.

They were facing each other, with both of their feet up in the chair opposite them.

"Could I stay for the night?" she winked at Carla.

"You wicked girl," Carla pretended to splash the wine on Helen's face. "You come bringing all those pretty toys, and now you're asking me that question."

She stood up and kneaded Helen's shoulders, massaging her nape and shoulders. It was her turn to make her happy. Helen stretched herself on the chair and closed her eyes, as Carla gave her a great back rub. They drank more wine as Carla then undressed Helen. Helen, not to be outdone, stripped Carla of her clothes as she fondled her tits and pussy, every now and then. They were taking their time teasing each other with a touch here and there, a smooch now and then, while the flames of their arousal slowly began to blaze as the night deepened.

"I'll race you to the other side," Carla challenged Helen, and they dived together into the pool.

Helen won by a large margin and they collapsed at the other side of the pool, breathless and energized. Helen touched Carla's nipples with her index finger. "I'm excited to experiment with our new toys." She brought down her tongue and sucked Carla's nipples.

Carla shivered and felt her body respond to Helen's expert touch. Being a woman, she knew exactly how to touch her, how much pressure she should exert, where the erogenous zones were, and when to fondle them.

Helen ran her fingers from Carla's breast to

her vagina—a feathery touch that titillated Carla. She did the same to Helen, exploring her body with her fingers. Their tongues met hungrily, their lips taking turn to suck each other. They were reclining on a plastic mat by the pool side. They kissed deeply again, twirling their tongues around, tasting each other, while their fingers were busy fondling each other's clits and breasts.

They wrestled on the mat, their naked bodies gleaming in the descending darkness. When they were hot with desire, Helen pulled Carla to her feet and they hastened to Carla's room. Helen brought out the strap-on dildo and ran it up and down on Carla's labia, teasing her and arousing her all the more. She had not strapped it on yet, as she sucked Carla's clit. Carla begged her to mount her with the dildo.

Helen strapped on the dildo and mounted her, hesitant to thrust at first, but when she saw Carla writhing beneath her and asking for more, she thrust faster and quicker.

"Yeah, faster please, yeah babe, faster...," she cried and lifted her pelvis towards Helen, as she humped her in deep, strong strokes.

"I'm cummminggg," Carla cried and shuddered as her orgasm came in great spurts.

Afterwards, it was Helen's turn. Carla, satiated as never before, showered Helen first with soft kisses all over her body. She sucked her tits alternately, circling the erect nipples with her thumb and forefinger lovingly, then sucking them again, rolling the nipples in her tongue. Helen rubbed her pussy under her as well, and she was aroused anew.

She went down on Helen, parting her labia to expose her red and raw clitoris. She ran her tongue up and down Helen's clit, and then down into the inner folds of her vagina. When Helen's pussy was wet, she sucked the dildo and lapped it with her tongue. She strapped the dildo on and, with a twisting motion, inserted it into Helen's craving vagina. She gyrated her hips as Helen moaned loudly, urging her to give it all to her. Helen had one hand on her clit, caressing it, as Carla rode her. She thrust the 9-inch pseudo-penis deeper and deeper until Helen was wild with pleasure; she had spread her legs wider and had lifted her feet as she came, convulsing in her orgasm.

"Oh god, that was incredible." She reached out for Carla and kissed her.

Carla's sexual abstinence for a year had now turned her days into a sexual bonanza that she welcomed. They decided to keep the double dildo for later use.

As Ken promised, he called up Carla, the following day.

"I'm still not free," she informed him.

"What about tonight?" he persisted. "I'll be leaving for Germany in a week."

"Hmmmm, okay," she hanged up.

"Who was that?" Helen asked.

Was it time to reveal to Helen that she knew her ex and that her ex had fucked her thoroughly? It was the perfect time, but still Carla hesitated, and she did not know why.

"A friend," she vaguely replied.

"Male or female?" Helen was curious.

"Male," Carla left Helen momentarily speechless.

Helen prodded no further as she was afraid she would alienate Carla. Their relationship was still in the development process, and Helen wanted to give Carla some freedom.

"I'll go to town this afternoon for some personal business. Want to come with me?" Helen asked her.

"No, I'll be finishing my story."

After Helen left for town, Carla presumed that she would proceed home, so when Ken called, she said that she can spare a few minutes to talk to him.

It was quarter to seven when Ken rang the doorbell. He was handsome in a blue polo shirt and gray slacks. He seemed even taller than 6 feet, as he stood there with his broad grin; curly, dark hair; and deep-set eyes. Carla felt her insides churn. She was definitely attracted to him inasmuch as she denied it.

"Hi, thanks for finally allowing me to visit," Ken greeted her. She is hot, Ken thought, and his desire started to stir. Carla was dressed in a simple tube blouse and a flowing skirt, but her voluptuous curves were noticeable.

"Hi, come in."

"Don't you want to go someplace?"

"I'll have to finish work," she pointed at her laptop.

"Oh, I see," Ken nodded. "You're really one busy person."

Carla chose not to answer. Her plan was to have a brief conversation with him and then send him away, but as they talked, she realized she had missed him, strange as it seemed.

His image towering above her, fucking her, kept flashing back into her mind. She felt her vagina become wet with longing. What was the matter with her? She had thought she could go on without sex for at least a couple of days because she had been so sexually gratified with Helen, but it was not the case. She was being aroused by Ken's simple gestures. The dildo was as big as Ken's—she then realized that, and she felt her pussy quiver in anticipation.

They talked about Ken's job as a system analyst. Carla learned that although Ken owned a villa in Ibiza, he still considered himself a tourist because he only stayed in Ibiza during summers.

After they ate Spanish muffins, they drank red wine, while the evening deepened. Then Ken's face became somber.

"I came because I had missed you," he blurted out, unable to control himself.

Carla remained immobile in her chair.

He covered the space between them in a flash, "and I wanted to do this." He kissed Carla, who was unable to move away.

Carla intended to avoid something happening again between her and Ken, but her body refused to cooperate. Soon, her hands reached out for Ken's neck as she clung to him and kiss him, making soft sounds, until the kiss deepened and their fingers groped for each other's private parts.

They parted, breathless, their hunger for each other imminent by the bulge in Ken's pants and the moistness in Carla's crotch.

This time, they were not drunk, and they were fully conscious of what they were doing.

"I've missed you a lot, babe," Ken pressed her body tightly to him and kissed her again, exploring the sensitive areas of her mouth. His fingers rubbed her nipples under her blouse. Carla did not reply, but her whole body responded to his every touch, her pussy eager to be filled up again with Ken's big and thick dick.

"Let's do it nice and slow this time," he said.

Holding Carla's hand, Ken led her to the bedroom. They kissed again, more passionately, while both of Ken's hands were busy. One was alternately caressing Carla's nipples, while the other was down her pussy, teasing and fondling her clitoris.

He sat on the bed and cradled Carla on his lap while continuously kissing her. Her back was to him, so he could rub her breasts and pussy at the same time. They were both in the stages of being half-undressed as they groped for each other hungrily.

Carla suddenly felt the urge to suck Ken's dick, so she turned around and pushed him down the bed, as she removed the last restrictive clothing from his muscular body. She bent to run her tongue along Ken's shaft. Ken moaned softly.

She licked his crown while her fingers enclosed the base of his penis. She then took him into her mouth while massaging the base of his dick. Carla's butt was up in the air as she continued to give Ken a blowjob. She moved her mouth and lips up and down his manhood while sucking him, as he lay there moaning softly.

Carla was completely lost in what she was doing such that she was startled when she felt her pussy being fondled from behind. She turned around to see Helen grinning impishly at her.

"Go on," Helen mouthed at her, soundlessly.

Carla bent again and sucked Ken's dick, thankful that Ken did not notice Helen in the shadows. Did Helen know? Carla felt the building pressure in her pussy as Helen repeatedly tweaked her clit with her tongue. Carla sucked at Ken's dick more intensely as the pleasure in her pussy increased.

Helen shifted and positioned herself under Carla's pussy so that she could freely eat her at her leisure. Carla's arousal was peaking, and just then, Ken turned her around to straddle her. He drew away when he saw Helen underneath them, gleefully enjoying his surprise. But it was only for an instant. He was nearing climax and was beyond stopping.

He pushed Carla into the bed and straddled her, entering her slick pussy with a couple of short thrusts. Then he grunted and moved in wanton desire, ramming his dick into her, going faster and faster, grunting with delight as his dick went in and out of Carla's tight vagina.

Helen kissed Carla and fondled her tits as her ex-husband humped Carla repeatedly, arching his back with pleasure as he neared climax.

Carla locked her legs across Ken's back as

she felt the deluge of desire ready to collapse. Helen's ministrations intensified her arousal. She sucked Helen's tongue as the sensation in her crotch increased. When Helen touched her clit as Ken fucked her harder, she came again and again, quivering in unmeasured ecstasy as thousands of pleasure points erupted in her body. Ken though continued fucking her, prolonging her orgasm, as she came again when Ken finally pinned her into the bed with grunts of fulfillment.

Helen, who was fingering herself, came a little bit later as she lay there beside them, touching their bodies and hers in one final sweep of joy. She sucked on Carla's lower lip again, as she climaxed.

Then Helen turned to Ken and said indifferently. "Hi Ken, it has been a while. Can we do it again?"

Ken turned to her, his eyes sorrowful, "Is Carla your new conquest?"

"Don't be bad," Helen was beside him, trailing his body with her fingers. "She's a friend, a special friend."

"Carla, did you know this rascal is my ex-husband?" she gave a gleeful laugh and stroked Carla's breast.

Carla was speechless. She did not expect this to happen, and she was at a loss why Helen seemed indifferent.

"We can make a threesome," Helen laughed again.

"You seem to misunderstand our relationship," Ken said tersely.

"It's you who don't understand ours," Helen cut Ken off.

"Then perhaps you can tell me," he said, sotto voce.

"Carla, will you do the honor?" Helen turned to Carla.

Carla turned to them both and said, "I'm not sure of what relationship I have with either of you. Please give me time to sort this out."

"Well, in the meantime, let's be a threesome," Helen winked at Carla and Ken. Carla shook her head and wondered if she would, indeed, be able to ride the waves of passion with Ken and Helen.

21 MOMENTS IN TIME PART 3

It was a tranquil, lovely afternoon so Carla Walker decided to stroll along the sandy beach. Her long blonde and curly hair flew in swirling waves around her face as she trudged, sandals in hand, watching the swimmers a few feet away.

A topless woman sat cross-legged beside the water, obviously in meditation. Was she able to concentrate? she thought. She sat on one of the boulders and stared into the vast, shimmering blue waters before her.

The naked image of Helen and her ex-husband, Ken, climaxing before her stirred a gnawing lusty feeling inside her. After they had a passionate sexual encounter, she had asked them both to allow her some space.

She met Helen first, and they had developed a special friendship that included sex. She had often wondered if they were actually gay. She had cherished her encounters with Helen because she knew exactly what she wanted and Helen gave this to her. Her body responded achingly to the thought. She had missed Helen terribly.

But she had missed Ken too. Ah... dashing, debonair Ken. Why did they divorce? Neither of them wanted to answer her question. And she wanted to find some answers before she could proceed with a relationship with either of them.

"A penny for your thoughts?"

Carla turned and came face to face with Ken. She started to rise, but Ken held her back.

"Please Carla, talk to me. I can't stand your silence."

"I have to go," she stepped away from Ken.

"If you want to know about Helen, I'll tell you everything," Ken implored.

Carla stood frozen on the spot, her heart beating wildly. "I'll tell you...," Ken murmured and led her towards his waiting car.

He drove in silence for a while around the bustling town center before he spoke, "Could we go to my place? We would feel more comfortable there," he said.

And make love afterwards? Carla couldn't help but re-live the passion-filled moments she had with Ken, his glistening rock-hard dick penetrating her deliciously. The scene flashed through her mind, and she was thrilled with the thought. She had decided not to have sex with either of them, but her resolve crumbles whenever she saw Ken.

She nodded in acquiescence.

By the time they got to Ken's place, it was

dusk; the brightly lit streets mirrored the festive ambiance of summer in Sta. Eulalia.

"Come. Let's have dinner first," Ken led her inside his cozy, well-furnished villa.

Carla's eyes went instinctively to the wall where she saw Helen's picture and found it to be empty. She felt a certain happiness settle in her soul. What exactly did it mean?

They enjoyed the scrumptious dinner prepared by Ken's cook. They ate slowly, relishing the steamed prawn in their tongues, and then drank coffee as they settled in the patio underneath the star-lit sky. Carla wanted to remember this moment forever. She felt happy just being with Ken, but felt the same way too when she was with Helen.

"Carl, I don't want to badmouth Helen. She had been my wife and she has still a special place in my heart...," he sighed deeply. "It's only you to whom I revealed this...," Ken hesitated.

"Don't worry Ken," Carla's hand shot to cover his own.

Carla's heart went out to him, and she wanted to hug him and tell him everything would be all right.

"Helen and I parted because she discovered later on in our relationship that she preferred women." Ken did not dare to look at Carla.

"You mean...," Carla stuttered.

Ken nodded.

That explained everything: Helen's attachment to her and her caring and loving attitude towards her. Helen actually acted as a "husband" since they started going out together.

Carla understood how Ken felt. It must have been painful to learn that your wife had stopped loving you because she wanted to be with a woman. Ken's ego must have been badly bruised too.

Ken looked at her then and said, "In the short time that we've been together, I have come to realize that I want more than friendship. Would you take that step with me?"

"I...I..." Carla was at a loss on what to say. "Please give me more time."

"Am I too late? Does my dear Helen have your heart already?"

Carla stood up, not knowing how to answer his question. "I have to go," she murmured.

Ken caught her hand and drew her close to him. "Please stay."

Carla opened her mouth to answer but Ken's covered it, crushing her lower lip into his sucking tongue. She resisted for a while, but when Ken's hands went down to her crotch, she sighed in surrender as her body countered what her common sense dictated.

She had to know what her true feelings for Ken were. What about Helen? Who reigned first in her heart? For that moment, her knees buckled, and her breath came in gasps as Ken carried her into the bedroom.

Their lips remained glued to each other as they sucked and savored each other's lips and tongue. "We could shower first," Ken undressed her slowly, caressing her luscious breasts and nipples with his palm. He led her to the shower while stroking the nipples. "You're so beautiful," he said in awe.

In the shower, Ken soaped Carla's body lovingly. He kissed her now and then while rubbing the sponge gently and tantalizingly slowly down her chest, back, and thighs, deliberately concentrating on her clit and tits.

Carla started moaning, as she reached out for Ken's already rigid dick. Oh, how I missed this, Carla thought. It was long and thick, and her pussy was moist with anticipation. She was not sure though if what she felt was love or lust. That was why she wanted to spend some time away from him and Helen, but it seemed impossible.

She started massaging Ken's dick, stroking smoothly up and down his hardened shaft.

"Would you mind soaping my back," he whispered into her ears.

Ken's sinewy body was soft to Carla's touch. She gradually sponged his rippling muscles and then knelt to leisurely rub the soft material in between his thighs. Ken's dick was at attention, yearning for fulfillment. After scrubbing Ken's body, they both stood under the shower, washing away the lathery soap, pinching and fondling each body area.

Ken held Carla's big round breasts and caressed them tenderly, pinching the nipples every now and then. He was breathless with want and lust. They kissed and played until their bodies were aflame with passion.

Ken turned the shower off and lifted Carla onto his throbbing, aching penis, carrying Carla's widespread thighs easily to bring her pussy down into his eager dick. Carla clung to his neck as she sucked his lower lip and rotated her hips to allow Ken's deep penetrations into her pussy.

The veins of Ken's neck and arm bulged with the pressure he was exerting, as he lifted Carla up and down his dick. Plopping sounds reverberated inside the bathroom as their wet and hungry bodies strained to meet each other and fulfill their cravings.

Carla's eyes were closed while she sucked on Ken's tongue every time she came down to grind her pussy into Ken's ramrod dick. Ken licked her nipples whenever she came down. The sensual sensations created by their mouths, tongues, and groins became too much to bear; they finally locked their groins as their orgasm made their bodies convulse into one music of joy and delight, their tongue meeting and grappling with each other.

They showered playfully again and raced to the bedroom to dry themselves up.

"Stay with me for the night," Ken suggested.

"What about Helen?" Carla could not help but ask.

"What about her?"

"Well, she's my special friend."

"You haven't decided yet?" Ken stated; there was a trace of sadness in his voice.

"That was why I wanted to stay away from both of you for a while."

"You came with me. Doesn't that mean anything?"

Carla was silent. Indeed, Ken was right. She could not resist him. Did it mean she had stronger feelings for him? If she stayed with Helen, did she intend to stay with her forever? Carla had never been in such dilemma before.

"Then I have to leave," Carla said, confused;

she started dressing up. Ken was beside her in an instant.

"Don't leave, Carl. I was just clarifying the issue." He pushed aside her dress and kissed her lingeringly on the lips, "but let's forget it for now. I just want to be with you."

Carla was helpless against Ken's charm over her; she simply was not able to resist when he started fondling and caressing her. Ken led her back to the bed naked. His phallus was already tumescent, eager to fuck again. He told Carla to lie down while he knelt astride Carla's navel, facing her. He held her two big breasts and then inserted his dick between them.

"So soft and warm, babe," he bent down to kiss her. Then he let his dick slide in and out between Carla's two succulent breasts. As the crown of his dick emerged on the other side, Carla sucked the crown and licked it with her tongue. Soon, Ken was totally wild; he increased the tempo while squeezing Carla's big tits.

"I'm cummiinnnggg," he groaned in glee as Carla sucked his crown and licked the drop that came from his penis. That turned him crazier, as he humped until his semen spurted into Carla's warm and waiting mouth.

By then Carla was hot as well. She had been playing with her clit while Ken breast-fucked her and her pussy was clamoring for Ken's dick. She sat up and pushed Ken to the bed, and then she was on top of him rubbing her petals into Ken's flaccid phallus. But she did not mind. She kissed him; licked his neck, shoulders, and chest; and sucked his nipples.

She licked the insides of his thigh until his penis became harder and erect.

Carla rode him then, sliding in and out of his shaft, savoring the full length of his rigid cock going in and out of her vagina. Ken reached out for her tits and squeezed them firmly, and then held her waist again to bring her down, again and again, into his waiting dick.

Carla's movement increased in pace as her arousal peaked, and she was riding him feverishly to satiate the need inside her groin and the folds of her labia, swallowing Ken's dick in hunger and delight. She slid forward, up and down repeatedly, until she moaned loudly and gasped as her orgasm came and flooded her burning senses. Ken came after a few moments and they savored their union as mountains of pleasure inundated their naked bodies.

Then Carla's cell phone rang, but they kept themselves glued to each other, not moving for a few minutes. It stopped ringing. They curled into each other's arms and basked in the warmness and afterglow of their lovemaking. It rang again, and Carla disengaged herself and picked up the phone.

"Hello."

"Where are you? I'm here outside of your door." Helen's voice was irritated.

Carla was not able to answer. There was also a pause from the other end.

"You're with Ken?" There was disbelief in her voice, and then, "No, you didn't."

"Yes, I'm with Ken," Carla confirmed, afraid of what Helen would say.

"Why? Don't you care for me? I'm coming over," and the lines went dead.

Ken said, "Helen's coming over, right?"

Carla nodded. "Let her come. She wants to join the party."

Within 30 minutes, the doorbell rang. Ken opened the door to an angry Helen.

"Come in, and join the party," Ken was smiling impishly. Helen's eyes grew wide, as she stared at Ken and his growing erection.

"Where is she?" Helen demanded.

"Calm yourself first, woman; she's not one of your possessions," he pacified her.

"Neither is she yours," Helen blurted out and marched to the bedroom, expecting Carla to be naked as well. But she was fully dressed and was sitting on the edge of the bed, lost in her own thoughts.

Helen hesitated on the door. "She's not one of your possessions," Ken's words echoed in her mind.

Helen approached Carla, while Ken was behind her.

"How are you?" she asked softly, her irritation simmering down.

"I want to be alone," Carla murmured; there were tears in her eyes.

Helen's heart went out to her and she reacted instinctively. She reached out and kissed her cheeks, wiping her tears with a finger. Carla drew away, but Helen's lips reached her own in a flash, searching her tongue and nibbling her lower lip. Carla tried to struggle, but soon Helen's expert fingers found their target and Carla's body responded like a violin to its master.

Ken just stood there and watched them, as his arousal mounted anew. Should he stop Helen? Carla was allowing it to happen and was obviously enjoying it. What right did he have to stop them? So he stared at them lustfully as he ran his fingers up and down his rigid phallus.

Carla was supine halfway on the bed then, and Helen was shredding her clothing oh so slowly, loving each exposed skin with her tongue. Helen's movement was deliberately slow, and as Ken watched his ex-wife making love expertly, he heard Carla groaned in pleasure. Helen was an expert with women, he thought, and preferred them.

His pride had been hurt at first when he learned about it, thinking he was inadequate, but later on, he realized that it was not his fault; Helen just preferred women.

Carla got hold of a bunch of Helen's black hair and moaned again as Helen was now buried between her thighs. Ken then joined Helen in providing Carla the sensual pleasures that she so deserved. He kissed her and massaged her breasts as Helen sucked her clit and explored her pussy thoroughly, leaving no area untouched.

Carla cried in ecstasy as Helen's familiar tongue raked on her clitoris, never letting go, maintaining the pressure. Ken's lips and fingers intensified the pleasures in her body.

Using his tongue, he sucked her upper and lower lips alternately, exploring Carla's inner cheeks and lips. They sucked at one another's tongue as the sensations amplified tremendously. Ken's tongue descended to her tits, and while the other is being fondled by his fingers, the other one was being played by Ken's tongue.

Ahhhh, what exquisite sensations, Carla thought as her arousal continued to increase, and all her nerve endings pulsated with joy with Ken's and Helen's expert ministrations. She was nearing climax as Helen sucked and licked the folds of her labia and her clit. When Helen inserted two of her fingers, Carla whimpered, saying she was coming. Helen concentrated her tongue on her clit as she finger fucked her until she climaxed and her juices trickled down her hands.

As Carla writhed in pleasure, Ken could not contain himself; he gently pushed Helen behind and mounted on Carla. Ken shoved his angry, pulsating dick into Carla's juicy pussy and they both groaned like animals in heat. Carla felt another gigantic orgasm coming. Her vagina contracted as Ken rammed her cock in and out of her slick and tight opening; the lips of her vagina buried Ken's dick in delight.

They were fucking wantonly now, their movements fast and wild.

"Oh, yes, yes, fuck me harder, harder please," Carla screamed in joy, while Ken, his face a beet red, humped furiously, savoring the extreme pleasure from Carla's suctioning petals.

Helen inserted her hand in between them

and fondled Carla's clit and Ken's balls when they separated momentarily to thrust into each other again. While doing this, Carla played with her clit as well. They came simultaneously, gasping for breath, crying each other's name as they slapped their groins against each other and rubbed and ground them together to savor the unequalled sensation. Carla closed her eyes to bask in such incredible pleasures.

They collapsed on the bed, entangled with one another with Carla between the two while they continued holding and fondling her. Soon, their breathing returned to normal, and they all fell asleep in Ken's large king-sized bed, still naked and sexually satiated.

Ken awakened in the middle of the night and stared at the two ladies who had meant something in his life. They were in a spoon position, with Carla's back to Helen, because Carla had been in a tight embrace with him. Ken's heart fluttered; did that mean Carla had finally selected him? He shook his head, thinking it wasn't most likely, and covered both of them with a blanket.

He proceeded to his study and did some of his paperwork until the wee hours of dawn before going back to bed.

When Ken awakened the following morning, the two women were nowhere to be found. There was a note propped on his bedside table.

"Thanks for a wonderful night." It was signed by both of them. He was about to throw it when he noticed a hurriedly written note on the other side: "Please don't visit me first. I have your number. I'll call you up when I'm ready. Carla."

Ken stared at the note for a long time. Carla wanted some time away from him. Was he shunned by Carla after all? His heart fell into pieces. It was then he realized that he has completely recovered from Helen and that he loved Carla. He read again, "I'll call you up when I'm ready. Carla," before tearing the note slowly.

Carla was back in her house with Helen. Helen had insisted in bringing her home.

"I would have to take some time away from both of you to sort out my feelings," she touched Helen's cheek. "You understand, don't you?"

Helen wanted Carla all to herself, but it has to be voluntary. Carla has to select one. It would be great to make a threesome sexual adventure, Helen thought, but the eventual psychological complications would destroy both relationships. Romantic relationships are between two people only, and three is always a crowd.

That week, Carla continued with her short stories, tapping at her keypads all day long, smiling here and there as her story developed and her characters took shape and interacted.

"I love you," Aaron whispered into her ears, as he pulled apart the string of her bikini.

"I love you too," Janine turned to look at him in the eyes.

Aaron's deft fingers traveled sensuously down her body, until it came to rest on the lips of her womanhood....

Carla's fingers stopped typing. If she

continued with this scene, she would end up calling either Ken or Helen, and she was not yet ready.

She sighed and stood up, rubbing her tired eyes with the back of her palm. She went over to her bed and lay down. Soon, she was asleep, dreaming of the time that she was finally settled and secure in her relationship.

She woke up feeling happy. In her dream, Ken was there, just like her first dream, but this time, he turned to look at her when she called his name. That gave her an unexplained sense of felicity. She knew then that she loved Ken more than anyone in this world, Helen included.

She showered, singing excitedly under the spray of water. She planned to call up both of them tomorrow to inform them of her decision.

The following day, Carla went to the nearby park to mull over her decision. Once she made it, there would be no turning back. She strolled around the park, admiring the spectacular landscape around her. Below her was the string of beaches along the outstanding coastline. From the distance, people appeared like toys while they splashed in the clear blue waters.

At the opposite side, rolling hills and verdant mountains greeted the eye with their natural beauty. The air was nifty and refreshing from atop, which contributed to the tranquility of the park. It was an ideal place to reflect and relax.

Carla sat in one of the benches as memories of Ken assailed her anew—Ken dashing in his navy blue polo, Ken laughing in glee, Ken's gleaming manhood as he shoved it relentlessly into her eager vagina. She loved all of them; she loved Ken. It would be heaven to bear their children, and that was what made her the happiest.

She knew telling Helen of her decision would be difficult. Helen was the first one who was able to assuage her loneliness. She would always have a special place in her heart. She couldn't imagine herself though spending her lifetime with Helen.

She went home reaffirmed that her decision was the right one. I'll call them up first thing in the morning, she thought.

That was what she did the next morning. First, she dialed Helen's number.

"Hello, it's me. I'm sorry. I decided to stay with Ken."

Helen was speechless at first, her heart bleeding. "Are you sure?"

"Yes, I have had enough time to think it over."

There was a pause, "I see, well... what can I say, good luck," and Helen hung up.

Carla did not expect that to be that easy. She sighed, relieved and exultant. Next she dialed Ken's number. It kept ringing but Ken did not pick up. She rang twice, thrice; still, there was no answer.

Carla's spirit dipped. Where was he? Was he so busy, or was he deliberately avoiding her call? She went about all day long dejectedly doing chores absentmindedly. She was not able to write too. What if Ken had decided not to pursue her anymore? Her heart sank all the more.

At 1PM, she was crying in bed, thinking she would have to endure loneliness once again.

Her phone rang, and Ken was on the other end of the line.

"Hello, babe. Sorry, I've just come from a meeting with top management. Are you okay?"

Carla burst out crying and laughing at the same time. "I love you, Ken," she managed to say amidst her laughter and tears.

"Hey, I love you more," he said in glee, almost tripping at the base of the steps. "I love you."

Ken hailed a taxi hurriedly and sped towards Carla's home, his heart exuberant in joy. Carla was waiting breathlessly at her front door, every nerve of her body screaming for Ken's.

It was not long before Ken stood there with his naughty smile and laughing eyes, looking straight at her. They ran into each other's arms and melded into one as their lips met in hunger, devouring and tasting one another in a heat of passion and love.

Hand in hand, they went inside and fell into each other's arms once again, their hands hungrily groping for their erogenous zones, knowing exactly how to fondle it. Ken stripped Carla of her clothes and Carla knelt to nestle his rigid penis in her luscious breasts. Then she held her thick, big shaft and licked its opening. Ken grunted and grabbed a handful of her hair as Carla sucked his crown and ran his tongue up and down his phallus. When Carla took all of him into her mouth, he moaned excitedly, as he thrust his engorged dick in and out of Carla's mouth.

Carla sucked and licked Ken's dick with slow, titillating movements that Ken's back went taut with his desire. She massaged the base of Ken's penis with her fingers, as her mouth covered the crown, continuously sucking and licking around and over the crown. Ken increased the tempo by prodding Carla's head with his hand.

"Yeah, baby, yeah," he crooned, his body ablaze with passion. Carla got almost choked when Ken shoved his dick all the way down, as his head went up in absolute surrender to her ministrations. Carla went on running her tongue up and down Ken's penis, sucking and licking it.

He pushed Carla to the floor and straddled her, groaning in pleasure as Carla's pussy enveloped his penis in a tight embrace. He started going in and out of her pussy, in and out, then faster and harder until he grunted and convulsed, and with one powerful thrust, they both climaxed, holding on to each other as their orgasms overcame everything else in existence.

22 MOMENTS IN TIME PART 4

Carla had chosen to be with Ken instead of Helen, Ken's ex-wife, and she felt contentment in her decision because more than anything else, she also wanted to have children who came from her own flesh and blood, like majority of women do. Although Helen was a loving and caring person, with her, Carla would always feel incomplete.

Carla and Ken planned for a simple church wedding where only close relatives and friends would be present. Carla closed her eyes, and she could see herself gaily walking the aisle, resplendent in her wedding gown. Daydreaming about her future with Ken, her phone rang. It was Helen.

"What happened, Carla? Weren't we happy?" she asked plaintively.

"I'm really sorry, but I can't go on with our relationship." Carla cares for Helen, but not as

Helen wanted her to.

"Did I do something wrong?" Helen asked, worried.

"No, you didn't, Helen, but I have learned to love Ken. I care for you too but only as a friend."

"Babe, I don't care how you feel about me. Just don't leave me," Carla could hear Helen sniffing on the other end of the line.

Carla was surprised by Helen's statements. When she had called her up previously to say that she wanted to stay with Ken, Helen had reacted well. Why was she making a fuss of it now?

"You'll find someone who would love you, just as much as you do," Carla comforted her.

"That's easy for you to say," Helen rationalized. "I'll be coming over so we could talk," she hanged up before Carla could object.

Carla didn't want Helen to come over because she knew they would end up in bed again. Helen knew how to arouse her that she would want to be satiated that very moment. She hurried into the bedroom to get her bag; she would go for a walk until Helen would leave, but just as she was rushing outside, she knew it was useless. Helen was a determined woman who gets what she wants at all costs.

"We'll have to talk," Helen's firm voice cut through the distance.

"You know how I feel," Carla met her eyes defiantly.

"Just for a few minutes," Helen begged then, knowing she had no alternative.

Carla sighed and went back inside. How could she make Helen understand that she loved Ken and that they're planning to marry? For sure, Ken would not want a third party in their marriage.

"Can we just continue with our relationship without Ken knowing?" I looked at her, unable to comprehend why she seemed desperate. Helen was controlling her tears. And Carla had thought she was the weak one.

"You can find someone better than me," Carla patted her arm comfortingly.

"Could you allow me to stay until I could move on?" Helen gripped her arm, "please?"

Carla nodded, thinking that once she and Ken got married, she would not be able to see Helen again. Helen brightened up a bit and announced: "I'm cooking 'afritada.'"

Helen was a good cook, and she usually spoiled Carla when she spent some time with her. They ate the delectable meal prepared by Helen and then proceeded to the patio for some wine. Helen served Carla like she was a queen, serving her first before sitting down to eat.

"Don't do that," Carla reprimanded her, but she did not listen. "I'm making sure you'd miss me when I'm gone."

"Silly woman," Carla exclaimed. "How could you say that? You'll find your soul mate too. "

"Who would have thought you'd fall for my ex?" Helen laughed out loud.

Carla gave her a penetrating look.

"What I mean is he's such a dearie, a perfect husband really. But I didn't know myself then. I had thought I preferred men; I was wrong."

Helen was stroking Carla's arm while she was talking. "Yes, you'd make an ideal couple," Helen acquiesced.

Then Helen leaned over and kissed Carla full in the mouth. Carla drew away from her, but Helen caught her hand and pinned her on the reclining chair.

Helen's right fingers went inside Carla's blouse and searched for her nipples; Carla had no bra. Helen's left fingers stroked the lips of Carla's pussy, lightly caressing and stroking it.

Carla's mind wanted to stop her, but her body won as she felt the same desires well up her groin. Helen was a temptress, an expert in what she was doing to lure Carla into her world of sensual pleasures. She sighed and her body relaxed as Helen sat her on her lap and simultaneously rubbed her clit and nipples. Carla turned her head around to kiss Helen, as Helen strummed her like a guitar, plucking her clit steadily and caressing her vagina sensuously.

Carla's blouse came off, and her two rounded, full breasts sprang joyfully forward and came to rest on Helen's ready palms. Helen alternately fondled her nipples, making quick movements from left to right, while her left fingers were exploring Carla's moist pussy. Helen's index finger flipped Carla's clit repeatedly, while her thumb and ring finger ran up and down her petals. Carla closed her eyes and savored the exquisite sensation coming from her pussy and tits. Helen knew Carla's body well and knew where Carla wanted to be touched.

"Does it feel good?" Helen would ask her.

Carla would then say, "Yeah, yeah," and she would moan with pleasure. That was how Helen discovered all her erotic spots.

Helen also knew when Carla was faking it or not just from her groans and sighs. Helen increased the pressure and speed of her ministrations as Carla writhed in front of her, and she shed the last of Carla's undies from under her legs.

Then she carried her to the bedroom, kissing her hard and long, exploring her mouth and tongue. She lay Carla on the bed and undressed herself. She was hyperventilating with passion and want. It has been days since they last satiated themselves sexually. Her lips went down directly into Carla's yearning petals. She brought out her tongue and ran it over and over her clit until Carla was crazy with desire.

Helen got the double-ended dildo and inserted it into Carla's hot pussy.

Carla moaned, "Yes, give it to me."

Helen inserted the other end of the dildo into her own aching vagina. Helen had lifted one thigh and they were both making strange little noises with each caress and stroke. When Carla thrust the dildo, Helen could feel it penetrating deep inside the folds of her pussy, her walls quivering and engulfing the false penis; it was some kind of succulent hotdog, with both of them on either side of it.

The dildo was about 14 inches long, and they seemed not to get enough of it as they gyrated their hips and thrust towards it any way they wanted it, moaning deliciously in the process. They fondled each other's clit to heighten the sensation, as they fucked each other with the dildo. After several minutes, they went insane with sensual pleasure and kissed and caressed their tits as they came.

"Oh, God, I'm commiiinggg, yeah, oh yes," Carla shrieked, and soon after, Helen joined in with the cries of ecstasy and delight.

They made love again at early dawn and showered together as they teased and caressed their bodies once more.

"We plan to get married before the summer ends," Carla informed Helen.

Helen did a mental calculation; she had less than a month to go before she would say goodbye to Carla.

"You would come to our wedding of course," Carla added.

"Of course, "Helen replied absentmindedly.

Helen visited Carla daily, while Ken usually fetched Carla to his house. Fate was perhaps good to them because they never came to face with the other. When Ken came, Carla would run immediately to him so they could leave while Helen remained cooped up inside the house. Carla felt guilty because she had not volunteered the information to Ken.

Ken and Carla started preparing for their wedding. The wedding invitations were designed simply with golden edges. The wedding dress was a shimmering shade of pink with a sleeveless top and a flowing skirt.

"Hon, we could buy your shoes later," Ken touched her cheek longingly.

Carla knew that touch, and she was thrilled

because it had been a while they haven't made love.

"Okay, hon."

And so, they sped to Ken's villa. Ken has been telling her to move in with him, but she said that she wanted to stay at her house for the last time. She wanted to be with Helen as well just for the last few days while she still can. She would never forget that it was Helen who came to her rescue when she had been lost and lonely. Helen will always have a special place in her heart, Carla thought.

She lost her train of thoughts when she felt Ken's hands inside her thighs. Their lower bodies were partly hidden from view to the driver, and Ken could not wait any longer. Ken found his target and rubbed it incessantly such that Carla had to move forward to allow him more access. Her hand flew to his penis, and she rubbed it underneath his pants. It was already engorged and ready.

They ran to the house, laughing, because Ken's erection is so big the driver might notice. Ken's villa was modest, but it sat amidst a large area about 20,000 square meters of land, so he was practically away from other houses. Ken preferred this because he was a private person.

In the living room, their mouths melded together like soldering irons, and their tongues sought and wrestled with each other until they were breathless. They were making soft, squelching sounds as their lips sucked and licked each other, their arousal mounting.

Their hands were busy as well; Ken's hands were caressing her tits and fondling her clit inside her undies. Carla's were on his dick. They were pushing against each other, hungry and aroused, until they fell into the couch.

Carla's blouse was gone and Ken exposed her creamy, voluptuous breasts and buried his head in their softness, licking and sucking her nipples. Carla had also released his bulging phallus from its constraint, and it joyfully sprang forward, pulsating and angry. Carla bent down to lick its crown. They were facing opposite each other, their heads buried in each other's crotch, devouring each other's jewels.

Carla quivered as Ken went down to her pubis, then to the lips of her pussy, then back to her clit. Carla was on top of Ken's face, grinding her wet mound into his face, moaning loudly when Ken focused on her clit. Carla had missed Ken's tongue. Helen's was soft but firm, whereas Ken's was hard but gentle. Each has a distinct delicious quality to it that Carla had enjoyed completely.

Ken parted Carla's labia and focused his tongue running up and down her clit. She always went wild with clitoral manipulation. He inserted three fingers into her pussy and he was delighted at the tightness that enclosed his fingers.

Carla cried, "Yes please, yes," and rotated her hips to Ken's persistent tongue.

Carla momentarily lifted her head to suck Ken's thighs as she savored the intense sensation from Ken's tongue. Then she bent again encircling his penis in her hand, teasing his balls with the other, and sucking his crown with his lips.

It was Ken's turn to moan with enjoyment. She ran her tongue round and round Ken's crown, then up and down the length of his shaft, and back again to his crown as Ken continued exploring her pussy. She then took his penis full in her mouth and had sucked him as her mouth moved up and down his distended dick. He grabbed a handful of her hair and prodded her to go faster. Carla's head bobbed up and down, sliding deliciously in and out of Ken's ramrod manhood.

With a grunt, Ken shifted his position to Carla's back. He was partly kneeling and standing, his right foot on the carpeted floor, while Carla was on all fours. He entered her from behind, shoving his aching penis into Carla's eager vagina. They both moaned in delight as Ken's dick was sucked into Carla's slick and warm love tunnel. Her vaginal muscles tightened around Ken's penis as he started pumping. Carla sighed with the insane pleasure she had never experienced with Helen. A man's real dick is still different from a dildo, she thought and closed her eyes at the intense pleasure invading her pussy. She felt that all the corners of her pussy were properly filled up with pure pleasure.

Ken started thrusting his dick in and out of her. He banged her, showing no mercy as he rammed his dick into her, going faster, and then still faster, his face suffused with passion as he basked in the incredible friction caused by her tight pussy. Carla matched his movement by pushing back against him with her ass and wantonly grinding her pussy into his penis as their groins slapped against each other in increasing tempo.

Carla climaxed first, and her cries of glee reverberated across the room; she was blinded by the intensity of the exquisite pleasures that inundated her body. Ken reached down to touch her breast as he climaxed in one big ejection that trickled down her satiated pussy.

They locked their groins together until the last of the wonderful sensations ebbed away. Ken carried her into the bathroom, where they playfully washed away their juices and started fondling each other again. They filled the bathtub up to their ankles and played with the geysers. Ken got one of the handy waterspouts and trained it at Carla's clitoris. The steady raining pressure of the water felt like a thousand fingers fondling her clit. Carla was aroused once again. She writhed and sucked on Ken's arm as she enjoyed the novel sensation. She grabbed Ken's head and kissed him hard, sucking on his lower lip as the sensation continued to deepen. Carla convulsed and climaxed again as Ken fondled her breast while the water drummed her clit and Ken's lips were on hers.

Ken's flaccid penis grew tumescent again in her hands, and when Ken lifted her on his lap to penetrate her, Carla came again as his penis slid down her already juicy vagina. Her legs were alongside him, as they kissed again, their saliva mixing sweetly as they twirled each other's tongue and savored their love. Ken had not reached his orgasm even, but Carla was having another climax again. He held Carla by the waist and lifted her up and down into his hungry penis, sucking her nipples or her lips as she came down hard on his dick.

Carla had thought she was satiated already, but to her surprise, another orgasm was incoming again.

"Hon, fuck me hard. I'm coming again," she moaned as she came down on him, his dick plunging deep into the folds of her vagina.

Ken lifted her again, and as she came down, her world exploded in one blinding flash of sensations as her orgasm assailed her body with sweetness she had never experienced before. Ken's mouth sought her own as he groaned like a wild animal and climaxed too; their wet bodies shuddered with the intensity of the sensations.

"That was incredible, hon. Thank you." Carla kissed Ken again as they remained locked in each other's embrace in the bathtub.

"Thank you, babe. I love you," Ken kissed her back.

"I love you too, hon," Carla nestled her head on Ken's shoulders.

They slept peacefully after their fierce lovemaking and groped for each other during the night, cuddling and staying close to feel each other's warmth.

They woke up in the wee hours of dawn and made love again until their bodies were fully gratified.

"Won't you move in today?" Ken asked

Carla.

"I'll do that after the wedding," Carla kissed him.

Carla was in the bath when her phone rang. Ken picked it up and saw it was Helen. His face clouded and he bit his lip. He did not receive the call.

A text followed, and he could not resist not to read it, "Are you with Ken, sweetie? I miss you. Do come home ASAP."

Ken read the message and felt his anger mounting. He had thought Carla bade goodbye to her. His ex-wife did have an effective way of hurting him.

When Carla came out of the shower, Ken confronted her with the message.

"You read my messages?" Carla was equally indignant as well.

"Don't change the issue. You didn't tell me you were still seeing her," he angrily retorted.

Carla had nothing to say because she knew it was her fault.

"We should call this wedding off until you decide what you really wanted," Ken stated and then left her speechless as he stormed out of the house.

Carla wanted to cry, but the tears weren't forthcoming. When she came out of the house, Ken was nowhere to be seen. She felt like the world ended for her, but her eyes were still dry.

It was when she reached home that the gravity of the situation struck her.

"We should call this wedding off until you decide what you really wanted," Ken's words echoed in her mind.

Helen was there sweetly smiling at her; that was when she burst into tears in Helen's comforting arms. In between her sobs, she told Helen what happened.

"I'm sorry, sweetie. I didn't mean to cause you this pain."

"I know," Carla cried again, as Helen caressed her hair lovingly.

And Helen led her to bed.

"Come, I'll let you relax. Forget about your problem first. We'll talk about it later," Helen comforted her.

Carla closed her eyes as Helen started massaging her toes.

"Relax, sweetie," Helen murmured as she started kneading her toes and heels. Her loving touch loosened up Carla and made her forget about Ken's anger.

Helen had always considered her first before herself; lucky is the person whom Helen loved, and that was her. Why would she not choose Helen instead?

Carla went around her chores listlessly during the days that followed. There were no calls and texts from Ken. He did not visit her either. Carla had begun to worry. Could Ken let go of her so easily? During the night, she cried herself to sleep. Helen insisted that she should move in while Carla was depressed. But Carla said that she is confused and needed more time to think it over.

Days passed, but Carla still did not hear from Ken. She was not able to eat or do anything but cry. There were dark circles around her eyes, and she lost weight.

"Sweetie, can't you forget him and love me

instead? Am I not lovable?"

"As I've told you, you have a special place in my heart, but I want a family with Ken," Carla wanted Helen to understand her feelings.

"We could adopt you know," Helen countered back.

"It's not the same, Helen," she reiterated.

On the 10th day, Carla dared to call Ken but found out that his cell phone was turned off. Ken had finally closed the door for her. She realized then that Ken had decided to go out of her life completely.

Helen saw her all messed up; her red-rimmed eyes bulging from their sockets and her unkempt hair emphasized her despondency. Did she love Ken that much? Helen's heart went out to her. She loved Carla so much she could give anything she would wish for.

That night, she stayed again, even when Carla said she was okay. Helen gently led her to the shower and bathed her as if she were an 8-year-old, gently soaping and scrubbing her unblemished skin and shampooing her hair thoroughly.

"You silly girl, you haven't bathed since yesterday, I bet," she pretended scolding her.

While she was bathing her, Carla's body responded to Helen's touch. Her nipples stood erect as Helen carefully sponged the area.

To help her forget Ken momentarily, Helen decided to allow her to take the lead. "Here, make me happy too," she said and guided Carla's fingers to her already hot pussy.

Carla fondled her where she knew Helen felt the most pleasure. She was gently fondling

Helen's clit round and round in soft, sensuous circles. Helen could feel the crescendo increasing.

Helen moaned in delight as Carla inserted a finger to penetrate her. She had learned very well the art of pleasing a woman, Helen thought.

Her breath was coming in gasps as she ground her pussy into Carla's fingers. Carla was exactly doing what Helen did to her in their previous sexual encounters that Helen was groaning in ecstasy.

Helen savored every minute of delight with Carla's fingers. They faced opposite directions and ate each other's pussy voraciously as if they were starving, slurping the juices and licking clean the folds of the labia. They started fondling and caressing until their arousal was at its peak. Then they went back again sucking and licking the head of the clit, the folds of their womanhood, until they both went insane with pleasure, shuddering and arching their backs with wanton delight. Their orgasms came and persisted as they continued loving each other's mound of pleasure.

Soon, when they were fully satiated, they collapsed on the bed and went to sleep; Helen had an arm around Carla's naked body as she had her back to Helen. Helen cupped her breasts and whispered to her ear, "It's gonna be all right."

The following days, Carla still was wallowing in her depression. Helen could not stand it any longer, watching Carla wither and die in front of her. She went to see Ken personally.

"Do you really love her, Ken?" she confronted him. "If you do, then please go see her. She needs you." Helen was lachrymose as she finally decided to let Carla go.

"I won't bother her anymore. I just want her to be happy."

Ken went to Carla right after. Unknown to both women, Ken had also been depressed knowing he could not survive without Carla. He had vowed to himself that if Carla would not make up with him after three days, he would go crawling back to her and would permit her to have relations with Helen, just so she would take him back again. But now, he was elated that Carla wanted him back.

Without delay, Ken sped towards Carla's house. His heart was beating wildly as he pressed the doorbell. There was no reply on the second buzz. Ken fished for his cell phone in his pocket and rang her up. There was an interminable ringing before Carla's voice came on line.

"Ken? Is that you?" her voice was incredulous, hesitant, and unbelieving.

"Yes, it's me, hon. Please open up."

Carla was ecstatic; she ran barefooted to the door, her eyes streaming with joyful tears. She would tell Helen that she loved Ken more than anyone else in the world—even more than her—and that she was ready to live with him for the rest of her life.

When the door opened, they rushed into each other's arms and held each other like there was no tomorrow. They kissed and kissed again, savoring each other's lips. The promising horizon was waiting for them to conquer. Their bodies became aflame with familiar sensations that only they could assuage, their groins aching to be one again in the delight of sexual pleasure.

"I love you, hon," Ken whispered passionately as their lips melded again into one.

"I love you more," Carla kissed him back, her tears mingling with her joyous smile.

Then they happily rushed inside, hand in hand, Carla leaning securely on Ken's shoulders, knowing they had all the time in the world to explore new worlds and pleasures for the rest of their lifetime.

AUTHOR'S NOTE

Readers: I want to expand a few of the stories to see where the characters can be explored further. If there are any of the stories that you would like to read more about again, I'd love to hear from you!

Visit my blog at http://www.julimateson.com

Join my newsletter for free exclusive previews
http://www.julimateson.com/in

Follow me on Twitter at
http://www.twitter.com/julimatcson

Like my page on Facebook at
http://www.facebook.com/julimateson

Discover my books at major ebook retailers everywhere.